BEHIND
THE CIGARETTE

BEHIND THE CIGARETTE

Jacqueline Grandey

atmosphere press

To Flowerpot, Debbie, Zane and Chad …thank you.

I smashed every last rose that was left on display.

It was a metaphor.

I was no longer under his control.

I was no longer imprisoned by my own insecurities.

... I never felt so alive.

CHAPTER 1

DALLAS

"Don't make a sound," Trent whispered softly in my ear. I kept my eyes closed as I released a smile as I laid there quietly on my stomach. *Ahh, this man leaves me breathless just by hearing his voice.*

I could feel a tingling sensation as his five o'clock shadow gently scraped my neck as he began to slowly give me butterfly kisses on my ear.

"Ooo," I whispered. My skin responded instantly as he started to lick my shoulder from behind, moving along my blades, and down my spine. I let out a subtle sigh. I could feel his thick black hair roll across each butt cheek as I just kept my eyes closed and just absorbed this surprise of affection at three a.m.

He gently spread my legs open as I rolled my neck in the opposite direction on the pillow.

"Ohhh," I moaned as Trent started to slowly lick my pussy. His warm tongue licked my folds up one side and down the other. My toes curled into the sheet. He then inserted one finger into me slowly sliding it in and out. I clenched my cheeks as I was starting to get moist.

3

"Ahh," I said, as I didn't want a complete word to slip out as he had instructed me not to make a sound, however, I couldn't help having the groan slip out as music played on from the bedside radio.

He continued a slow rhythm as I was becoming aroused. With his hard morning erection, he then eased himself into me.

Accepting his fullness, Trent moved back and forth, filling me.

My legs tightened underneath him as he laid on top of me, quietly groaning in my ear.

"You're so wet, Alex," he whispered while he licked my ear and continued to thrust in and out from behind. He pushed a little deeper as my breathing became rapid as I whispered back.

"You're going to make me come with that pace Trent," I warned him as I could feel his facial hair against my neck as he smiled.

"I like this pace. I want to come with you Alex. Will you come for me?" he asked. I just squeezed the pillow and nodded my head yes to his invitation. Trent kept the pace slow but thrusted a little harder, a little deeper.

"I love when you're inside me," I whispered back towards him.

Trent pushed deeper as I felt his warm breath in my blonde hair and his damp chest on my back.

I couldn't hold out much longer as I began to quiver hard against his dick while he released inside me. "Happy Valentine's Day," Trent whispered in my ear after we climaxed.

This is definitely a piece of heaven on earth, I thought to myself as Trent slowly pulled out, stood up, and headed towards the bathroom.

I just laid there trying to decipher if this was real or just a damn dream. I could not believe this man came back for me. He drove from Texas with my best friend Tyler and my brother Austin to 'save me' in Miami. I giggled as I envisioned all the dozens of roses I smashed all over Gage Heston's house as my final encore as I exited that toxic relationship.

Trent opened his home to both me and Tyler as he simultaneously handled our situations. Me with my physical and emotional wounds and Tyler with his detox and his infamous collapse on stage.

Plus, he handled all the band's affairs, trying to rebuild Tyler's image. He loved me enough to take on the two of us, and I just couldn't believe he was that brave.

I smiled as I rolled over onto my back, watching the candle's flame flicker, while my favorite Deftones song "Change" (In the house of flies) played on in the background. As the song belted out the words '*I feel so alive*,' I stretched and hollered out, "I feel so alive!"

Trent started to laugh as he walked towards the bed and crawled slowly back in naked next to me. I straightened up our pillows as we leaned against the black iron-rod headboard and continued to listen to the Deftones.

"You know what this song is about, don't you?" Trent asked me as he lit his clove cigarette and shook out the match, inhaling a much deserved cigarette. I shrugged my shoulders as I looked at him.

"It's about you and that Mr. Heston." Trent took another puff as he looked over at me.

"Gage?" I questioned him as I rolled my eyes.

"Ew. That's going to ruin the song for me," I pouted as I kicked my leg out from underneath the crisp white sheet. Trent laughed.

"Seriously, Gage broke you down, he pulled off your wings, he laughed while you changed for him. He hurt you over and over, which caused you to lose your self-confidence and become insecure." Trent continued, "He stripped you of everything you were, everything you want-ed to become, and he enjoyed every fucking minute of it." Trent paused.

"Your relationship wasn't a loving relationship—it was fucking ownership. He put you on display. But, you changed, Alex. You grew wings, hence those intense lyrics, which is why you feel so alive. Give yourself the credit." He smiled at me as he inhaled another puff.

"I love the end of the song, though." Trent paused and flashed a devilish grin.

"His guilt catches up to him and he wants to give you his gun so you can blow him away, which is what I would love for you to do," Trent growled.

"Humm. A bullet for the old valentine," I said as I let out a long breath of relief.

"I guess I still like the song then." I smiled as I grabbed Trent's cigarette and inhaled slowly as I listened to the song's *Aah, aah, aah...*

A few hours later I hollered up towards the loft where Trent was still lying in our bed.

"I'm fixin' to make pancakes. You hungry?" I smiled as

I stirred the batter.

"I'm fucking starved!" I heard a voice from behind me say.

"Oh, hi Tyler. Sorry, did I wake you?" I asked.

Tyler, my beautiful disaster of a best friend, was once again standing in my kitchen.

"Did you sleep well?" I asked him as I looked up towards the loft for a second time, wondering if Trent fell back asleep.

"Is the mattress comfortable enough for you?" I asked while I smiled at him, watching him raid the fridge in search of orange juice in his shredded Alice in Chains tee shirt, unbuttoned black jeans, and smeared guyliner.

"I passed the fuck out last night. I really think mine and Olivia's relationship is over. It's fried, died, and laid to the side." Tyler smirked as he headed for the cupboard to retrieve a glass.

"I really liked Olivia, but you cannot run around with *Whip-ettes* and expect her to smile, pat you on the head, then get on her knees." I laughed as I pictured WHIP's groupies flirting with the frontman.

"You are welcome to stay as long as you need to." I offered him a place to stay as I smiled at Tyler, knowing damn well that he hates to be alone, so I need to face up to the fact that I just took on a roommate.

Trent walked into the kitchen with our cat Ernie in his hands.

"Look who wants pancakes too." He smiled as he set Ernie by his bowl of kibble then walked over to me and kissed me on the head.

"Smells delicious, Alex. What can I help with?"

Trent is so thoughtful. "I'm fine, sugar. Just finish setting the table, and I'll bring over the pancakes and fruit."

I licked my lips as I watched him begin to set the table in no shirt and ripped jeans, baring his olive-skinned inked chest.

"I saw that!" Tyler teased.

"Here, you can have the syrup to sweeten up that thought." Tyler tossed the syrup at me. I just laughed, knowing his mind was always in the gutter and that I was so busted for lusting after Trent.

I placed the syrup on the table, then brought over the pancakes and fruit. I sat down at our wooden four-top table with metal chairs that I scored at the local thrift store. Trent placed a few pancakes on my plate, on his, then passed the dish to Tyler. I was just filled with joy as I watched my two favorite people in the whole world dig into our breakfast.

CHAPTER
2

After breakfast, Trent left to go hide in his recording studio that he set up after moving from Louisiana to be with me here in Texas called *Head Rush*. Tyler had the job of writing some new lyrics before he met up with their band WHIP this evening.

I, on the other hand, had my freelance graphic design work to attend to. I still maintained my position as the lead designer for WHIP's old record label. It's the one Gage Heston tie I could not sever just yet, which didn't please Trent.

Gage agreed with the other record label executives that business was business and that I was good for his music business. He kept our personal affairs out of the way. Business was business and personal was personal, which I tried to respect.

But, no more sticky cubicles at the D-towner for me! I had my own schedule and deadlines that I needed to meet. Freelancing gave me a sense of freedom: I could choose which gigs I wanted to take on with what client as I built my own independent list. Ultimate *bliss*. I paused as I was booting up my laptop that was covered in WHIP stickers and looked around at the new industrial loft that I had just

9

purchased, and was quite pleased with myself.

Job, check! House, check! And, significant other, check, check! I laughed as it was the first time I'd ever felt so grown up. What could my mother really bitch and complain about now? I laughed aloud.

Tapping my fingers on the table, I glanced around the loft, searching for Tyler. I assumed he was hiding in the spare bedroom, writing some of his intense poetic lyrics. But I was secretly hoping it wasn't some sappy, I-miss-Olivia bullshit that could send him into a downward spiral.

It'd been months since all of us returned from the 'Florida-Louisiana' chapter of our lives. I was leaving Gage in Florida, and Tyler was rehabilitating in Louisiana. Tyler was still so fragile.

I'm very proud of the progress he has made, and I do not need one fucking 'suicide girl' rock reporter to fuck it all up. She was cute, career driven—I'll give her that. But Tyler, on the other hand, just needed to kick his addiction and get his vocal career and stage persona back on track.

I think that's why a part of me is really at peace with him staying here. I've been his only family ever since his mother left and his father beat him over it. Tyler really needed his best friend more than ever now, as well as the help of his bandmates to keep him sober and focused.

After a few hours of knocking out some lame logo design for a local bank, I was bushed. I got up from the kitchen table, stretched, and wandered over to my favorite corner of the loft space.

I had my easel, a gift from Trent, set up with a canvas leaning on it. I had my metal table on wheels for my other art projects to create. I also had a roped laundry line attached to the wall with metal clips to display my sketches—most of them were Trent—and all my finished pieces were leaning on the adjacent wall. I was bursting with creativity ever since Trent helped me set up this space for my art.

When I was with Gage, he told me that my paintings sucked, and then he just stowed it all away in his garage... not a very inspirational space, I might add. I just smiled as I headed over to the fridge to pour myself a glass of sweet tea to dissolve the taste of Gage in my mouth. It was so hard to let everything go after leaving a toxic relationship.

My mind was crunching again. I had to stop neurotically fixating on the past with Gage. I left him. I chose Trent. End of story.

Swirling my ice around in my glass, I noticed Tyler's door was partially open as I headed over to check in on him.

"Hey, how you holdin' up, Ty?" I asked Tyler as he was stretched out on the unmade bed with a notepad on his lap and a pen in his hand.

"Grrrr, I can't fucking concentrate. How can I write a radio-worthy song when all I hear is Olivia's high-pitched voice screaming at me!" Tyler tore up the piece of paper and chucked it at me.

"Hey, I'm not Olivia! Don't toss your trash at me!" I scolded Tyler.

"I'm sorry blondie," Tyler pouted.

"You need a cigarette," I suggested.

"I need a fucking drink," Tyler snapped.

"You're so fucking edgy, dude. Not cool. Call your sponsor or something!" I snapped right back.

"You are my sponsor, baby girl. I only need you. I'm so grateful to you for just being you. You understand me, you push me, you accept me, you just fucking love me for some fucked up reason. Olivia wanted to change me—not as drastically as Gage wanted to change you. Nevertheless, it's a control issue, and I'm a dominant, so good fucking luck with that!" Tyler got up off the bed and stretched.

"Let's go outside and sit on the balcony. I need to clear my head," he said as I picked up the balled up paper of lyrics and tossed it into the trash as I followed Tyler out onto the balcony.

Sitting on our wicker chairs, I watched Tyler light up a cigarette and scratch his messy black hair.

"Your hair is growing out." I smiled at him.

"No more Sid Vicious. I like it longer and messy. You look kinda hot, Ty." I laughed.

"Stop trying to cheer me up, baby girl. Think the *Whip-ettes* will like my new do?" he asked as he scratched his head once more.

"You know I need to line up another warm body to lie next to?" Tyler questioned while he flicked an ash into an empty plant pot.

"Oh, the infamous *Whip-ettes*. How are those dirty girls?"

I stuck out my tongue as both Tyler and I hollered out in unison, "Sluuuuuts!" We laughed.

"Good, I got you to laugh." I said as I let out a breath as I leaned back in my chair.

"Look, this ache for Olivia... it'll pass. You're so talented..." Tyler rolled his eyes.

"Stop, really. It sounds so cliché, but you're really fucking talented, Ty. Put that stage arrogance on and fucking fake it till you make it. I mean act like Olivia hasn't got to you. You're still a rockstar—act like one!" I laughed.

"I did, and that's what got me into trouble, baby girl," Tyler corrected me.

"Look, if you loved her so much, then you wouldn't have acted the way you did. She deserves better, but her eyes were wide open from the beginning. She toured with you, she knew you took drugs, she played with the other *Whip-ettes*. Honestly, the last thing you need is a relationship right now. You need to focus on the next album, pick up the tour where you left off, and figure out what and who you want in your life. You'll get through this. Melancholy madness always makes the art better." I smiled as I reached for his hand. Tyler accepted it and squeezed it while just holding it for a moment.

Later that afternoon, after hopping in the shower, I was getting ready to meet up with Trent at *Head Rush*.

I adjusted my matching black lacy bra and panties, slipped on my cotton black knee length dress, fastened the western belt and sat on my bed to pull on my cowboy boots.

I placed my right foot in one, then the left, but then I felt something stab my toe. I pulled the boot off and shook it, and out fell a small black box on to the floor. I leaned over, picked up the box, and opened it. It was a Valentine's Day gift hidden in my boot from Trent. I laughed.

I opened the box and discovered a sterling silver artist palette charm for my necklace. I squealed.

"He's so amazing!" I mumbled to myself. Not only was I woken up to incredible sex this morning, but he also found time to place a charm in my damn cowboy boot. I love that man. I relished the thought of him for a minute. I then grabbed my brown vintage leather coat and skipped down the stairs over to Tyler's room.

"Are you ready to roll, rockstar?" I asked while standing on my tippy toes, still amped up from my little black box gift.

"I'm ready," Tyler huffed as he stood there shoving cigarettes, a lighter, a cell phone, and keys into his black leather biker jacket. He motioned for me to turn around as we both headed downstairs to my truck.

The recording studio was located off Dragon Street, which wasn't far from our loft. I pulled into the alley and parked 'Axl,' my truck, right next to Trent's motorcycle.

"It looks like everyone is still here," Tyler said as he yawned while rolling up my passenger side window.

"Cheer up, Ty," I huffed. Tyler then jumped out as I grabbed my bag and stepped out of the truck, slamming my door. *He's not ruining my Valentine's Day with his damn manic depressive mood swings.* Sometimes, I think I liked him better on cocaine.

I followed Tyler into the studio, which from the outside looked like an old brick building with graffiti and leaky pipes. However, from the inside, it was beautiful.

The sitting area had a burgundy red area rug laid on the original wood floor with a black L-shaped couch perched on top of it. Leather ottomans were scattered on the floor. A black antique trunk was used as a coffee table with candles on it. There was also a long corridor that led to the small kitchen and bath that had framed pictures of WHIP during their live shows lining the wall. The lighting was dim and the vibe was chill. One room to the left of the sitting area was for their rehearsal, and one room to the right was their recording studio.

Walking into the studio, you had your socks knocked off with the impressive Neve console that had Pro Tools MAC plugged into it. Trent had his Korg Triton Studio 88-key workstation set up next to the console and his Waldorf Q synthesizer in yellow, one of my favorite colors, set up against the wall.

Looking through the soundproof window in front of the console, you could see the drum kit and bass guitar set up alongside a collection of electric and acoustic guitars that hung from the wall. Amplifiers and cords were littered everywhere. The vocal booth was in the center—which was Tyler's world.

The whole musician's creative space was quite impressive.

Now, I understand why Trent hides in here a lot. I laughed to myself.

"What are you smiling about, my pretty little Valentine?" I heard Trent come up from behind me and kiss my neck.

"Hey sugar," I turned around, grabbing my necklace and kissing the little artist palette charm he surprised me with this morning.

"Thank you," I said as I then kissed his soft lips.

"You're welcome, baby. I'm glad it made you smile."

Trent stepped back and opened a can of soda. "How's Tyler holdin' up on the big V-day?" Trent asked me while he took a sip out of the can.

"No one's affection can warm him right now. His ego is still bruised." I gave a pitiful look to Trent, and he just understood.

"Well, after we wrap up in the studio, we're all heading to *The Broken Hearts Club*, if he wants to join us, that is," Trent offered as I just stood there watching Tyler bop his head around while holding on to the sides of his Sony headphones.

"He'll join us," I assured Trent.

CHAPTER 3

After the boys wrapped up a quick session at the studio, some of us headed over to *The Broken Hearts* club. I walked hand in hand with Trent as Tyler followed behind me talking with the bass player. I knew a nightclub wasn't the best environment for a recovering addict, but he was with the band, he was with me, and a glass of wine wouldn't send him back to rehab in Louisiana. We couldn't take everything away from Tyler. He needed to feel some sense of control. *Cigarettes and a glass of wine will settle him down tonight*, I assured myself.

We walked into the intimate club where every table had black linens and candles burning on them. There was a small stage in the dimly lit place where musicians sat on stools playing only acoustically.

The guys and I slid into a booth against the wall as a waitress scurried over to take our drink order. Trent ordered a bottle of red for the table and then helped me get out of my coat. Tyler smiled at the waitress, then took a cigarette out of his pocket and used the table's candle to light it as he watched the guitarist strum a love song.

"Fucking sappy love songs tonight? Great." Tyler blew out his smoke, pouted, then looked over at me.

"Don't start," I mouthed to him. He rolled his eyes, then leaned back as the waitress set down the wine glasses.

"Happy Valentine's Day guys!" she sang sweetly as she poured everyone a drink. I took a sip of the wine then kissed Trent.

"Thank you, it's good," I purred. He smiled as he slid his hands between my thighs and softly stroked their interior. I purred a little closer to his ear.

A fellow musician friend then came up to the table and began talking to Trent, so I leaned back in the booth and just listened to a cover of "These Arms of Mine" by Otis Redding.

I glanced around the bar, and it was starting to fill in with people. Everyone's eyes were on the center stage; it was a rarity to listen to such talented musicians just sing and play acoustically. Our booth started to feel a bit snug as the rest of WHIP showed up from the studio to join us. Tyler was unusually quiet as he smoked and stared off aimlessly. I felt a little sad for him that his broken heart was sitting in *The Broken Hearts Club* on Valentine's Day.

I became distracted with the drummer and his girl-friend when Tyler got up from the table and went over to another booth. They were filling me in on a few ideas the band had about staying in the moment, possibly a shot to write the music for an upcoming movie soundtrack, anything to keep their career in motion. I was enthralled with the conversation when suddenly I heard a few girls clap their hands while a few other guys whistled with their fingers.

I sipped my glass of wine and looked around, wondering what all the commotion was about. There, up on the stage, was Tyler sitting on a bar stool behind the microphone stand between two other acoustic guitar players. The room fell silent as he started to sing very softly. I turned my ear towards him as I continued to listen. I quickly recognized the lyrics.

Wait, oh my god, Tyler was singing "Nothing Compares 2 U" by Prince. My mouth dropped open as I listened intensely. He sounded so profoundly sad and so fucking beautiful at the same time, my heart just sank. Tears started to surface as I sat there admiring his guts to get back up on a stage, even though it was small, after his arena stage overdose performance and just sing something again. I really missed watching him perform.

The adoring crowd showed their appreciation for the acoustical performance as they stood on their feet in awe just quietly waving their lighters and cell phones back and forth. He managed to get through the entire song without cracking once.

When the song came to an end, the small crowd erupted with hand clapping and more whistling.

Tyler flashed a half polite smile then shook each of the guitar players' hands, walked off stage, and walked straight out the front door of the club.

Trent tapped my leg and pointed at the exit. I huffed, crawled over him, and went after Tyler.

When I got outside, I looked around and did not see him anywhere.

"Ty?" I called out. I heard some coughing from behind

the club. Tyler was vomiting wine into the trash can.

"Eww, are you okay?" My eyes started to water. Tyler wiped his mouth and sat down on the concrete. "That was so beautiful Ty, I love that song..." I paused.

"Why are you so fragile? Are you really hurting that much?" I let out a subtle sigh.

"Alex, I'm just a fuck up. I just don't know any more. I mean everything is making me so sad. I miss being on stage. I feel like I've just let everybody down... you, the band, Olivia..." Tyler started sobbing. I crouched down on the concrete and wrapped my arms around him so tightly as tears began to stream down my face as well.

"It's okay, sugar." I patted Tyler's back and squeezed a little harder.

"You've come so far. No drugs. No hard liquor. The treatment is over. You're with me and Trent. You're not alone in this. We love you." I looked up and began to wipe his tears. Then I brushed his hair behind his ears as I kissed his cheeks over and over.

"Healing takes time. Throw in a broken heart to boot on top of all this crazy bullshit you've been through, no wonder you're so upset. I get it, believe me," I said as I sadly looked up and tried to comfort him.

"Yeah, but you have Trent," he sniffled while he fished for a cigarette in his pocket.

"I have you. You and I will always have each other," I reassured him.

"You are my constant comfort and inexhaustible strength, Alex," Tyler said as he blew out some smoke as I wiped his smeared eyeliner from all the tears.

"Let's go home, Ty. You just need a good night's sleep." Tyler nodded his head 'yes' as I stood up and pulled him to his feet.

The next morning, I was too wound up and decided I needed to go for a run to clear my head and release some of my anxiety.

Trent rolled over in bed and asked, "Where are you headed, baby?" He rubbed his eyes as he tried to focus on me as I was lacing up my tennis shoes.

"I'm going to go for a run. Do you want to tag along with me?" I asked.

"Sure, babe, give me a minute to throw something on." I smiled as I watched him roll out of bed naked and head into the bathroom.

Tyler was in the land of the dead sleeping downstairs, so I quietly grabbed Trent's shoes and whispered, "I'll meet you downstairs. I'm going to pack us some water and some protein bars." He smiled as he walked out of the bathroom and started to get dressed.

I fed Ernie, packed some snacks, then grabbed my truck keys just as Trent met me in the kitchen.

"I just need to clear my head after last night. Tyler is a lot for me to handle emotionally at the moment. I just need a good run to reset myself," I said as Trent smiled then kissed my head.

"I get it, babe. I need to clear my head as well. It'll feel good to get some exercise. Where do you like to run?" he asked sweetly as he lightly pulled on my ponytail.

"Ow," I laughed.

"Does the Santa Fe trail sound good to you?" I asked.

"Sounds perfect. You lead the way." He gestured for me to head out the door. I turned and paused in front of Tyler's room as Trent patted my butt.

"Let him sleep, Alex. Let's go." I nodded my head and followed Trent outside to the parking garage.

Arriving at the Santa Fe trail, I hopped out of the truck and took in a deep breath.

"Ahh, doesn't it smell wonderful out here?" I asked as Trent laughed while he shut the truck door.

"Wow, no one is really out on the trail this early in the morning," he said as he looked around at the empty trail.

"Yeah, Katy is much busier. I prefer the peace and quiet this trail offers. I run clear down to that bridge." I pointed to a bridge that was in front of the downtown Dallas city buildings.

"Beautiful, huh?" I asked as Trent nodded.

"So, are we ready?" I asked as I called over my shoulder, getting a head start in front of Trent.

"Hey, wait, I'm coming!" he laughed as he caught up to me.

"I have one question I need to ask, then I'll bite my tongue the rest of the run, I promise," I said to Trent as we kept a steady pace alongside one another.

"Okay. What's up?" he asked.

"I think Tyler needs an antidepressant. What do you think?" Trent whistled, then released a breath.

"Well, after last night's meltdown in the back of the *Broken Hearts Club*, it might not be such a bad idea. Have you brought it up to him?" Trent asked with sincerity. I stopped mid-run and looked at him.

"Ugh, not yet. I was a little hesitant, but you're right. After last night's episode, I need to suggest something to him. He's just so vulnerable right now. He feels like he just let everybody down—me, Olivia, the band. Maybe I will bring it up to him later today," I said as I started to pick up my pace again alongside Trent.

"I can take him to the clinic downtown where I get my birth control," I said as Trent laughed.

"The place where they give out funky colored condoms?" he asked as I nodded my head.

"Yeah, there," I said.

"I think it's a good idea. Just be careful how you suggest it to him—he might get a little defensive," he said.

"That's what I was worried about, but I need to make sure he gets his head back in the right place before he spirals downward," I said as Trent agreed with me.

"Okay, enough about Tyler. See that pedestrian bridge over there?" I asked.

"Yeah," he said.

"I'll race ya!" I hollered as I took off towards the bridge.

Trent finally caught up to me as he put his hands on his knees, breathing hard.

"I'd cut back on the cigarettes if I were you," I said as he laughed as he tried to catch his breath.

"What's all this?" Trent looked around at the dozens of locks securely hanging from the bridge. "Beautiful, huh?" I asked as Trent nodded his head, walking over to the bridge and touching a few.

"They symbolize love locked together. When a couple is in love, they bring a lock to the bridge, attach it and throw away the key into the water down below," I said as I glanced over at him.

"Huh. What an amazing little gesture to how you feel about one another," Trent said as he looked over the bridge at the water flowing down below.

"I know. Do you believe that love is locked forever?" I asked.

"It's just a symbol, like wedding rings are. I believe in it." He flashed me a grin as I shuffled around into my running jacket pocket and pulled out a small black lock and key that was tucked away from who-knows-when.

"Look, I have one for us!" I said as Trent walked over and took it from my hand.

"Awe, I love it!" he said as he admired it, then bent down and clipped it to the bridge.

"We're love-locked, baby. You're stuck with me, so toss the key!" he said as he looked back over at me.

I released a breath, closed my eyes, then threw the key over my shoulder. Trent stepped in and grabbed a hold of me and swung me around as I laughed happily.

"Love you babe," he said as he set me down.

"You're all dewy!" I laughed as I leaned up and kissed him.

"Love you back!" I smiled as I gazed back at our black lock on the bridge.

An hour later, when we arrived back home, Trent went straight upstairs to shower and get dressed. "Where are you headed off to, handsome?" I asked him as he gave me that weak-in-the-knees grin of his as I walked over and kissed him softly on the lips.

He answered, "The recording studio. I have a few things I still need to iron out. Hey, I really needed that run this morning, thank you." He smiled as I just stood there watching him as he buttoned up his black jeans and reached for his black TOOL t-shirt.

"It was refreshing to get outside. It was good to clear my head and process a few things." I paused as I lowered my voice.

"Oh, by the way, I was talking to some of the guys from the band last night at the club, and they were all amped up about some rock and roll film coming out? Does this film need a band for their soundtrack or something? Do you know anything about this?" I questioned Trent as he rolled his eyes then sat down on the comforter.

"Yeah, I do know something about that. The film needs an actual vocalist to sing the parts of the lead actor, while the entire soundtrack will be dedicated to that particular band that's chosen." Trent swallowed hard.

"Wow, did the film company consider Tyler as the vocalist? Is WHIP even considered?" I immediately perked up.

"That would be such a comeback for him after the Atlanta show drug overdose incident!" I cheered. "What label is handling it, WHIP's?" My voice went up an octave.

Trent shushed me to lower my voice.

"No, baby, it's not ours. It's Mr. Heston's deal," he said as my stomach turned. Just hearing Trent say the name Mr. Heston made me want to puke.

"Gage? Really? Shit." I pouted.

"Drop it, Alex. I'll find something else for Tyler to fixate on. You work on getting him on his happy pills." Trent gave me a goofy smile as I just laughed and dropped the subject.

After Trent left for the studio, I jumped in the shower, then went downstairs to check in on Tyler.

"Knock, knock. You awake rockstar?" I peeked my head into the room in search of Tyler, but he was busy in the bathroom. As I sat on the bed for a minute and waited, I noticed the balled up paper I put in the trash bin yesterday. I got up, retrieved it, then snuck out and went to the living room to read it:

BETRAYAL

You drained my heart.
You put an ax into my back.
It's hard to forgive when you're constantly attacked.
I'll always fall to my knees when the weakness gives in.
I'm trying to flee from our overwhelming sin.
Every time I run back to you, you'd just slit my
  wrists again.
Burn the memories... Burn the love... Burn what
  made us, us.

We need to let go of this forbidden love, when the
  blood stars shine in my favor.
I'm leaving this toxic mess and moving on from this
  destructive behavior.
I've tattooed over the scar, but I still feel the same
  about you.
There was never pure love, just betrayal, that showed
  itself through.

Burn the memories. Burn the love. Burn what made
us, us.

Piece together the afterthoughts. Tie up the emptiness.
I'll never forget the pain you brought as I surface
from this mess.
Can't believe the truth. Can't believe I've failed.
You ripped my heart out. The final sign of betrayal.
Burn the memories. Burn the love. Burn what made
us, us.

Holy shit. I sunk into the couch as I digested this poem that I was sure was written for Olivia.

Tyler then opened his bedroom door and joined me in the living room.

"Whatcha doing, baby girl?" Tyler asked while he stood there scratching his head.

"How are you feeling, boo?" I asked while I handed him the paper.

"What's this?" Tyler asked while he started to read the wrinkled up piece of paper.

"It's good. Some Valentine's Day poem, eh?" I laughed.

"Nah," he replied. "I'm just venting through my stupid poetry." Tyler rolled it back up and tossed it back to me.

"That's how you heal, Ty. You write it all out," I chastised him.

"Heal, schmeal," Tyler said while making a jerk-off motion with his hand.

"You suck." I got up and went to the coffee maker.

"I'm fixin' to make coffee. You want some?" I asked the tormented artist.

"Yes." Tyler followed me and sat at the breakfast bar

and watched as I started the coffee.

"What's on your mind, Alexandria Leigh Rae?" Tyler pried while I searched the cabinet for sugar.

"Alexandria Leigh Rae?" I responded as I turned around and faced him.

"Are we in serious mode now, Tyler Xavier Black? Can I talk seriously to you?" I stopped what I was doing and looked Tyler straight in the eye.

"Is this a heart to fart convo we're about to have?" Tyler stuck out his tongue.

"Yes, it's a heart to heart," I said as I took a deep breath.

"Would you consider taking an antidepressant?" I bit my lower lip as the coffee brewed behind me. "You want to numb me out, huh?" Tyler pretended to clean crumbs off the bar in front of him.

"Fuck off. I'm not trying to numb you out. I'm trying to help you get a grip on the situation. Crying and vomiting wine behind a nightclub is not what I consider getting a grip. I wouldn't suggest it if I didn't think you needed it." I paused to see his reaction.

"I don't know what I need anymore, baby girl." Tyler's eyes started to well up as I took his hand, leaning towards him.

"A light dose of something to help take the edge off for a little while will help you. I'll take you to the clinic that I go to and we'll talk to a doctor. Then you can focus on your music and not let this whirlwind of emotions get in the way." I sensed Tyler would trust me and come around to the idea of taking a chill pill.

"Okay," he said.

"Okay." I tapped his hand.

After our coffee, I texted Trent that Tyler and I were headed to the clinic. He responded that he was happy to hear it and that it was a good move and that I should meet him at the recording studio later after everything was said and done with Tyler, and I agreed.

CHAPTER 4

Tyler and I pulled up to the community clinic, and I parked my truck in the lot.

Shutting off the ignition, I asked, "Do you want me to go inside with you?" He gave me a half smile.

"Nah, I need to do this alone," Tyler huffed as he opened the door and dragged his feet as he headed into the clinic. I rolled my window down, leaned back in the driver-side seat, closed my eyes and let out a deep breath. This was the right thing for Tyler to do—anything to help lift the cloud of melancholy that had been hovering over his head lately.

Forty-five minutes later, Tyler was walking back towards my parked truck.

"Yeehaw!" he hollered out, startling me as I sat up and just laughed. Tyler walked up to the vehicle and slapped a prescription for Prozac on to my front windshield and said, "Let the healing begin, baby girl." He rolled his eyes.

"Yee-F'n-Haw is right. I'm so proud of you, Ty," I praised Tyler as he hopped in the passenger side and I started up Axl.

"The good news is that the Doctor recommended the antidepressant but also said it was okay to smoke fucking marijuana. Some fucking multimodal approach? I do have another favor to ask of you," he said.

"What now?" I asked.

"I just need to make two stops, baby girl. One to the pharmacy and one to my dealer. Is that cool?" he asked.

I just smiled, nodding my head yes and hollered out, "Let's blow this popsicle stand!" as I started the truck. Tyler just laughed as he rolled his window down and turned up the radio as I peeled out of the clinic's parking lot.

After dropping Tyler off at the loft, I drove down to *Head Rush*. I missed Trent already even though I just saw him this morning. I parked in the alley once again next to his motorcycle and let myself in the back door.

There, sitting on the leather couch reading a copy of *MIX* magazine, was my Trent. He was lost in his thoughts while Velvet Revolver played in the background.

"Reading anything interesting?" I smiled at him as he looked up from the magazine and smiled back. "Nothing as interesting as what just walked into my studio," he said as I laughed and rolled my eyes.

"Come here, cowgirl, you look spent." Trent motioned for me to come over and sit on his lap as he tapped his thighs. I obliged.

"How's our tormented frontman? Is he on the verge of slitting his wrists?" Trent mocked Tyler.

"Stop." I put my hand over Trent's mouth. "He'll be okay. Wounds take time to heal." I released my hand from his mouth.

Trent whispered, "I'm sorry." I leaned into him as he hugged me.

"It's okay, Tyler can be so draining. But, I don't want to talk about Tyler anymore. In fact, I'm tired of pep-talking him. Can I just put my tongue to better use?" I stuck out my tongue as Trent laughed.

"Give me that tongue," he teased as he leaned towards me and slid his wet tongue into my open mouth. He began circling my tongue with his and my whole body turned to jello.

"I've missed you," he said softly. He then grabbed a hold of my waist and pulled me closer on his lap. I released a moan.

"You taste like a candy cane, Alex. Your mouth is such a treat," Trent whispered as he licked my bottom lip, slightly biting it, then thrusted his tongue back in my mouth, circling a few more times.

I started to pant as I leaned back and Trent licked the glistening skin on my neck down to my first button on my flannel shirt. He slowly unbuttoned one button at a time, as my moans encouraged him to continue.

He reached for my cotton bra and slowly unhooked the front clasp, leaving my breasts to fall open to the air, my nipples immediately peaked. I moaned heavily. He then held one breast at a time and sucked on each peak until I started to squirm in his lap.

I leaned forward, grabbed his black TOOL t-shirt, and pulled it up and over his head, exposing his fully inked chest. I licked my lips in appreciation of his defined body as I unfastened his black jeans.

"I want you inside of me, Trent," I said as I slipped off his lap and pulled his jeans down. I then feverishly pulled my jeans off while Trent leaned back against the couch, admiring me. I watched his hard penis spring up as I crawled back on to his lap.

Trent licked his fingers and rubbed them against my slit. I moaned once more as I ached for him to be inside me. I was wet. I raised my hips up as he slowly held me open and entered me. His thick shaft filled me as I let out a hungry gasp.

Trent slowly pushed deeper and deeper as I began to feel like I was falling through space. He worked his cock slowly, but deeply within me.

"Oh, Trent!" I said, as I accepted it fully. Trent slipped his tongue back into my heated mouth as I grabbed his silky hair, giving it a tug. I couldn't hold out much longer. I rocked forward and backwards on his pulsating cock till I slowly released an intense orgasm.

"Oh my god, baby," I said as I closed my eyes, feeling the orgasm flush through me.

Trent was smiling and said, "Baby, it's my turn." He slid out and flipped me onto my back against the cool leather couch. He spread my legs open with his warm hands and slid himself back inside of me. I held my breath.

He fucked me so slowly as beads of sweat began to form on his forehead. I whispered to him,

"Come for me Trent, I need this. Come with me." My heart picked up its pace as Trent picked up his and we both climaxed together so hard, but so sweet. *Oh, how I needed this release after today*, I thought as I laid there holding on to Trent.

A few weeks had passed while I kept busy with my freelance work and Trent worked in his studio. Tyler continued to move forward with his therapy of an antidepressant and lyric writing. Prozac really seemed to keep Tyler's highs and lows at an even keel. He made a promise to me, but most importantly, to himself, not to take hardcore drugs. I felt so proud of him.

One evening when Trent was out with the other bandmates on his motorcycle, Tyler and I had the loft to ourselves. I decided to make a light dinner for us and play some vinyl.

Every time I was cooking up something, Tyler seemed to surface.

"Are you hungry?" I asked my skinny-as-a-bicycle friend.

"I'm marinating some chicken if you want to heat up the grill and join me?" I asked as I flipped the chicken on my dish and smothered it with olive oil.

"Yum! Fajitas! I'm so in!" Tyler squealed as he headed out to the balcony and turned on the grill. I stood there chopping peppers and singing along with Willie Nelson while he played in the background. Tyler stood on the balcony, watching the grill heat up, and lit up a joint.

"Does my music inspire you?" I hollered out towards the balcony.

"Want a hit, baby girl?" Tyler asked while he coughed after taking his first drag.

"Why... yes I do." I grabbed the peppers and the marinated chicken and headed out to the balcony.

"You know pot makes me too fucking honest," Tyler said as he handed me his burning joint. I accepted it as we both stood side by side, sharing the joint as our dinner cooked on the grill.

"Alex, I saw something about this rock and roll film coming out that's auditioning singers for its soundtrack on social media today," he said.

"Oh, yeah?" I responded as I took another hit.

"Yeah, I want to audition for it. Some amazing new director is involved, but..." He paused.

"But what?" I acted stupid like I didn't know where this conversation was headed.

"Hand me the peppers," I said as I took the dish and asked Tyler again.

"But what?" Tyler stood there and stretched.

"It's our old label auditioning singers." He put his hands in his jean pockets and looked over the balcony to the ground.

"Fuck you. The answer is no." I knew exactly what he wanted. I turned the chicken and pushed the peppers around.

"You dumped that shit label because of what that douche bag Gage Heston did to me, and now you want me to reach out to him and ask for a favor? What the fuck, Ty! Not cool." I was starting to lose my temper.

"Settle down, baby girl. Your healing process seems to be way more in control than mine, because you are not alone. I thought that after the dust settled that maybe you could ask Gage Heston for a favor for me? I really need this," Tyler pleaded.

"I'm still very hurt, Tyler. Do you remember what I looked like when I showed up at Atlanta General to visit you? Or was it because you were so fucked up that you don't remember collapsing on stage? I was bruised, I was brunette, and I had ugly clothes on. You didn't even recognize me physically, emotionally... anything. You promised me that you would leave his label that instant while I figured out a way to leave him. I was that important to you.

That man beat me down, but he never broke me," I huffed.

"That controlling piece of shit seems to keep surfacing lately—what the fuck. It's like he's haunting me!" I blew out a breath, turned off the grill, grabbed the chicken and went inside.

Tyler followed me.

"I knew it was a long shot, but I thought I would ask," Tyler sighed as he sat down at the table with me.

"That's asking a lot of me right now, Ty. That's pretty fucking selfish of you. I know you need something to jump-start WHIP again, but no, I just cannot entertain the idea of facing Gage. Please do not put me in that position." I looked down as I sliced the chicken. Tyler nodded his head and stayed quiet as we ate our dinner.

CHAPTER
5

"Guess who lined us up with a show in Houston?" Trent stood there waiting for his coffee to brew. I sat at the breakfast bar and quietly chewed my toast.

"Who?" I mumbled as I wiped my face with my napkin.

"Zack! Man, our new tour manager fucking rocks! We're splitting the bill with Gravity Kills. How insane is that?" Trent looked over his shoulder as he poured sugar into his mug.

"Hello? Did you hear me?" Trent laughed.

"Sorry hun, I heard you. When? I love that band—that'll be a kick ass show." I took a swig of my iced tea and swallowed my toast.

"Are you okay, baby?" Trent asked with sincerity.

"I'm okay. I just have a project on my mind that I need to take care of, that's all." I smiled at him as he blew me a kiss. I had a project alright. It was not work related though—it was Tyler.

"Hey, why don't you bring your sidekick to the show?" Trent suggested.

"My sidekick? It'll set off the metal detectors at the venue with a vibrator!" I started to laugh.

"Not that sidekick, you pervert. I'm talking about Nova." Trent smirked at me.

"I'll text that bitch and ask her to join me." I laughed.

"Maybe we can invite my little vibrator sidekick to our bedroom later?" I licked my lips.

"Little is right," Trent responded.

"It's a date," Trent said as he stirred his coffee as I fished around the breakfast bar for my cell phone so I could text Miss Nova.

Long time, no hear, WTF girl? I texted Nova. I immediately got a response.

How are you and the leather twins holdin up? she asked as I laughed.

Those rock stars have another gig lined up in Houston, you game? I invited her then waited for her response.

I'm game. Text me the details later. I had a long night at Vanity and man do I need my beauty sleep. I laughed as I set my cell phone down.

Ugh, good ol' Vanity. I do not miss that smokey strip club where I worked as an exotic dancer. I picked my phone back up and responded, *sluuuut.* She would get it and laugh. I set my phone back down and went searching for Tyler.

He spent a lot of time in his room alone lately.

"Hey Ty." I peered my head in his doorway.

"Hey blondie," he answered back.

"I heard y'all had a gig lined up down in Houston? Are you fucking amped?" I figured that would get his mind off the soundtrack audition and that he would be stoked to perform once again.

"I said, are you amped?" I asked for a second time.

Tyler looked up from his notepad.

"I'm fucking amped," Tyler replied sarcastically.

"What the fuck, Ty? You'll be up on stage, singing with all that swagger you've got, having all the *Whip-ettes* cream in their panties once again for you." Tyler smiled.

"I saw that frontman! I'm so excited y'all are playing a gig. And... y'all are splitting the bill with Gravity Kills, dude!" I made devil horns with my hands and waved them in the air. Tyler laughed.

"I'm nervous. I want to fly straight, but this is going to be one hell of a test for me. I'm just nervous, that's all. What if I fail?" Tyler set his pen down and leaned against his headboard.

"Fear regret and not failure," I said. "It'll be a good trial run for you. Take one gig at a time." I tried to sound encouraging.

"Live shows are a lot different from studios. Since I've been recovering and hiding out, singing live scares me a bit. I've never been like this before." Tyler's voice lowered as he confessed.

"You mean, you never performed sober? You can total-ly do this, dude. It's one show." I didn't want to rev up his anxiety level, so I dismissed the thought of telling him that it might turn into a small tour if all went well. Tyler had built up some kind of reputation in the music industry, kinda like another Scott Weiland, so the new label was watching him a bit more closely.

"Well, I'm excited for you! I'm going to bring Nova with me, so you'll at least have two groupies in the audience!" I cheered as Tyler flipped me the bird. I then rolled my eyes, turned around, and headed out of the room.

Later that evening I was lying up in the loft on my bed, curled up with Ernie, reading when Trent came home.

"Hi beautiful, I'm home," Trent hollered up the stairs towards the open loft. *I love all these little pet names he calls me like baby, cowgirl, beautiful... they all just make me smile. Anything is better than Angel.* I started laughing to myself as I recalled the stage name Vanity's smutty little manager called me when I worked at that smokey strip joint.

"What are you smiling about?" Trent asked once he reached the top of the staircase, looking in on me. "You. I'm smiling over you. I've missed you today." I set my book aside and shifted my legs.

"It's warm up here," Trent said as he headed over to the window above our bed and cracked it open.

I felt the breeze instantly blow through my hair, which gave me goosebumps.

"That's better," Trent said as he sat on the bed and began removing his Doc Martens.

"I've been thinking about you all day." He drifted his eyes up towards me.

"Oh, yeah?" I questioned him.

"Yeah." Trent tossed the boots towards the closet and turned around to face me.

"I was thinking about what you and I discussed over breakfast." I started to laugh as I pressed my knees into my chin. Trent picked up Ernie and set him down on the floor then crawled towards me.

"I've been fantasizing about opening these legs all day today at the studio." Trent pulled my knees away from my chest as he slowly opened my legs. I smiled as I watched him crawl a little closer towards me.

"I wanted to kiss your tasty lips." He leaned in and softly kissed my lips. I allowed him to give me a few kisses as I giggled.

"I wanted to taste your wet tongue." I let out a light moan as he slid his tongue into my mouth and circled my tongue a few times then pulled out.

"Oh, you taste so good," I said, as my breathing became ragged.

"What else were you thinking about?" I egged him on as the wind blew in from my window, causing my nipples to harden under my braless tank top.

Trent leaned in towards my ear and whispered, "I want to tease you with your sidekick. I want you to get wet for me, then I want to fuck you, Alexandria." His words left me breathless.

Distracted by his words, I fumbled as I reached my arm over to the nightstand, opened the drawer, and pulled out my vibrator. Trent leaned back, pulled his tee shirt over his head, and shook away his hair off his forehead.

I smiled as I leaned myself back against my black iron-rod headboard, legs still trembling as I kept them open for Trent and slowly unbuttoned my jeans. Trent grabbed two loops from my pants and pulled them down and off my legs, tossing them to the floor. I giggled.

Trent lit two candles on the opposing nightstand while I watched him shake out the burning match and run his fingers through his silky black hair. Teasing, I tossed the vibrator on the bed. Trent snatched it up and turned it on while moving cat-like towards me.

He then lightly started rubbing it up and down the out-side of my panties. I released a breath as I asked. "Is Tyler home?" I bit my lip with excitement.

"Why? Do you want him to join us?" Trent teased as I rolled my eyes and stuck out my tongue.

"No. He's not here, baby," he said quietly.

"It's just you and me, so scream as loud as you want to." He laughed.

I swallowed hard as Trent continued to slowly move the vibrator along my inner thighs until he reached my pussy once again. I cried out a little louder this time. He pulled my satin pantie outwards and slid the vibrator in. Throwing my head back in ecstasy, Trent continued to push the vibrator inside of my pussy as I started to get wet.

His rhythm was slow at first, but then he picked up the pace once I pulled on his hair, encouraging him to play harder and faster.

"I want you inside of me!" I shouted as I tried not to come on this object stroking me.

Trent whispered, "Not yet."

As he pulled the vibrator out, he then moved it slowly up under my tank top. He began rolling it over each erect nipple, then up my neck and across my lips. I just smiled back at him. I sat up, reaching for his jeans to unfasten his belt, but Trent stopped my hands, unraveled the belt himself, and reached forward for my wrists. I let out a "ummm" giving him permission to continue.

Trent wrapped both of my wrists with his belt above my head then tightened it against the iron rod headboard. I was officially turned on as Trent slid back down to my panties and tugged them off while spreading my legs a bit wider.

I cried out, "Fuck me, Trent." Trent inserted the vibrator once again into my pussy as I gyrated my hips to his thrusts.

"You're going to make me come," I shouted.

Trent then pulled the vibrator out and grabbed his erect cock as he opened my slit and began to slowly fill me with his thick shaft. My legs squeezed around him as I felt every inch sliding into me.

My hands stayed tied as I submitted myself to Trent while he fucked me harder and harder.

I started to climax as I screamed out, "Trent, you feel so amazing!" as I panted. Trent continued to fuck me as I broke myself free of the tightened belt, grabbed his tight ass, and pushed him deeper in to me.

I kept coming as Trent slowed his pace down and then rolled me over on top of him. My legs felt like noodles.

"I want you to come again, Alex," he demanded as I smiled while sweat began to drip down my back. I leaned towards Trent and licked his damp neck, breathing in his intoxicating cologne.

"I want you to come with me," I insisted as I was acting like the dominant one now as I leaned towards the night-stand and grabbed a candle off of it. I sat up and straddled Trent as I slowly dripped the hot candle wax on to his inked chest. Drip. Drip. Drip. Trent moaned in ecstasy. I trailed the wax down his chest, over his abdomen, until I reached his pubic hair. Trent grew harder as the wax turned him on.

I quickly tossed the candle, grabbed his cock, and slid back down on it.

Trent hollered out, "Fuck me, Alex, fuck me hard!" I flipped my hair back, gripped myself, and rode him hard until we both climaxed.

Afterwards, we both laid back on the bed, naked, catching our breath.

"I love fucking you," Trent said as I smiled, rolling my head in his direction. He was satisfied, and I was very pleased with that feeling.

He slowly intertwined his legs with mine, and as we relaxed we both drifted off to a much-needed sleep.

CHAPTER 6

HOUSTON

This was the weekend of the first big show WHIP was performing live once again. I had butterflies in my stomach as I helped Trent pack his bag. The guys were all going to meet over at *Head Rush*, where the tour bus was parked, then all head down to Houston in time for sound check. I was driving down separately with Nova. I didn't want to crowd my guys, plus I needed a little time with my girlfriend. All the male hormones were smothering me.

Nova arrived at the loft that afternoon. I was chilling on our balcony when I heard a banging on my front door.

"Hey Mama, let me in!" Nova was here.

"Hold on, girl, I'm coming!" I raced to the door, opened it, and both of us just screamed as we hugged each other.

"It's been too long, bitch. I've missed you so much!" Nova squealed. I just held her for a minute. Nova was one wild, uncontrollable, independent woman whom I'd come to adore.

"I've missed you too." I stepped back to take a good look at my friend.

"Come in, come see my loft." I took her hand and walked

her into the place.

"Wow! Girl, this is definitely a step up from that dump in Deep Ellum!" Nova's eyes widened as she looked around in appreciation. "I figured I would be walking into a dungeon of some sort with that damn metal cage that we danced in at WHIP's show set up in the middle of the living room."

I laughed. "Nah, the only thing metal in this place is my headboard, which I'm tied to every once in a while." Nova laughed.

"You and Trent are a pretty hot ticket eh?" Blushing, I laughed once again.

"Oh that man, he's so good to me, Nova." Nova nodded in agreement.

"I see you still have your shadow living here as well." Nova walked over and peeked into our spare bedroom that Tyler was now occupying.

"He's healing. It's been an emotional rollercoaster for our frontman. Between Olivia breaking his heart, overcoming addiction, figuring out his role in life—it's just been pretty tough for him," I defended my fragile best friend.

"Please." Nova rolled her eyes.

"I'm glad he has you, girl. No one else could take this shit from him." I just swallowed and realized that she was right.

"Are you ready to hit the road?" Nova asked.

"I'd like to get to the hotel, get gussied up, hit the bar, then head to the show if that's alright with you?" I agreed to the plan.

"Let me grab my bag, feed Ernie, and lock up. I really need this night out, girl." Nova smiled.

"Me too, girl, me too." I agreed.

Heading on to the interstate in Nova's Mercedes, I toiled with the radio as she kicked the car into gear.

"Yeehaw! See ya later, Dallas!" I hollered as I looked outside my passenger-side window, watching the city fall behind us. Pearl Jam's song "Yellow Ledbetter" came on and Nova started singing,

"On a ceiling, I hung there as if I was wasted. I saw her and I wanted to leave." I started to laugh uncontrollably.

"Girl, what are you singing? Those are not the lyrics!" Nova sang a little louder.

"No one knows the lyrics. I doubt Eddie even knows the actual lyrics!" I shook my head in agreement. *Nova always sings songs incorrectly—hums to her own tune.* I just went along with it.

A few hours later, we arrived at the five-star hotel in Houston.

"We're here!" Nova let out a breath as she put the car in park right in front of the valet stand.

"Good afternoon," the valet said as he opened my passenger door.

"Hi sugar!" I responded as I hopped out of the car and stretched for a moment as I glanced around at the beautiful hotel.

Waterfalls were on both sides of the entrance sliding doors to soothe the travelers as they walked into the hotel.

"I'm here," I mumbled under my breath as my stomach did a quick somersault.

"Grab your bag, girl," Nova directed me. I retrieved my bag and followed her into the hotel's check-in counter. Nova grabbed the hotel key and waved it in front of me.

"Ready?" she asked.

"Ready," I replied as we made our way over to the set of gold elevators.

"What a stunning room!" I praised the room in amazement as I looked around at the two king-sized beds and the to-die-for view of downtown Houston.

"Only the best for my best girl." Nova walked up behind me and put her arms around me. I swayed with her until she spun me around and kissed my lips, making a loud smacking noise.

"Want some X while we get ready?" she squealed.

"Sure." I shrugged my shoulders as I laid down on the plush cream-colored bed comforter. Nova tossed a colored pill at my head as I caught it, sniffed it, and swallowed it.

"See y'all later," I said as Nova laughed while almost spitting out her water as she swallowed her ecstasy pill.

Within one hour we were in our black mini dresses, black studded leather high heels, and red lipstick.

Nova brushed my hair as I threw my head back.

"That feels so amazing." I grinned as goosebumps flashed along my arm.

"Everything feels amazing on X, girl." Nova smacked my butt with the brush.

"Yeah, that's the point. Let's head down to the hotel bar. Are you ready?" she asked as I reached for my perfume, misted my wrists and neck, then grabbed my studded clutch.

"I'm ready sluuut," I laughed as I rolled my tongue behind my teeth.

Nova took my hand in hers as we headed to the hotel's downstairs bar.

We sat on mahogany high-back bar stools just gabbing like two schoolgirls. I missed partying with Nova.

"Hey girl, hot man alert. My pussy is getting all moist." She took a swig of her drink and pointed to the young man walking towards the bar. He had sandy blonde hair, a nice build, and incredible blue eyes. I laughed as I looked over my shoulder.

"You're nasty, girl. Every man gets you wet. The valet driver probably gave you an instant orgasm. You're worse than the band with their groupies!" I smacked her bare leg.

"He's behind you." She nodded to me.

I swiveled my stool around to see who it was and smiled.

"Hi Zack," I greeted the good-looking guy as Nova tapped my hand with excitement.

"Oh, Zack, this is my girl Nova." He extended his hand to shake Nova's hand.

"Nova, this is Zack. He's WHIP's new tour manager," I said as I winked at Zack.

"Hi girls!" Zack greeted us.

"I wanted to check and see if you are all set for tickets and backstage passes?" he asked while shuffling around in his interior jacket pocket.

"Yes on the tickets, no on the passes." I blushed just thinking about touching his athletic chest. I wanted to touch everything possible on ecstasy. He fished out two passes, then set them on the bar.

"Big night tonight," he said as we both nodded yes as we undressed Zack with our prying eyes.

"Well, I got the drinks," he said to the bartender as he slapped some cash down on the bar.

We replied, "Thanks dude," in unison.

Zack smiled then said, "I better be heading over to the venue. I need to check the band's rider once more and make sure no liquor is stocked in Tyler Black's dressing room." I frowned.

"He'll be alright," I reassured Zack as he let out a deep breath.

"See you girls after the show?" he asked as he turned to head out.

"I'll make sure of it!" Nova hollered after him.

I just sank into the barstool and pouted.

"No pouting, princess." Nova pinched my side.

"Stop worrying so much about fucking Tyler. He's such a drag." She rolled her eyes as she knew exactly what was on my mind. *He's got more damage than a soul should ever see,* I thought to myself. I then elected to keep my mouth shut; there was no use bringing Nova into another conversation about Tyler—she just didn't care.

"I have to pee," I said to her as I slid off the bar stool and headed to the restroom.

Fixing my lipstick in the restroom mirror, I bobbed my head to the house music playing in the bar.

I was excited to be with Nova again and to see my favorite band tonight. I was in a good mood. I smoothed out my dress, checked myself in the mirror one last time, then headed back to the bar.

When I returned to Nova, I noticed the back of a man wearing a navy pin-striped business suit and my jaw dropped open. It couldn't be? My good mood just perished into thin air as I stopped in my tracks. I'm assuming my eyes must have been the size of two giant soup bowls as Nova waved me over, giggling wide-eyed herself as she pointed to the man laughing.

"Look who's in H-town Alex? Good ol' G-man!" Nova motioned for me to sit down. The man stood up, turned around, and faced me. It was Gage Heston.

"Hello Alexandria Leigh Rae." he said as I stood there blinking my lashes.

"The label tells me good things about your design skills. I'm very proud of you." He let those words melt on his tongue like sugar.

"I'm very grateful to the label, Gage—you know that—and of course I'll do my best when it pertains to my work," I said as he frowned at me. *What? Was my bashing every rose on display in his condo a too subtle of a goodbye for him? What did he want? A fucking thank-you and a 'good riddance' note from me?*

He interrupted my toxic train of thought as he said, "Well, at least you're grateful to the label unlike those pretty boy rockstar boyfriends you seem to still run around with." I rolled my eyes as I shifted my weight in my heels. He always hated Tyler Black.

"I've been thinking a lot about you lately. I've missed you. I'm truly sad that we never got to say goodbye in Miami," he huffed under his breath as he tried to sound sincere. Nova gave me an empathetic look as I dismissed her. *Gage doesn't have a sincere bone in his body.* My own body started to tense up as I tried to digest the words 'I've missed you' as Nova got up, pulled on my arm, and tried to get me to sit down.

"Nova, we better get going." I pulled my arm away from her.

"Gage, here's my Miami goodbye." I flipped him the middle finger as she waved me off. Gage let out a deep laugh.

"Still classy, eh?" he said.

"Still leaving!" I grabbed my clutch a little tighter.

Gage hadn't changed. He was still tall, dark, chiseled, and forbidden. I could not face this demon on a bean tonight. I just could not handle him. The bad girl within me, however, wanted to trace the pinstripes on his pants with my tongue even though he was still the enemy. That's really what the drugs wanted me to do, but I needed to stay focused and get my butt back over to the band and away from this asshole.

"Do you need a lift to the concert venue?" he asked politely as I snapped my thoughts back to reality. I started to shift my weight once more in my heels as I flashed Nova the dirtiest look.

"We'd love a ride, G-man." Nova accepted his offer as she gulped the last of her drink down and hopped to her feet.

"No," I mouthed to Nova.

Gage finished his usual drink on the rocks, set the glass on the bar and said, "Let's go," as he took Nova's hand. *Why does she fall mouth first on to any man wearing a dress suit? She cannot control her inner stripper.* This was not cool. My temper was fuming. My heart was racing. My thoughts suddenly shifted to Tyler and the fact that HE needed me tonight: not Gage, not Nova, just my best friend Tyler. I followed the two of them hand in hand out of the bar as we headed to the valet station.

Climbing into his car, I felt sick. My emotions were

swirling all around me. Anger towards Nova. Unknown guilt towards Gage. Worry for Tyler. I just wanted to go home. I didn't like this game anymore.

"Why are you going to the show tonight, Gage?" Nova asked him as she flirted while she rubbed his arm as he put his car in drive. I rolled my eyes as I looked out of the back seat window. I couldn't help noticing Gage staring at me through the rearview mirror every ten seconds.

"I'm handling Gravity Kills," he answered. *Of course he is*, I thought to myself. Looking down, I watched my heel dig a hole into his new car's carpet as I continuously kept rubbing my legs. That label of his sure had a long roster of clients. I reflected for a moment. WHIP's new label wasn't as big; it was considered an indie label amongst the musicians.

"Good for you," I mumbled under my breath.

"What's that?" Gage asked as he glanced once again into the rearview mirror at me.

"Nothing," I responded.

"WHIP is very happy with their new label," I said. Bam! One jab for me.

"They're a small label, right? What's their name again?" he responded sarcastically. Bam! One jab for Gage. He was right. WHIP was starting over now with the branded bad boy reputation Tyler had built for himself. No big label wanted to deal with his shit—this was why Tyler was so wound up about proving himself. This was why he wanted the fucking soundtrack. I suddenly felt guilty. Once again, the all-to-familiar guilt feeling was consuming my breathing space.

CHAPTER
7

As we arrived at the artist's entrance, I thanked god we made it as I watched Nova primp herself in the mirror then get out of the car. I'm still pissed at the fact that she let Gage drive us here but, it is what it is. I'll just sideline the pure hatred for him tonight so I can support Tyler; keep your friends close and your enemies closer was the mantra of the night.

So, I mustered up a smile as Gage opened my door. I was relieved to be at the venue.

"Here you ladies go, VIP service," he said with a sardonic smile. He then took my hand and helped me out of the car. I just swallowed my smile.

"It was a pleasure to see you girls again," he hollered towards us as Nova and I hooked arm in arm, making our way to the backstage door. I ignored him.

Opening the artist's entrance door, a hefty security guard with a shaved head and a teardrop tattoo under his eye checked our tickets and passes then motioned for us to come into the building.

Entering the venue, I could hear the crowd's chatter as

Nova squeezed my arm.

"It looks like the VIP section is over there to the right," she yelled loudly as she pointed at an area of seats just right of the front of the house console that was sectioned off with red velvet rope.

"I want to grab a drink first," Nova hollered at me.

"Want anything?" I shook my head no. Beans were all I could handle at the moment.

Alone, I made my way to my seat, adjusted my black cocktail dress then took in a deep breath. I paused. *I'm finally here. I'm not going to let the sight of Mr. Gage Heston rattle me tonight.* WHIP was too important to me. It was, however, inevitable that I would run into that man sooner or later.

As I glanced towards the stage, I saw WHIP's banner hanging from the lighting rig. I still loved that logo I created for the band. I patted myself on the back, kudos to me.

The house lights remained on as the stagehands kept working tirelessly as they wrapped cable, adjusted the drum kit, and tested the microphones. I just watched in awe, a thankless job.

Just then Nova was excusing herself as she pushed past everyone in our aisle with her drink in her hand. "Okay, Mama, I'm back." She sat down out of breath.

"So, it looks like our boys are up first!" She cleared her throat as she took a swig of her drink, acting like catching a ride with Gage Heston was nothing but normal. I dismissed it.

"Yep," I agreed as I watched fans wave their signs and blow whistles with their fingers.

Suddenly, there was a tap on my left shoulder.

"Alexandria?" I turned around and another security guard with a headset on asked if I could follow him. "What do you need? Am I in trouble?" I asked as I stood up and looked at Nova, shrugging my shoulders.

"Mr. Black needs to speak with you," he said with his deep voice.

"Tyler?" I asked as I handed my clutch to Nova and followed the gentleman towards the backstage dressing room.

Walking into the 'singers only' dressing room, I felt a chill roll down my spine. Tyler was sitting shirtless on a chair, hand in his hair, staring into the mirror on the vanity while tapping his foot.

"Ty?" I whispered.

"Hey blondie." He leaned back while continuing to tap his foot on the floor. His bag was opened on the vanity with dress scarves spilling out, bits of clothing were scattered everywhere, and Tyler was not dressed.

"Um, dude, you guys are first on the bill. You need to get ready," I said as I walked over to the suitcase and pulled a scarf out. I threw it around Tyler's neck, leaned in and gave him a kiss on the lips. Tasting like an ashtray, he laughed as he reached for the scarf and gave it a slight tug.

I suddenly dropped to my knees in between his legs and grabbed his arm.

"What is this?!" My eyes started to well up.

"Are you cutting, Tyler?" I asked frantically.

"Self-mutilation is not a very sexy accessory," I said in shock as I stared at the blood-dried red slits on his inner arm. I did not want to shame him; I was just concerned. He just pursed his lips and shook his head.

"I needed some relief from my emotional pain. Plus, all this pressure to perform at my best tonight. I do not want to be rejected," Tyler said with a lurking sense of sadness while rubbing his arm. This was more than I could take. I grabbed his hand that was rubbing his wrist and kissed it.

"You won't be rejected, Ty. You should see some of the cheesy signs I read that your fans are waving around out there. Lord Jesus, those *Whip-ettes* are horny!" I said with enthusiasm as Tyler smiled.

"My beautiful best friend, you are not alone tonight. I'm here. No cocaine, no pills, no alcohol was invited to this party. You can totally do this straight edge. Fuck it, just put it all out there!" I was trying to encourage him as I lied, knowing X was invited to mine.

I stood myself up and walked over to Tyler's suitcase and pulled out a white V-neck t-shirt and slipped it over his head. I then grabbed two more black scarves and wrapped them around his neck.

"Sexy!" I blew an air kiss at him.

"Yum! You look like Steven Tyler now," I purred as he started to laugh once more.

I began humming "Sweet Emotion" as I grabbed a few leather punk rock bracelets off the vanity and slid them over his wrists to cover the small cuts on his inner arm.

"Oh, one final touch." I reached for his black eyeliner and applied it to his sad eyes.

"Fucking hot," I reassured him as I kissed his pouty lips once more. He stood up, took a look in the mirror, and stuck his tongue out.

"Not bad, blondie, not bad." He smiled as he ran his

hands through his hair once more.

Suddenly, there was a knock on the door that startled us both.

"It's okay," I said as I squeezed Tyler's arm, "I'll get it." I opened the door while the stage manager was standing there holding his walkie talkie.

"Is Mr. Black ready? I need WHIP up in five." I smiled and turned around to face Tyler.

"Looks like you're up, rockstar!" He nodded his head as I mouthed okay to the stage manager and closed the door.

"I'm going to go find my seat so I can watch the show. I'll be right back here when you are finished. You've so got this, Mr. Black." I was boosting his confidence as I gave him one last kiss and headed back to my seat.

The house lights dimmed and the crowd roared. I stood up, clapping my hands as Nova whistled.

A haunting melody drifted from the amplifiers out over the audience. The crowd silenced. Soft lighting lit up the Korg Triton as Trent played. My cheeks flushed as Nova poked my arm with her elbow. I just stood there staring at Trent, listening to this mystical, eerie intro WHIP created.

Then, my wounded friend walked out on stage. The crowd erupted once again. He gripped his microphone while my heart raced as I held my breath, waiting for his mouth to open.

He began singing, *"You drained my heart..."* I let out the breath I was holding. Once again, he sounded so painfully beautiful.

"Wait, I know this song, Nova!" I nudged her back.

"It's 'Betrayal.' Oh my god, he made that poem I found rolled into a ball an actual song. I can't believe it! It sounds so beautifully haunting." Nova shook her head yes as she listened.

"*Every time I run back to you, you'd just slit my wrists again*," the song went on as Tyler's vocal chords stretched a little higher.

"*Burn the memories... Burn the love... Burn what made us, us.*" He continued to belt out.

The fans must have agreed with me that this song was amazing because the screaming and clapping continued, and I knew at that moment that their appreciation would feed Tyler's bruised ego.

"My god girl, Tyler looks sexy." Nova licked her lips. I laughed. I then glanced over at Trent and my pulse started to race.

"That is sexy to me!" I pointed to Trent playing the keyboards. She laughed.

"I know, Alex, but he's spoken for." I smiled.

"He is so good to me," I said with appreciation. I knew that the man playing the keyboards was a confident, gifted musician as well as a tender, pleasing lover and that he was all mine. I stood there, shoulders back, head up high, and proudly watched the two loves of my life perform.

When WHIP's set came to a close, I grabbed Nova's hand and headed once again to the backstage area.

As we made our way through the clutter of road cases, stage crew members, and backstage guests, I found Tyler standing there drinking his bottle of water. He quickly tossed the water in a bin, ran over to meet me, picked me up and swung me around.

"I did it, Alex!" he screamed as he was so amped up. This was the Tyler I knew.

"Oh my god, you were amazing!" I said as he hugged me once more.

"Dude, 'Betrayal'... are you kidding me? You couldn't have picked a better opener!" I sang in a high-pitched voice.

"That was a surprise for you." Tyler smiled.

"A surprise for your fans! They fucking loved it!" I was so elated to see Tyler excited again. He was on a pure endorphin high right now, and so was I now that Molly had left the building.

We continued to celebrate as Gage Heston walked up to us and congratulated Tyler as he reached out his hand to shake Tyler's hand.

"You sounded real good out there, my friend. Too bad we had to part ways." Tyler glanced over at me.

"Thanks Gage," he gulped as he returned the handshake.

"Well, I need to check on Gravity Kills. I'm trying to decide if this is the right band for the film soundtrack we're producing. See ya." He grimaced as he walked away.

"Bam! Another jab for Gage Heston," I muttered.

"What are you talking about?" Tyler looked intensely at me. I let out a long huff.

"Gage and I are having this verbal boxing match tonight."

Tyler put up his hand. "Wait, you spoke to him?"

I pouted. "He gave me and Nova a ride to the venue. Please do not tell Trent. That fucking bitch Nova accepted a ride from him, and I'm not very happy about it, but I'll deal with her later. Again, please don't tell Trent!" I pleaded once more.

"I won't baby girl, but are you okay?" he asked with sincerity.

"I'm okay. Let's drop it." Tyler nodded as I just stared off at the band members in a group huddle all chatting amongst themselves.

I shook my body, releasing all the bad vibes Gage left on me, then headed over to see the rest of WHIP. They were all in their notorious black clothing and black eyeliner, celebrating what a success the show had been. These guys had been patiently waiting for another live gig as Tyler went through rehabilitation. What a relief to everyone, including Zack, the new tour manager. The new label would be thrilled about tonight's performance. Trent turned around as I approached him from behind.

"There she is!" Trent smiled as he opened his arms and wrapped himself so tightly around me. I just melted as I inhaled sweat and cologne.

"You're all sticky!" I laughed as I looked up at him, pushing aside a strand of wet black hair behind his ear. He leaned in and kissed me with his warm, wet tongue. I stood there accepting his tongue and returned his affection with twice as much intensity.

"Yum." Trent smiled as I peppered his mouth with light kisses.

"I wish I could make love to you right now," he whispered in my ear as I blushed.

"You were amazing tonight, baby. What a thrill, huh?" He shook his head in agreement and just gleefully smiled.

"Tyler did it," he said with relief.

"No, WHIP did it," I corrected him as I smiled at the band.

Just then, Zack made his way over to his band and distracted Trent as I stood beside him, tightly gripping his hand, watching Gage from a distance talk to his band Gravity Kills.

"Hey baby"—Trent interrupted my toxic train of thought—"the band is going to head back to the hotel. Some of the guys are heading to a party. Tyler is heading back to his room. Are you up for a late dinner, just the two of us?" He asked me while he nodded his head in Nova's direction who was hanging on Zack, yearning for his affection. I laughed.

"I'll dump the broad. It'll be just you and me at the hotel restaurant," I assured him. He kissed me softly one last time as we parted ways with a promise to meet at the hotel restaurant.

CHAPTER
8

I walked into the quaint restaurant alone, asking the host for a table for two. He led me to a table by the window covered in white linen with a candle lit in the middle. I smiled as I welcomed the peaceful setting, thanking him while he pulled out my chair. He handed me a menu and placed one down for Trent. I leaned back and gazed out the window at the bustling city of Houston. I was spent—Gage, Nova, and Tyler all depleted my energy tonight. I needed a quiet dinner to help me unwind.

As soon as I settled in, I noticed Trent standing at the host stand looking for me. I waved him over to our table.

"You clean up nice," I complimented him.

"A shower felt good," he said as he reached for my hand.

"How are you holdin' up, cowgirl?" he asked as I squeezed his hand in return.

"I'm famished," I said.

Just then the waiter stopped by the table and set down two glasses of wine. We ordered a light dinner, then I picked up my glass and raised it to toast.

"To WHIP." He grinned.

"To WHIP, we did it. Thank you for being here," he replied. I blushed as I took a sip of wine, feeling its warmth comforting me.

"I mean it, Alex, thank you. I know Tyler needed you, and I did not want to crowd him tonight." I blinked.

"And..." He lingered on the *and* part.

"And, I know Gage was there tonight, which could not have been easy for you." Trent sipped his wine, waiting for a response.

"It was inevitable. I was bound to run into Gage Heston again, Trent." I quickly dismissed the 'Gage conversation' at our dinner and continued. "But, Tyler... I'm getting motion sickness from this emotional rollercoaster he is on."

Trent let out a slight laugh.

"I mean, he was cutting tonight." My eyes welled up as Trent's hand covered his mouth in disbelief. "Yes, my best friend was looking for some relief from his emotional pressures. He was hurting himself to feel anything but his own tormented feelings. That's so fucked up, Trent, and it's really scaring me." I wanted to be open with Trent about Tyler. He was the only one juggling both of us in Louisiana—me with my emotional and physical wounds and Tyler with his addiction.

"I thought we were getting past all this." I started to cry as Trent stood up, walked over to my side of the table, knelt down and wiped my tears.

"Baby, this takes time," he said.

"What does?" I interrupted him.

"Healing." He kissed my forehead, then slid back into his dining chair.

"It took a long time till I was able to forgive my father and the bullshit he put my family through. We were living in a house of pain for years. Look, Tyler has come this far. He did the work, he went through detox, he started Prozac, he made it through his first live set in eight months. Give him some credit. Tyler needs to redefine success." I nodded as I sniffled in agreement.

"He is also nursing a broken heart," I said quietly.

"Everybody at one point or another has had a fucking broken heart. It's just all the people he's worried about disappointing. He needs to focus within, not just on the fucking frontman persona." Trent took another sip of his wine.

"I agree." I sat there with my hands folded in my lap.

"Hey," he said as I looked up.

"You're doing an amazing job yourself, baby. You've broken free of the chains that bind you, you got this kick ass job, you dumped that smut pedaling club you worked for." He paused.

"You have me." His voice lowered as he scratched his head and looked out the window.

I looked up, batting my lashes.

"I have you." I felt a sense of calm wash over me. He let out a breath as he pushed my plate a little closer to me.

"Here, eat something, baby. Then we'll head upstairs, hit the hay and head back to Dallas in the morning." I smiled as I picked my fork up and stabbed a piece of broccoli.

Trent kissed me at my hotel room door, then turned and pushed the button for the elevator.

"I'm going to check on Tyler for you." I smiled, then waved as he walked into the elevator.

"See you in Dallas," I said.

"See you at home, baby," he said as I blew him a kiss, then opened the door to mine and Nova's room.

Walking in, I was taken aback when I heard a man laughing. Zack jumped up off of Nova's bed and began pulling up his jeans in a hurry. I rolled my eyes.

"Hi guys, good night guys. I'm bushed." I landed face down on my bed, kicked my heels off, and tried to go to sleep. Nova giggled as she walked Zack naked to the door and said her goodbyes.

"Holy shit girl! That man is something else!" she whistled as she leaned against the door.

"I really don't want to know right now, girl. I'm fucking exhausted. Tyler drained me tonight." Nova rolled her eyes as she crawled back into her bed.

"Okay, we'll talk about this whole evening on the ride home," she said as I gave her the thumbs up and passed out.

The next morning, Nova was casting a shadow over me as she held a cup of coffee in her hand.

"Hey, sleeping beauty, it's time to get up."

I moaned, "Officer nooooo." Nova laughed, clearing her throat. I then rolled over and tried to focus on her. Nova was back in last night's cocktail dress, smeared liner, and holding my cup of joe.

"Thank you," I said as I sat up and rubbed my eye while taking the coffee from her hand.

"Zack? Nova, come on!" I groaned.

"I couldn't help myself," she laughed as she sat on the bed.

"Are you ready to head back to Dallas?" I nodded my head yes as I took a much needed sip of coffee.

"Do the guys need a lift?" she asked nicely.

"No. But maybe Gage Heston can give them a lift," I said sarcastically with an attitude.

"Oh, I'm so sorry about that, Alex. I really am. What a bonehead move on my part. I was flirting and trying to smooth everything over between y'all. I'm truly sorry. Do you forgive me, girl?" Nova blinked her lashes as she asked for forgiveness. I then stuck my tongue out at her and just dismissed it.

"No, the guys are good. They are taking the tour bus back to Dallas after their gear gets loaded up this morning." I took another sip of my coffee.

"Okay then, let's do this walk of shame in last night's dresses, girl." Nova hopped up.

"No walk of shame for me, girl. Zack?" I had to harp one more time.

"Yes, Zack." She smacked my foot as I swung my feet around to slide off the bed.

Once I arrived back at my loft, no one was home. *The guys must be unloading their equipment*, I thought, so I flipped on the kitchen light and found Ernie sitting on the breakfast bar as he meowed his hello.

"Hi Ern." I dropped my bag as I walked over to pet my cat, check his litter box, and then headed straight to the shower.

Opening the bathroom door to let out the steam, I heard the door slam and a grunt come from downstairs as I scurried to the loft to look over. Tyler was walking into his room.

"Ty?" I hollered down.

"It's just me, Alex. I'm so exhausted!" he moaned as he flopped onto the bed.

"Where's Trent?" I asked.

"Um, he's with Zack having coffee. I think they're lining things up for a radio interview or something?" "Good," I yelled back downstairs.

"Come here!" he whined. I slipped on my jogging pants and my Depeche Mode t-shirt and headed down to Tyler's room.

Standing in the doorway of the room, I smiled as I looked at my best friend spread out on the bed.

"Baby girl, I did it." He let out a sigh.

"I feel like I have a fucking hangover even though I had nothing to fucking drink." Tyler rolled into a fetal position on the bedspread, exhausted.

I saw the small red cuts on his inner arm starting to scab over as I sat down gently on the bed.

"Move over, string bean," I demanded as I pushed his hips out of the way. I crawled into bed and curled up with Tyler, holding him as the two of us drifted off to sleep.

Later that week, Zack had a radio interview all set up for WHIP. Their record was still selling even after Tyler's collapse on stage, WHIP breaking the major label's contract and signing with a smaller Indie label out of Austin. These boys were hell-bound on making WHIP a success.

I decided that I wanted to tag along since my projects

were all completed for work that week and I needed a break. Trent texted me the address as I grabbed my purse and headed out to my truck.

Pulling into the radio station parking lot, I turned off the ignition and let out a breath. I opened the door and instantly saw red. It wasn't the color of my truck I was fixating on, it was Gage Heston.

He was standing outside the station talking on his cell phone. He was still flaunting his expensive business attire, the typical dark gray suit to complement the dark eyes and his dark soul. I frowned as I slammed my truck door.

Gage then looked over at me, ended his call, and walked towards me,

"I thought you might show up here." He flashed me a grin. *Why does he toy with my emotions? I cannot take this shit on right now.* One basket-case to deal with was all I could handle at the moment.

"What are you smiling about?" I asked him as he moved a little closer, invading my personal space as I leaned against Axl, trying to give us some distance.

"This ugly truck—can't seem to let this beast go, huh?" He frowned at my truck as I laughed and tapped my truck with gratitude.

"I wanted a moment alone with you so I could tell you that I really regret how I treated you in Miami." He shoved his cell phone into his interior jacket pocket as I let out a "Ha" and rolled my eyes. Did his guilt finally catch up to him?

"I tried to change you into something you are not, and I apologize, Alexandria." He stepped toward me as I looked to the ground.

"I can do it right this time. Look at you, you're all grown up. I have to admit I must have been some kind of influence on you," he said proudly as he lifted my chin with his hand and stared into my eyes. "Apology noted," I muttered as he laughed just to relieve his own guilt.

"I gave you a job, and I even let your pretty boyfriends out of their contract without a fucking lawsuit; that should count for something, eh?" I brushed his hand away from my face.

"Look, Tyler really performed well the other night. If he keeps it up, I can do so much more for him." He was dangling Tyler's career right out in front of me.

I paused for a second then asked, "What about this film you are involved with?" I wanted to ask for my best friend who was trying to rebuild his image. Gage squeezed my arm a little too tight for my liking.

"Are we making a deal?" he inquired slyly as I rubbed my arm, feeling a bit queasy. I knew the old Gage would show up again.

"Call me so we can have dinner. You know, discuss Tyler, see where things go." I bit my lower lip as Gage stepped back and headed for his car. *I cannot let him slither back into my life. He's just too toxic.*

I shamed myself for even standing there listening to some lame apology. I paused for a moment then locked the truck and headed into the radio station.

Upon entering the building, I saw Tyler leaning against the fire extinguisher in the hallway as I walked up to him.

"We just saw Gage, girl," Tyler said as he fished in his pocket for a cigarette.

"I seem to see him more now that we're not dating than I ever did when we were dating!" I huffed. "Here, step outside with me so I can have a smoke." I nodded as I turned around to follow Tyler outside.

Leaning against the building, I shyly said, "He apologized for how he treated me in Miami, dude." Tyler lit up his cigarette then inhaled a puff.

"He did? Are y'all cool with each other now?" He was hopeful for himself, not really for me.

"Are we cool!? Please, that man is so toxic—like those fucking frogs, toxic!" I shook my head in disbelief.

"Ribbit," Tyler said as he blew out smoke.

"That man has always been a frog, a toad, what have you, never a fucking prince." I pouted as I kicked the brick wall with my cowboy boot. Grabbing Tyler's cigarette out of his hand, I inhaled it.

"Ribbit," I responded as Tyler laughed and took back his cigarette.

"You wanna get out of here?" he asked as he tossed his cigarette and stomped it out with his boot.

"What about the radio interview?" I asked nervously.

"Ahh… the boys can handle it," Tyler said as he stretched and put his arm around me.

"There's a tattoo shop next door. Let's go check it out!" I wrapped my arm around Tyler's waist as we headed to the tattoo shop.

CHAPTER
9

"I want wings!" I shouted as I traced the outline of a sketch of angel wings hanging on the wall.

This tattoo shop was definitely an artist's dream.

"Look at all these drawings!" My eyes were about to plop out onto the floor one by one as I stood there admiring all the art.

"I want a piercing!" Tyler hollered over to me from the black leather bench he was seated on, leaning against a wall smothered in band posters.

"What's wrong with the piercings you've got?" I asked while a petite redhead with tight leggings and heavy cleavage nervously approached Tyler asking for his autograph. I laughed.

"I want my tongue pierced." Tyler stuck out his tongue to his fan as he signed her *Revolver* magazine. She smiled and scurried out the front door.

"Ooo, that'll be sexy, Ty. Do I have the honor to kiss you first with it?" Nothing screams sexy like a silver barbell pierced right through the middle of your tongue. I laughed at the image.

"No one else but you, blondie, I promise!" Tyler said as he jumped to his feet just as the body piercer stuck his head out from behind a black curtain, asking who was next.

"Me bro," Tyler said as he turned and gave me the devil horns. I giggled as I stood there still trying to decipher if I wanted ink. This would be something I would definitely talk to Trent about since he rocked the most ink. The wings could symbolize that I was free just like Trent reminded me after making love to me on Valentine's Day. *That I am free… free to make my own damn decisions.*

I blushed, never feeling so alive.

Tyler walked back out to the lobby waving cleaning instructions in his hand.

"Wow! That was quick!" I said as I stood on my tippy toes, trying to open Tyler's mouth.

"Let me see!" I demanded as Tyler opened his mouth and I traced the little silver barbell in the middle of his warm, swollen tongue.

"I like it, Ty." I licked my lips.

"Yeah?" he asked, looking for a vote of confidence.

"Yeah," I agreed as I licked my lips once more and pulled my hand away from his mouth.

We then made our way back to the radio station where WHIP had already finished the first half of their two-part interview.

"Where the fuck did you go dude?" the drummer yelled out as Tyler and I approached the band standing outside taking a quick break.

"You have obligations, dude." The bass player chastised Tyler as well.

"Ob-li-gations..." Tyler rolled his eyes. I skipped over to Trent.

"Hi baby." He leaned down and kissed my chapped lips.

"Where did you guys go?" He was concerned. I stuck my tongue out, then pointed over at Tyler.

"The tattoo shop next door," I said as Trent shook his head.

"Zack is trying real hard to keep this band on track. He set up this interview, so we need to have Tyler in there, babe." I blinked my lashes, feeling guilty.

"Alright," I said with a heavier than usual southern accent.

"He was okay. He was with only me. Just go back into the station and make him do all the talking this time," I said as I nudged Trent.

"Punish him by making him talk with his freshly pierced numb tongue as it drools all over their microphone." Trent started to laugh as he gathered up the guys and they went back into the station to finish up part two of WHIP's interview.

"I didn't see his face. I saw yours," Trent said, standing in our kitchen. I gulped as I took the orange juice out of the refrigerator and set it on the counter. My heart just spilled out onto the floor as I turned around to face him. I was so busted, as I knew exactly what he was referring to.

Like an idiot, I stood in the radio station parking lot listening to Gage's pathetic apology when I shouldn't have even been giving him anything but my middle finger again. Trent shook his head in disappointment as he turned and headed straight for the bedroom stairs.

Pausing, he turned back around and said, "Be careful there. Just remember what that man put you through, Alex. I wouldn't give that asshole the time of day. You know how he is and how he can make you feel so small and so insecure. He just dangles that graphic design work in front of you, and it's really kind of hard for me not to interfere with your work," he said as he turned and walked up the stairs.

I poured myself a glass of orange juice as I heard Trent holler from the bedroom, "But, I will not entertain the idea of you having any other form of a relationship with Gage Heston. Got it? Tyler is one thing for me to handle, but not Gage. Not now, not ever," he said as he looked over the loft down at me as I took my juice and slumped onto the barstool feeling guilty.

"Got it," I mumbled under my breath. I allowed Gage Heston to once again weed his way through my life somehow tonight. I was inconsiderate of Trent's feelings. It was so pitiful how I could be so solipsistic at times.

The next morning when I awoke, I rolled over to an empty bed. No Trent. The cat wasn't even there to show me warmth. The loft was empty.

I wondered if my heart was really in the right place. I questioned myself. My pathetic plan was really to keep Gage at arm's length so I could continue my design projects for some of his musician clients, but I also really wanted to help WHIP with the possibility of landing the movie soundtrack. The guys really needed the boost, and Tyler's guilt at hurting the band's image destroyed him.

My feelings set aside, should I blame Tyler for his state of fragility as he tried to rebuild his rockstar image? I longed to help him. Was that really so bad? Even if Gage was involved, I felt like I could somehow handle him this time around. I contemplated my empathy for Tyler when suddenly, there was a text alert on my cell phone from Trent:

Pack your bag, cowgirl. We're going to a Memorial Day party at the lake. I paused.

Remembering WHIP's guitarist owned a cabin at the lake, I texted back, *Good. Sounds like fun. Y'all need a break.* I pushed send.

Trent replied, *No break, WHIP is celebrating! We've got a ten city tour lined up with Gravity Kills. Zack is the man!* I gulped.

I knew it wasn't Zack. It knew it wasn't even Tyler's amazing vocal performance the other night in Houston. It was all Gage Heston; he was pushing the band away from me so he could slither back in. *That's fucking awesome! I'll pack the party hats! HA HA,* I responded.

I wasn't going to deflate all the air out of Trent's balloon; I was going to let him enjoy this.

Meet me at the studio at six...baby I'm so excited! I agreed as I set the phone down and headed for the closet to pack a bag.

Six p.m. sharp I pulled into *Head Rush* and saw Trent rolling his motorcycle into the studio. I parked and waited while I tapped my hands on the steering wheel, singing L.A. Guns.

Trent walked up to my driver side window and leaned in to kiss me. He gave me a light peck on the lips as I pulled his head in towards me a little closer and slipped my tongue into his mouth. Circling a few times, I then released and kissed his lips once more.

"Yum," Trent whispered.

"Congrats on the tour, baby," I whispered back.

He smiled and asked, "What are you listening to?" I laughed.

"It's my one vice, hair bands." Trent shook his head.

"Hey, no hatin' on the hair, baby!" I defended my choice of music. "Especially from a guy who wears eyeliner!" I stuck my tongue out at him.

"Touché, my love. Touché," he said as he walked around to the passenger side screaming, "*What happened to Jayne?*" as he got into my truck. I giggled knowing he liked the song. I just beamed as I put my truck in reverse and took off towards the lake.

Pulling into the driveway of the lake cabin, I felt a buzz even though I hadn't even started drinking yet.

It was dusk when we arrived, and I hopped out of the truck, admiring the lovely lake in front of me.

"Pretty, huh?" I called over to Trent as he walked up behind me and tenderly wrapped his arms around me.

"Umm," I purred as he nuzzled his lips into my neck.

"I'm sorry," I said, surprising him. He stepped back as I turned around and faced him. He bit his lower lip and stared back into my eyes.

"I love you Alexandria. You know that, right?" I let out a deep breath.

"I do," I whispered as a sense of relief washed over me,

knowing Trent was no longer cross with me about Gage.

Walking hand in hand towards the cabin you could hear the Black Crowes playing while guests drank their beer in front of the burning fire pit. The smoker in the back of the house let off a mouthwatering aroma as we both said in unison, "Yum, brisket!" I laughed as we approached the guitarist.

"Beers are in the cooler, liquor inside, and brisket is in the smoker if y'all are hungry. Oh, there's a mighty fine game of Texas Hold 'em going on in the house as well if y'all want to join in. Or, just fucking chill out here and listen to tunes while you admire this view." He turned towards the lake and saluted it with his Shiner Bock beer. Trent nodded to him then grabbed my hand and led me to the front porch step.

"Here, sit down here, baby. I'll go get us a plate of food and something to drink. You just relax. Hey, are you warm enough?" he asked with sincerity. I only had on a crop top, jean skirt, and cowboy boots. "I'm good hun, thanks." *I smiled as I watched him walk away. I hate to see him go, but I love to watch him walk away.*

"Hey, I thought I was the only one drooling around here?" Tyler questioned me as he interrupted my fantasizing. I busted out laughing.

"How is the tongue?" I asked him as he popped a squat next to me on the step.

"Let me see it," I demanded as Tyler opened his mouth while I inspected his piercing.

"It looks all healed up, Ty. Have you kissed anyone with it yet?" I nudged him with my elbow.

"Noooo. I promised you, baby girl." He exaggerated his no.

"You did promise me now, didn't you?" I smiled.

"Well fuck it, come here!" I ordered Tyler as he stood up on the step in front of me, leaned down and slowly pushed his way into my mouth. I parted my lips and accepted his tongue while he circled a few times, feeling the steel barbell roll against my tongue as my skin flared with goosebumps. Circling a few more times, I then pulled my tongue out as Tyler pulled his away, wiping his lip.

I said with appreciation, "Thank you, that felt fucking awesome." We both laughed.

"Now, I just need to find a *Whip-ette* at this party to suck face with." Tyler laughed as he rubbed his palms together as he looked around.

"Welcome back, Mr. Black." I gleefully smiled at the sexy frontman.

"Oh yeah, baby girl." Tyler leaned in and whispered in my ear, "I'm not drinking tonight. I smoked a little bit of pot, but I'm trying real hard here, Alex." I softly kissed his lips.

"I know you are, beautiful, I know you are. I'm proud of you." I softly touched his cheek, trying to soothe his anxieties.

A few hours into the party, the cabin, the lawn, and the lake were all littered with musicians and fans. This guitarist really knew how to throw down a shindig. Trent walked away from the band pow-wow at the firepit and approached me while flashing his devilish grin.

"Hi baby, are you having fun?" I stood up on my toes and kissed his lips.

"I am. This must be an all-nighter because people just

keep showing up! I did see a few other bands here. How cool is that?" Trent laughed.

"It's cool, baby." I kissed him once more.

"I saw some guys from the band the REVENUE, and they were doing coke in that RV over there." I pointed to an orange colored retro RV parked by the guest house.

"I've never tried cocaine, Trent, have you?" I glanced once more over to the parked RV.

"I have. A very long time ago." He smiled as he answered.

"How'd it make you feel?" I was intrigued.

"I mean, I've seen Tyler on it, and he fucks a lot on it. Does it really make you feel sexy?" I asked as

Trent nodded his head yes.

"Yes, it makes you feel sexy," he said as I licked my lips.

"Ooo... can we try a little taste together? Come on, we're celebrating your ten city tour! I haven't had anything to drink except a beer with the brisket hours ago. Plus, we're not going anywhere. We're supposed to crash at the cabin tonight, remember? Well, at least that's what I was told," I squealed with anticipation as I pulled on his t-shirt and tried to get an answer out of him.

Trent took in a breath as he hesitated.

"Please, I only want to try it if you're with me. I trust you and know you are looking out for me," I pleaded as I blinked my lashes and flirted with him.

"Sure. Come on," he huffed as he gave in to me while taking my hand and leading me over to the REVENUE's parked RV.

Tyler stopped us on the way asking, "Where y'all going? I'm so fucking bored!" I grabbed a hold of his hand as well.

"Bored?! What? I'm going to try cocaine," I squealed

once more as I swung their arms as I glanced over at Trent.

"Now how's that fucking fair?!" Tyler shouted in agony. I knew damn well that he wanted to join in on the party tonight.

"Well, since we're at a party and you are supervised," I laughed, looking at Trent for permission, "come do a little. But, you have to promise to stay with me and Trent if you do."

Tyler flicked his cigarette, yelling, "Hell yeah!"

I caved. Shame on me. I wanted him to enjoy the celebration like everyone else, so I caved in for him.

Trent, Tyler and I stepped into the RV and sat down at the table with our fellow musician friend.

"Hey guys, this is some pure shit here." He pointed at the table.

"Want to do a line?" He rubbed his teeth with his index finger as he pushed over a silver tray with three equal lines of cocaine in the middle and a sharp blade to the left next to a straw. I squeezed Trent's leg.

"You go first." I nudged Trent as he looked at me with disbelief.

"I can't believe you're trying coke." He paused.

Tyler then grabbed the tray, pulled it closer to him, and said, "Fuck it, I'll go first." Tyler licked his lips, put his nostril to a straw then started from one end of the powder and snorted the entire line up his nose in one swift motion. After leaning his head back, he just grinned.

"That's it, baby girl, that quick. Whew! That felt so fucking good. Hallelujah!" he hollered out.

"Now you go, Trent." I nervously pushed Trent to snort the second line. With the same intensity, Trent leaned down with the straw and snorted the second line.

"Holy shit," Trent said as he leaned his head back and smiled.

"Looks like I'm up, boys!" I said with excitement, then followed suit. I grabbed the straw from Trent, leaned down, and with my nostril I snorted blow. I couldn't believe it.

"That'a girl!" Tyler laughed as he clapped his hands as I shook my head, rubbing my nose.

"My fucking nose is burning!" I laughed uncontrollably as Trent shook his head while still leaning back.

Within a few minutes I never felt more awake in my life! This was why Tyler was always jumping on furniture in the green room at the concert venues. I then started to feel flush as my body temperature rose a few degrees and my heart started to beat faster.

"This feels good y'all." I looked down at the empty tray as Trent and Tyler started to laugh. I began to rub on both Trent's and Tyler's legs simultaneously.

"I so want to fuck right now. I'm so warm. I need to get naked!" I shouted as I started rapidly fanning myself with my hand. Trent and Tyler looked at one another, shaking their heads in disbelief.

"Damn, you lil hormone. Coke agrees with you, girl!" Tyler roared as he kissed my lips.

"Thank you for this, Alex," he muttered as he pulled his lips away.

The cocaine had given me instant confidence as I stood up and grabbed both Trent and Tyler's hands. "Come on you two, follow me," I instructed. We all three thanked the dude for the drugs and we stepped back out of the RV into the crowd of lakeside party guests.

"I want you two to fuck me!" I said excitedly as I spun around outside the RV. I'd seen Trent and Tyler kiss before on the dance floor, but I'd only slept with Trent. I felt I could trust my best friend Tyler tonight because I was high and wanted to have a little fun. So, I made the decision for the three of us that we were crossing boundaries and that we were going to have sex.

I then pulled both Trent and Tyler by the hand as I led the two sexiest men I'd ever let myself become close with towards the lakeside guest house.

CHAPTER
10

The summer wind was blowing in as the screen door closed behind us. In the dark, we entered the guest house, noticing that the only piece of furniture laid out in front of us was a king-sized four poster bed with white sheers hanging from the frame.

"Sexy, isn't it?" I turned around to look at Trent and Tyler who did not say a word. *I'm guessing I'm the ringleader in this circus now.*

The music outside transitioned into a slow, sultry tone, which mixed with cocaine, kept me in the mood for sure. I started to slowly sway my hips to the music as I pulled off my crop top and tossed it to the floor. I then unbuttoned my mini denim skirt and wiggled out of it, tossing it aside as well.

I stood there for a moment in a matching set of deep purple lacy panties and a bra, absorbing the admiration of these two sex symbols.

I flipped my hair around as I let a single bra strap fall off my shoulder. I blushed. I leaned towards Trent as I slowly pulled off his black t-shirt. Licking my lips wet, I honed in to lick his nipple as he let out a groan. I let my tongue drag from his chest up all the way up to his soft lips, pushing my warm tongue into his mouth. Trent moaned as he returned the kiss. He was calm on cocaine as I felt him slide his tongue slowly around mine once more as I pulled my mouth back.

I then moved over towards Tyler who was a little more edgy as I pulled off his t-shirt and started licking him from his navel slowly up to his neck. Tyler purred as he pulled on my opposing bra strap and slid it down my shoulder as he gently kissed my neck all the way up to my lips. He then slid his newly pierced tongue into my mouth and circled it around mine as I let a slight moan slip out. He tasted so fucking good.

I pulled away from Tyler's hungry lips and kept myself planted between the two sexy rockstars.

With a devilish grin, I grabbed each one of their jean buttons and unfastened them at the same time.

I slid my damp palms inside their pants and rubbed up and down on their hardening cocks, and I could feel myself starting to get wet. *What Whip-ette wouldn't want to have a threesome with these two men?* I laughed to myself as I continued to rub them.

I blinked my lashes up at the two of them as I then leaned back onto the cool mattress and spread my legs into a V-shape. Motioning Tyler to come here with my finger, he stepped up to me, grabbed a hold of my purple panties and slipped them up my legs and off my ankles. I made a scissor motion with my bare legs, exposing my glistening pussy. Tyler bent down and with his barbell pierced tongue he began to lick me from the bottom to the top.

"Oh Tyler, that feels like heaven!" I called out, encouraging him to continue. Then he flickered the barbell against my clit as I moaned in appreciation as he really turned me on.

Trent stepped forward as he pushed a white sheer aside and crawled into the bed joining the two of us as he swiftly unfastened my bra, releasing my breasts and tossed it aside. I started panting heavily.

He leaned in and started sucking one nipple at a time, smiling as they hardened for him.

"I love how this excites you, Alex," Trent said as he licked me. I threw my head back in ecstasy as Trent licked my breasts and Tyler licked my pussy.

"I want to be fucked by both of you!" I screamed out as I embraced the overwhelming sensation the two of them were giving me as I laid there, burning me with desire.

Trent laid down next to me, stroking my arm up and down as Tyler backed off the bed and removed his jeans slowly. I released a breath as I watched him. Tyler crawled back in bed naked towards me as flashes of our PDA blurred my vision. I had only kissed and played around with Tyler; I never actually slept with him before. There was this unspoken bond between the two of us that no one could take away.

Tyler then spread my legs and with his hard, endowed cock he slowly entered me. I became hysterical with emotion. I couldn't believe my best friend was inside of me. His hard cock fucking me felt so amazing on cocaine.

Tyler pushed up on his palms, leaned into Trent and slowly started kissing him as I just laid there watching Tyler's barbell flicker inside Trent's hot mouth. *Oh my god, these boys are sexy!* I shook my head in disbelief at what I was witnessing.

He then leaned back down towards me and started to kiss me very intensely as I now was officially fucking turned on. I began to really let myself lose it as I pushed him deeper into me while his hair fell across my face. He thrusted hard, and he thrusted fast.

"Oh, Tyler!" I cried out as he started to come instantly.

I then pushed Tyler over to my side as I rolled onto the bed on all fours, gyrating my hips. I needed to come. I wanted to come. I motioned for Trent with my finger once again to be my evening boy toy as he stood up, slowly pulled off his jeans and stood behind me.

"Fuck me Trent!" I pleaded on all fours as he grabbed his hardened cock and slowly entered me and began fucking me. My mouth fell open as he pulled on my hair and started to get himself off.

"You feel amazing, Trent! More!" I called out as I could feel his cock pulsating harder inside of me.

"I'm going to come!" I hollered out just as I released my orgasm. Trent kept fucking me until he pulled his cock out and came on my backside, letting out an "ahhh." I smiled as I could feel the hotness all over my ass.

"Oh my god you guys look so fucking hot!" Tyler whispered after he watched the two of us having sex as he leaned back on his pillow and lit himself a cigarette. I collapsed on the bed after Trent climaxed and flopped on top of me, nuzzling my hair.

"Oh, Alex, that felt so good, baby," he said, basking in the moment.

Exhausted, I laid there feeling the sweat of Trent's chest sticking to me as I rolled my neck over to smile at Tyler next to me. He blew out smoke from his cigarette and said, "I like you on coke, baby girl."

All three of us started to laugh.

Even though it was only a few hours, I felt like I slept like a rock. I was refreshed as I tried to focus my eyes on the screen door that was still ajar from last night's sexual adventure.

I glanced over to my right and smiled as Trent laid there passed out cold. I then looked to my left as Tyler rolled over towards me and opened his haunting dark eyes.

"You wouldn't believe the dream I had!" he shouted.

I shushed him and pointed at the door. Tyler slowly got out of bed, pulled on his jeans, and stepped out onto the porch. I then rolled out of bed, grabbed Tyler's t-shirt and my panties, got dressed quietly and slipped out the screen door as well.

The balmy morning felt refreshing as I stretched and stared at the lake. Tyler took out a cigarette and lit it as the two of us sat on the porch step. Blowing out smoke, he said, "I dreamt of death." He kept his head forward, looking at the lake, then took a second hit.

"Death? Ahh," I whispered.

"Dead in your dreams just hints that you're at the end of some negative cycle. You're mourning the end of something. You are sooo over being judged by others," I assured him.

"I am so over all this fucking anxiety about my choices, about Olivia, about performing with WHIP." He paused as he took another drag when I interrupted.

"Death isn't always a bad dream. Some part of your past, either your relationship with Olivia or your father, the detox, what have you, is fucking dead over." I nodded my head yes.

"That kinda makes fucking sense." Tyler shook his head yes as he agreed with me.

"You need to take that as a sign, Ty. You need to be the strongest, most powerful fucking lead singer anyone has seen. Take this tour and use it as a way to show off live and improve your rockstar image. Show all those assholes who fucked with your self-esteem that they knocked you down but did not break you. No drugs. No alcohol. Even Olivia..." I paused as I apologized.

"Sorry, but you are so moving on from that hot mess."

Tyler let out a subtle laugh. "I thought I did move on last night?" he laughed.

"You know you were the first girl I've slept with since Olivia?" My mouth dropped open.

"For real?" I was shocked. My best friend was such a man-whore.

"Do you regret last night?" I asked shyly.

"I do not," Tyler said as he stepped on his cigarette to put it out.

"If you take this dream as a sign and really focus, I'll make you a promise." I smiled.

"What?" he asked.

"I'll get you that damn soundtrack gig like you asked me to." I nudged his arm with my elbow.

"You'd fucking do that for me?" Tyler was a little shocked that I came around to the idea of dealing with Gage Heston once again for him.

"Of course I would. What haven't I done for you?" I asked him.

"Nothing. You're too good to me." Tyler leaned in and kissed me lightly on the cheek.

"I promise: no alcohol, no drugs, no cutting—I'm making a comeback. Just tea and honey to soothe my throat," he laughed.

"Well 'tea and honey,' leave Mr. Heston to me. But, for now, I better go wake up Trent so we can hit the road. Y'all have a meeting with Zack about the tour, and I have a design project that I need to finish. Plus, I need to feed Ernie!" I tapped Tyler's shoulder as I stood up and went back into the guesthouse to wake Trent.

CHAPTER 11

A few weeks into June flew by as WHIP was getting ready to hit the road on their summer tour.

I actually wasn't a melancholy Molly like I thought I would be with WHIP leaving again. I think a little distance between me and the famous duo could do me some good.

As I walked through the loft, I did not feel as alone, ignored or abandoned like I did when I was in the relationship with Gage. I'd come such a long way. So, I decided to sit down and write two letters that I would slip into Trent and Tyler's packed bags, letting them know that their lil cheerleader was rooting for them and that they were going to perform great.

That night, Trent came home exhausted from the studio, so I knew I shouldn't make any plans for us and that I should just let him rest. I decided to run him a bath. I lit a few candles, grabbed his favorite wine off the wine rack in the kitchen, and met him upstairs.

"Come on, sexy lover," I smiled as I stood in front of him, pulling off his t-shirt and tossing it onto the floor. I then unbuttoned his jeans and slid them down to his ankles while he stepped out of them. "Underwear too," I demanded as Trent slid them off and stood there bare naked in front of me.

What a mouth-watering image, I thought to myself as the reflection of the candles danced across his olive-colored inked chest and sexy V. I handed him a glass of wine and went to test the bath water.

"Are you getting in with me?" he asked sweetly as he stepped into the tub.

"Do you want my company? I know you are burnt out, baby. I can see it in your eyes." I set my wine glass down and stripped out of my clothes. He took a sip of his wine then held up his hand so I could steady myself as I joined him in the bathtub. Gage never wanted to soak in the tub with me; he was always too busy sifting through sluts on the internet.

"Now that's better, baby." He smiled at me as I grabbed the soap and started to massage his hands.

"I bet these babies ache from all that composing you're hung up on creating." I blushed as I rubbed each finger and knuckle out, while Trent sighed as he leaned his head back and closed his heavy eyes.

"That feels so good, baby, thank you. What am I going to do without my personal masseur when I hit the road? Playing keyboards makes my hands pretty sore from time to time." He smiled.

"Ice. Very cold ice. No fucking masseur—I don't care how hot she is!" I laughed.

"I can always join the tour as your personal massage therapist if you need me to?" I offered sweetly, as Trent opened his eyes.

"We would never leave the hotel room." He let out a subtle laugh.

"Can you grasp just how much I'm going to miss you out on the road?" I put my hand up to stop him from talking as I scootched in closer so I could kiss him. I lightly pecked his lips, then I slid my warm tongue into his mouth, aching for more as I swirled it around his. He returned the gesture as he kissed me back, letting a slight moan escape. I could not only feel his passion and love for me, I could taste it.

Not wanting my eyes to start watering, I withdrew my kiss. There was enough water in the tub; I didn't need to add to it with all my boo-hooing.

"This is what we do, right?" I asked Trent. "You're the musician. You need to travel to perform. This is what we do as a couple. I went into this with my eyes and heart wide open. Please do not feel any pressure, any guilt whatsoever. Do your best on the road, and I'll still be here waiting for you." Trent let out a much-needed breath as I leaned back as we just soaked in a comfortable silence.

Trent suddenly broke the stillness as he whispered, "Baby, I want to make love to you." I bit my lower lip and held my breath.

"Do you have the energy?" I laughed as I splashed a little wave in his direction.

"I'll muster up the strength," Trent vowed as he stood up with a loaded erection and stepped out of the tub. He then turned and grabbed my hand and guided me out of the tub and straight over to the bed.

As I laid back on the soft feather pillows, I could still enjoy the ambiance of the candles flickering from the bathroom as Trent crawled into bed, casting a shadow over me. He paused as he looked deeply into my eyes then leaned down and gently kissed my neck. A tingling sensation just rippled through my body.

"I want to be inside of you, Alexandria," he whispered into my ear as he continued to softly kiss my neck then licked my lower lip with his warm tongue.

"Ahh," I moaned.

"To hell with foreplay," I said as Trent laughed while slowly spreading my legs wide open. I gasped as he entered me.

"Ahh" was still the only word I could generate as I accepted his fullness.

My legs started to tremble as he slowly pushed deeper into me. I ran my fingers through his wet hair as drops of water ran down my chest, turning me on. Leaning my head back in ecstasy, he began to steadily rock me slowly in and out. I let a tear slip as it ran down my face as I felt his rapid heartbeat pound against mine. Trent grabbed my hand and squeezed it as I whispered, "You feel so good, baby. I'm going to miss this." Trent paused and looked into my eyes.

"I'm going to miss you," he said as I leaned up to kiss him while he continued to make love to me until we both climaxed together.

This part sucked. I really did hate it when he had to leave for a tour. I hated saying goodbye. I secretly pouted to myself as Trent pulled out and rolled over onto his back.

"I'm going to miss you way too much," I whispered as Trent glanced over at me and just blinked his dreamy dark eyes, and I knew this kitten was smitten.

The long awaited day was upon us. WHIP was heading out on their ten city tour. I had a whirlwind of emotions cutting right through me as I drove my truck over to the studio to say my goodbyes.

Just as I pulled in, the band were in the middle of loading their equipment onto the tour bus. Trent smiled at me as I parked my ride and jumped out.

"Whatcha doing here, baby?" Trent asked while he loaded an amplifier.

"I wanted to say goodbye to y'all." I looked around at all the scattered gear the guys still needed to load. "I won't stay long," I promised as I watched Tyler step off the bus.

"Hey string bean!" I hollered.

"Hey blondie," he laughed as he walked towards me.

"Are you all set?" I asked as I grabbed his hand and squeezed it.

"I'm nervous, but I need to do this straight," Tyler said as I nodded my head in agreement.

"Please call me from every fucking city," I demanded as Tyler nodded his head and mouthed,

"Yes ma'am," as I shuffled around in my bag, pulling out a jar of honey and a package of tea.

"Don't call me ma'am, and here 'tea and honey,' take these with you." I pushed the goodies into Tyler's chest. He laughed as he tossed the tea and honey into his backpack.

"Hey, I brought my camera. I want a picture of the three of us before y'all split." Tyler nodded as he grabbed Trent's arm and pulled him towards us.

"Here." I handed the camera to the drummer.

"Take a pic of me, Tyler, and Trent, please." I squeezed in between Trent and Tyler—my two favorite people in my world—as the three of us posed for the camera.

"Thanks, now let me get one of WHIP in front of the bus, and then I'll go," I ordered as the band all rallied together and stood in front of the bus and posed while I snapped a picture.

"Got it!" I yelled as I set my camera back into my bag and shrugged my arms.

"That's it," I huffed as I began to hug each one of them one at a time, the guitarist, the bassist, the drummer, Tyler, then finally Trent.

I headed back towards the truck, making devil horns with my fingers and sticking out my tongue as the guys all returned the gesture, laughing. I jumped in and started up Axl.

As I pulled out of the studio, I glanced up into my rearview mirror at the bus, and tears just started to stream down my face.

CHAPTER 12

VANITY

Buzz buzz... "What?!" I yelled as I fished for my phone still hibernating under my comforter.

"Hello!" I hollered breathlessly into my cell.

"Good morning to you too, beautiful." I paused.

"Trent?" I sat up, beaming with excitement.

"Hi baby. Who'd ya think it was?" he laughed on the other end of the line.

"Oh, no one. I was just balled up in my blankets missing you." I could hear him smile through the phone.

"How's the tour? It's been too long," I asked as I sat up in our bed.

"It's pretty fucking good I must say. Zack is running a tight ship, and I admire that. He's not putting up with any bullshit from us or from the venues either." I smiled.

"You mean Tyler?" I said as he laughed.

"How is our bruised frontman, really?" I scratched my head as I listened for a response.

"Hello?"

"I'm here, babe. I stepped away for a second. Tyler is kicking ass," he said as I hollered, "Thank you Jesus! I needed to hear that! When we chat it seems like he's just a ball of nerves. Is he taking his meds?" I inquired.

"He's taking his medication regularly, drinking tea with honey. He's on time for soundcheck. I'm pretty fucking proud of him. He's trying real hard to turn things around. He's even great with the reporters, and he even goes back to the hotel room alone..." I interrupted Trent.

"Wait, no *Whip-ettes*?" I laughed.

"No *Whip-ettes*, baby," he assured me.

"Good. How about you?" I shifted my focus to Trent.

"Well, I'm on no meds, I'm not drinking tea, I'm never on time, and fuck the rock reporters," Trent laughed.

"Stop it!" I pouted. "Be serious!" I huffed.

"No, I'm good babe. My gear is holdin' up, I haven't fucked up on stage. In my professional opinion, I feel WHIP is kicking ass." I smiled.

"Good. Umm, no *Whip-ettes* either?" I teased.

"No *Whip-ettes*. I can only handle one *Whip-ette* at a time, and my only *Whip-ette* is balled up in our comforter at the moment," he teased me as I laughed.

"Well babe, I just wanted to check in to let you know I was thinking about you and wanted to thank you for my lil note that I found tucked away in my bag." I giggled.

"You're welcome, lover," I whispered.

"Well, we are heading out to get some breakfast." He paused.

"I love hearing your voice," I purred into the phone. "Well, you're welcome, and go eat. We'll chat later. I love you Trent," I said.

"Ditto beautiful." He said as I clicked off the line and just savored that moment.

Trent and Tyler were safe and were kicking ass. I relished the thought then hollered, "Well that's that. I guess I need to hold up my end of the promise that I've made to Tyler on the porch step at the lake house!" I chewed on my fingernail for a second then said, "To hell with it, I'm calling Gage."

I scanned through my contacts on my cell and searched for Heston. I had no idea why I kept his fucking number locked in my phone, but I did.

I opened up a text message and typed out,

Soundtrack still on the table? I'd love to discuss. I hit send. I knew that asshole would respond immediately. *Ding!* My cell phone went off.

Glamour boys out of town, eh? I'm available tonight. He responded. Dismissing the glamour part, I paused before responding.

Meet me at six? I hit send.

Where? I sent Gage the address of a coffee shop over by the recording studio. I could park safely at *Head Rush* and walk to the coffee shop from there. I then clicked off my cell.

"Game on, Mr. Heston!" I hollered out as Ernie surfaced from under the comforter and meowed.

"Game is definitely on, Ern," I shouted once more as I hopped out of bed, knowing just what I had to do.

Six p.m. sharp I was standing outside the coffee shop enjoying the summer breeze blowing on the back of my neck, which always seemed to calm me. I elected to wear something 'Gage appropriate,' which was a black form-fitted dress that stretched clear down to my mid-calf and had slight cleavage with my black Milano Blanc high heels and my hair pinned back in a bun. I looked suitable and pretty by Gage Heston standards.

Within minutes a sleek black town car pulled up curbside and honked its horn. I rolled my eyes as the driver got out and held the backseat door open for me. Gage reached his hand out and guided me into the cold leather seat beside him.

"Good evening, Alexandria." Gage perked up as he nodded, approving my choice of attire for this evening.

"Hello Gage," I replied, feeling the bile rise in my throat.

"Where shall we go?" Gage asked as the driver looked into his rearview mirror, waiting for my response. "Northwest Highway," I said directly. The driver put the car into drive and headed towards the interstate.

"How are you holdin' up with your boyfriends being out of town?" Gage asked while giving me a smirk. "Fine," I said with my sweet southern accent just letting that question roll off my back.

"I know you do not like being alone, Alexandria." I huffed as I turned towards him.

"You seem to love it though, Gage. That's the difference between us. I wanted a relationship with you, and you just wanted a relationship with yourself. Do not start with me tonight." My temper started to flare up as I turned back towards the window.

"Never mind that, Alexandria," Gage insisted as we rode in silence until we approached our exit.

"Take a left and Vanity is down on the right," I directed the driver. He nodded his head yes as Gage looked over at me.

"Vanity? How do you know of such a place?" He asked with curiosity.

I mumbled to myself as I looked out the window, "If you only knew, Mr. Fancy Pants." I laughed to myself.

We entered the strip club parking lot as the driver pulled up to the valet to drop us.

"I'll text you when we're ready to leave," Gage said to the driver as he nodded his head yes as he held the door open for both Gage and me to get out. As the doorman opened the club door for us to walk into the venue, Gage handed him a hefty tip. I smiled with appreciation.

"Oh, don't you worry, Mr. Heston. You'll be spending money tonight," I assured him as he just laughed while he tucked his money clip back into his suit pocket.

Upon entering the club, the all-too-familiar scent of cheap body spray and cigars hit me all at once, making me feel dizzy. The DJ was tucked away in a booth playing the same "Girls Girls Girls" track that'd haunted me ever since I stopped working here. I tried not to gag as I looked around the familiar surroundings.

All three stages had exotic dancers performing on them, and not one empty seat was available on the floor. I then grabbed a hold of Gage's hand and made a beeline for the staircase leading up to the VIP section. Gage happily followed me up the staircase.

"I like where this is going," he said as he squeezed my hand a little tighter.

We passed the metal bird cage that I once auditioned in for my exotic dancer job as my stomach did a somersault. I then found an unoccupied room and motioned for the first busty brunette waitress I could find to come join us. Gage would drool over my selection as the flighty waitress pranced over to take our order as she lit the candle on the table.

"Hi y'all," the waitress said as she looked at us while fishing for her pen out of her hair to write our order down. She then did a double take as she set her eyes on Gage then back on me.

"Hi Angel," she giggled. Gage never picked up on the greeting.

"Hi. We would like a bottle of champagne, an old fashioned on the rocks, and in twenty minutes please send over Mercedes," I requested sternly as she nodded her head yes while her cleavage jiggled right along with her nod, making Gage smile.

"Wow. I like when you take charge like that." Gage rubbed on my arm as he moved a little closer to me on the purple velvet loveseat.

"No you don't." I rolled my eyes.

"You are the dominant one with all your 'conditions.'" I made air quotes with my hands. Gage smiled as he seemed to enjoy this truthful banter between us.

"Well, Mr. Heston." I paused.

"Condition number one tonight is this soundtrack we need to discuss." Gage nodded in agreement. "Okay, let's discuss." He smiled as the waitress reappeared with his drink in her hand. She set it down on a cocktail napkin while a floorman entered our private room to set up the champagne bucket with three glasses. I was relieved to see alcohol arrive at this point. I was much in need of a drink sitting next to Gage Heston alone. He stood up, tipped both the waitress and the floorman, then thanked them as they turned and walked out.

"Okay Alexandria, you have my attention." Gage took a sip of his drink and rubbed my arm once more. "Please tell me the contract is still open, that you haven't booked a vocalist, let alone a band for this project?" I batted my lashes, hoping Gage would cave in for me one last time as I asked for a favor for Tyler and for WHIP.

"It is still open, and yes, as hot as WHIP is performing, I'd love to have Tyler."

Wow. I was speechless for the moment. *That was too easy*, I thought as I furrowed my brow.

"Can we call your attorney and have him meet us here tonight for you to sign it? I not only want you to say it, I want you to sign it." I bit my lower lip, waiting for a response. Gage was surprised at my request.

"What do I get in return, Alexandria?" he asked while he shook the ice around in his drink.

"You get the hottest vocalist out there..." Gage interrupted me.

"I do not give a flying fuck about Tyler Black. Quit trying to sell me Tyler." Gage swallowed a piece of ice. "I want you back, Alexandria." I grinded my teeth together, not knowing quite how to respond to that statement.

"I miss you," he said as I gulped my champagne.

Suddenly, there was a knock at the door. Then Nova walked in.

"What the hell is Nova doing here?" Gage asked as he watched the two of us hug.

"It's Mercedes, G-Man," Nova corrected him to use her stage name.

"What a fucking surprise, girl!" Nova hollered as she reached over towards the champagne bucket and poured herself a glass.

"Mercedes is going to entertain us tonight, Gage," I said as I took another sip of my champagne and toasted Nova.

"It's your night. I should have known Nova worked in a joint like this." Gage let out a deep laugh as I knew he was putting everything together in his head from her condo, to her clothes, to her damn Mercedes car. Gage just shook his head as he started to relax.

"We're celebrating Gage's record label signing Tyler and the guys from WHIP to their rock and roll movie soundtrack deal!" I stuck my tongue out at Nova.

"Are we now?" She glanced at Gage as he nodded his head yes as I let out a breath.

"Well then, if we're celebrating the rockstars, then let's act like fucking rockstars!" Nova squealed as she raised her champagne glass.

"I'm going to dance for both of you to start this party!" Nova insisted as she stood up in front of the loveseat we were all seated upon and started swaying her hips. I glanced over at Gage, trying to judge where his head was at. He leaned back and loosened his tie. Moving closer to his side, I inhaled his familiar scent of cologne. I was in Vanity, I played this stripper act before. I needed to start fucking acting like one. I mentally chastised myself.

I began to squeeze Gage's leg as Nova turned herself around and asked Gage to unzip her dress. Gage obliged as Nova wiggled out of her costume like she was Marilyn fucking Monroe. I laughed.

She then slowly turned around and brushed her hands through her hair as her breasts were exposed one by one as the dress slid off of her and hit the floor. I kept glancing at Gage while he gave Nova his undivided attention. Nova leaned over his lap and rubbed her boobs in his face as I just kept squeezing Gage's leg acting like this whole charade was turning me on. I knew that Nova would catch on to what I was up to and play her part. She was getting paid for it, so why the fuck would she mind? Nova slowly gyrated on Gage's lap to sexy techno music, and I wasn't bothered by it one bit.

I played with Nova's panties. She licked my fingertips as Gage continued to get turned on by the playfulness between the two of us. The waitress peeked in from time to time to see how we were holding up, and I just kept ordering another drink for Gage.

Four drinks later, Gage was holding both mine and Nova's hands, shirt untucked, tie around his forehead, smiling.

"Let me get William on the phone," he said as he pulled out his cell and dialed his attorney.

"Billy my boy, sorry about the hour, but since I do have you on retainer, I guess fuck the hour, right?"

Gage laughed as he toyed with his young attorney on the line.

"The soundtrack agreement, ummm, can you swing by the club Vanity so I could sign it tonight? Just fill it in with the band WHIP—everything else should be in order. Also, I have two beautiful women waiting here that would love to meet with you as well." He smiled as he tried to persuade the attorney to work that evening.

I motioned for Gage to hand over the phone as he said, "Hold on buddy, my girl needs to chat with you." Nova grabbed

Gage's cheek and started to kiss him. He then handed me his phone while he started sucking face with my stripper friend. I stood up and stepped out of the room.

"Hi William, this is Alexandria," I said into the phone. "I'm sorry for the inconvenience this may cause you, but we need you to please add something to the contract." I was whispering, looking over my shoulder to make sure Gage wasn't coming for his cell phone.

"The vocalist is Tyler Black. The only band involved with this deal should be WHIP. And..." I paused.

"WHIP retains full rights to the songs as well as any money made on this film soundtrack. It shall go to WHIP and their new label exclusively." I let out a breath.

"Is Mr. Heston okay with that?" He sounded a little unsure.

"He's good with it. Believe me, we're celebrating this contract tonight. So, please fill in the correct information and swing by Vanity to join us. Say, one hour?" I asked, as William huffed.

"I'm on it. See you in one hour," he said. I intensely bit my lip as I clicked off the line, then held my breath for a second as I chewed on how I was going to keep Gage entertained until the contract arrived.

One hour later, William walked into our VIP room and waved the envelope with the contract inside.

"Billy my boy!" Gage stood up, stumbling a bit as he shook William's hand.

"I have the contract right here, Mr. Heston." He fumbled through the envelope, then took a pen out of his jacket pocket to have Gage sign.

"Now, it says..."

Gage interrupted, "I know what the fucking contract says. I had you draft it up for me." Gage was a little hostile with William.

"Yes sir, but..." Gage grabbed the pen.

"Just point to where I fucking sign so my girl here..." He glanced over towards me. "... my girl can focus all her attention back on me and not that fucking band." He leaned down on the table and signed the contract.

"Good sir, I'll have a copy sent over to you as well as to WHIP's manager tomorrow." Gage took another sip of his drink, then sat back down and looked at Nova.

"Is she happy now?" he asked as Nova nodded her head yes.

"Yes, our girl is happy," she answered. I took a deep breath in then offered William a drink. He pleasantly declined as he grabbed the envelope and left Vanity in a rush. I was relieved that he said no. The longer the contract stayed in our presence, the easier it would be to destroy it. I leaned my head back on the velvet seat and just smiled as thoughts of Tyler danced in my head. He was so going to love this. I wasn't so proud of how I acted to get the contract, but whatever the fuck it takes. Gage then grabbed my arm as he jolted me back to reality.

"Hey, I need to pay these bitches, then you and I are out of here." He let go of my arm as he sifted his pockets for his credit card to hand over to the waitress. I rubbed my arm as I looked over to Nova and frowned. He then tossed Nova a wad of cash as she gladly accepted it with a smile while stowing it away in her clutch. I kissed her cheek as I pulled her into my embrace.

"Thank you," I whispered as I squeezed her.

"I roofied Gage with some valium so he'll pass out on you on the way home," Nova whispered back into my ear. I held my breath as I stepped back and looked at her mouthing *what?* After all his drinking, my fake flirting, feeding his ego tonight was all too exhausting. I was actually afraid to drive back home with him alone.

Nova kissed Gage one last time before she left the VIP area. Gage looked over at me and said, "I'm texting the driver to pick us up." I nodded okay as I followed him out of the club.

The driver opened the car door as I slid into the backseat. Gage tipped the driver extra as he asked him to put up his soundproof window. Gage then slid into the seat next to me and slammed his door shut, startling me.

"Did you have fun tonight?" I asked while I removed Gage's tie off his head. He nodded yes as he tried to steady himself on the seat.

"Give in to me baby," he whispered. "I signed a contract for you. Both the band and I will make some money. I gave in to you. Now it's your turn to give in to me." He grabbed my pinned up bun and pulled my hair out. I huffed as I collected all the pins that scattered all over the seat. He laughed as he tugged at my dress while trying to push it up.

"Don't Gage, stop it," I whispered, looking up at the driver.

"He can't hear us, baby." He feverishly grabbed my wrists and held them down as he licked my neck. I shook my head no as Gage laughed.

"Why are you playing so hard to get? I want to fuck

you, Alexandria. It's been too long," he demanded as his voice slipped an octave lower.

"Gage, you're drunk. Stop it!" I kicked my legs as he rolled on top of me, ripping my dress. He leaned back, trying to unzip his pants as I kicked him with my heel. Gage then fell backwards and started to sway as he tried to get up.

"You knocked the wind out of me, bitch!" He laughed as he pulled himself up to the seat and sat down.

"Are you okay?" I asked, knowing that the valium must have been kicking in. I let out a quiet breath, thanking Nova.

"Lean back." I pushed Gage back in his leather seat and cracked the window for some air. He leaned his head back and as his eyes started to close he said, "That feels good," then nodded off to sleep. I then cracked my window and felt relief as light rain drops began to lightly hit my face as the driver drove me back to *Head Rush.*

CHAPTER 13

The next morning I woke to a head-pounding nightmare.

"Ugh, champagne," I moaned as I stood in front of the bathroom mirror. Once again after an evening with Gage, I looked like shit. *How does Nova do this four times a week at Vanity? I would not have the strength.*

After splashing my face with water, I headed straight down to the kitchen to brew some much needed coffee. I went to the refrigerator to grab the milk when I suddenly paused to stare at the two snapshots stuck under a magnet, one of WHIP in front of the tour bus and the other one of me, Tyler and Trent.

My heart sank. I really missed them.

I went through last night's shenanigans all for them. My stomach did a quick nervous somersault.

Zack should receive the contract tomorrow morning, I thought as I grabbed the milk standing at the counter, debating if I should spill the beans to Tyler or not.

"Hum..." I pondered.

Ernie's meow broke the silence as I bent down to pet him.

"Fuck it," I said as I made the impulsive decision. *I'm going to call Tyler.*

I went over to the sliding glass doors to let the summer air in as I sat on the couch with my Art Institute mug in hand. Sipping my coffee, I dialed Tyler.

"Yeah," Tyler answered with his groggy morning voice.

"Good morning, sexy rockstar," I greeted him as I heard a deep laugh on the line.

"How was last night's show?" I sipped my coffee once more.

"It was cool. I wish you were there though, the fans really love the song 'Betrayal.'" He said as I smiled.

"I knew they would. And you just had that lil piece of magic rolled into a ball in your trash bin." I laughed.

"I have a question." I paused.

"What if you use that tune for the movie soundtrack?" I asked while grinning from ear to ear.

"That'll be the day that asshole gives me anything," Tyler groaned, referring to Gage Heston.

"I'm giving it to you." Tyler could sense my excitement.

"No, you didn't, girl?!!" Tyler hollered out.

"Yes, I did!" I hollered back.

Tyler let out a "Yahoo!" as he screamed with excitement.

"This is going to catapult me to the moon! I mean, what a fucking gig! You really hooked me up, baby girl? I smell music awards!" Tyler was shouting on the other end of the line.

"Keep your leather pants on, now settle down!" I laughed.

"I kept my end of the deal, right? Did I keep my lakeside promise to you?" I asked sweetly.

"Yes, you did," Tyler agreed.

"As did I, I , I," he softly sang into the phone. Tyler kept his promise to me of not abusing, taking his medication every day and just focusing on his career during this leg of the tour.

"I know you did, beautiful. Trent told me. I'm so proud of you. You better fucking enjoy this gift. Just wait till you hear what I had to go through, ugh," I groaned as I smiled into the phone while listening to Tyler lighting up his cigarette on the other end of the line.

"Thank you," he said as he blew out smoke.

"Did you tell anyone else yet?" Tyler inquired. I knew he meant Trent.

"No. Just you. Gage Heston's attorney, William, is sending over the contract to Zack as soon as Monday, so get ready!" I gleefully sang back into the phone.

"Wait, do I even want to know how you put this all together?" Tyler took another hit of his cigarette. "Does it really matter?" I asked.

"You're the real fucking rockstar, Alex! WOW. I'm so fucking happy!" he said.

"Then it was worth it." I leaned back and decided to let William handle the details.

"Well, Mr. Movie Vocalist," I teased Tyler.

"I'm taking a recovery day." I let out a sigh.

"You deserve it, baby girl. Damn, I can't believe you hooked me up! Have I told you how much I love you? Really?" I rolled my eyes.

"I know you do, Tyler," I said as I clicked off the line then finished my coffee and felt well-pleased at the efforts I went through last night. It was all worth it.

Later that afternoon I was still in my pajamas. I cleaned. I organized my design projects. I even listened to music.

Everything to keep me distracted from Gage and the anger he would certainly not control when he found out what he signed last night. I gulped at the thought of him having one of his fits. *What's done is done.* I centered myself as I decided that I was going to take a hot shower and a power nap.

A few hours later, my cell phone buzzed as I saw Trent's name flash across the screen. My butterflies finally awakened in my stomach again.

"Hi," I answered.

"Hi. How's the love of my life holdin' up?" he asked me as I just smiled.

"I'm holdin', sugar. How are you holdin' up?" I boomeranged the question.

"I'm lonely and I'm so horny, baby," he groaned into the phone. I laughed, letting out a breath. He was in a good mood. I wasn't so sure how he would react, knowing I had my hand literally in Gage's last night as I put this contract together for Tyler and WHIP. I dismissed it and shifted my focus back onto my boyfriend.

"Lonely in St. Louis, huh?" Trent laughed.

"I wish you were here. I'm alone in my hotel room. This bed is just too big for one." I could hear Trent tapping the mattress. I laughed, knowing what he was suggesting.

"Are you lying back on the bed, Mr. Keyboard player?" I asked slyly.

"I am," he responded.

"What are you wearing, cowgirl?" I giggled at his cheesy question.

"Only a smile!" I said, teasing him.

"Actually, just my red lacy panties." I could hear Trent moan.

"Oh, I love your lacy panties. Can you pull them down a bit for me?" he asked, initiating phone sex.

"I'm holding them, Trent, and I'm sliding them slowly off my hips, down to mid-thigh, as I want to expose my moist pussy for you." Trent sighed.

"I'm slowly trailing my fingertips down my blonde landing strip and spreading my lips for you." I started to breathe a little heavier into the line.

"Now, what are your fingers doing?" Trent asked with his deep throaty voice.

"I'm inserting one finger inside me as I slowly finger-fuck myself, wishing it was you," I said.

"I like that. Keep the pace slow, Alex," Trent ordered as I obeyed.

"My nipples are hardening for you, Trent, and I'm starting to get very wet for you," I was teasing him. "Ohhh," I could hear him groan on the other end of the line.

"I'm pulling my red lacy panties allll the way off while I'm lying in my bed completely naked and hungry for you." I began breathing ragged into the phone.

"I'm inserting my finger slowly once again, but deeper, Trent, much deeper. Can you join me?"

I closed my eyes as I heard Trent unzip his pants.

"Pull out that hard, horny cock you have hidden in those tight jeans," I instructed.

"You make me so hard, baby. I want to fuck you," Trent said as he let out a deep breath.

"Now, I'm finger-fucking my moist pussy, and I want you to stroke slowly for me. Just like when you make love to me," I instructed.

"I am baby, I'm stroking for you. Ohhhh." I could hear Trent getting excited.

"I'm picking up the pace baby. I have two fingers inserted and I want to come while I listen to you stroke yourself good." I licked my lips as I rubbed myself off. I could hear Trent masturbating on the line, and I just started to enthusiastically orgasm on my fingers.

"I'm coming Trent, oh I'm coming so hard for you!" I cried out.

All I heard in response was "ahhh" as I knew he was having an orgasm too. A minute later, he whispered, "I really miss you Alex." Groaning as I grinned, I rolled over and shoved a pillow underneath my neck. "I miss you so much, Trent." I pouted.

We then stayed on the line with each other for about an hour after phone sex as I listened to every exciting detail he was experiencing on this ten city tour.

The next morning I felt refreshed. I hopped out of bed with a new lease on life. Phone sex is not the real thing, but it was good enough to hold me over until I physically saw Trent again. I needed to know that he still longed for me while he was out on the road. I smiled as I stretched then jumped out of bed to start my day.

Around noon, Tyler called me as I was working on a design project.

"Hi baby girl, I'm here at the hotel with Trent, and we're heading to Zack's room for a quick meeting with the band." Tyler sounded amped.

"Why am I tagging along with you two?" I curiously

asked as I continued to type on my laptop.

"I said we are heading towards Zack's room, just hang tight. Shhh..." Tyler shushed me on the line.

I shut my laptop down and stretched while I patiently waited to hear something on the other end.

"Knock. Knock," I heard Trent say loudly as he banged on Zack's hotel room door.

"Hey dudes." The drummer answered the door as Trent and Tyler entered the room. Zack had his phone on speaker while he paced around the hotel room waiting for papers to print off from his laptop.

"Okay guys, I have Mr. Heston here on the line, and he has some exciting news. Listen up," Zack ordered.

My stomach spun as I waited to hear Gage's voice on the speaker through my cell phone.

"So, we meet again boys," he laughed as I cringed just hearing that demonic laugh.

"Listen, I'd love to have WHIP on the film soundtrack if your manager, Zack, feels we can work together once again. Mr. Tyler Black, your voice will be singing all the leading actor's singing parts. The rest of you members of WHIP, you will record the songs for the soundtrack. William, my attorney, will send the contract over to Zack shortly, if we're all in agreement." He paused.

"I think we're all in agreement," Zack said.

"Good then. The contract's yours. Good luck," Gage growled on the line. The band all started to cheer as I leaned back in my chair and just listened intensely.

Zack was wrapping up the call as he said, "The boys are really ecstatic. I'm so glad we could work together on this. Thank you again. This is really good, Gage." Zack paused as he waited to hear Gage's response.

"Yeah, it's good," Gage said.

"She fucked me good. She fucked me real good," Gage laughed then clicked off the line.

The room fell silent. I held the phone, shaking my head as I called out, "Tyler?"

"Tyler? Are you there?" I repeated as I held my breath.

"Hold on, Alex," Tyler answered.

"Trent is flashing me a look of disdain. Holy shit!" Tyler yelled as he dropped the phone. I quickly stood up.

"What the fuck, Tyler?!" I looked down at my cell, wondering if I lost the call. Tyler got back on the line.

"He fucking punched me, Alex!" he yelled.

"Who punched you? What the fuck is going on there?!" I screamed into the phone as I heard a door slam, assuming someone left Zack's hotel room.

"Trent, that fucking asshole. What the fuck did I get a sucker punch for? I didn't fuck Gage! Look, Alex, I'm going to need to call you back." *Click.* Tyler hung up the phone.

Dead silence was all that lingered. I dropped my phone. Oh my god, the boys think I fucked Gage Heston for the contract. I bent down to grab my phone and fell over, landing on my butt. Pulling my knees into my chest, I just started sobbing.

Reality struck me like a bolt of lightning as I immediately thought of Trent. I so fucked this up for Trent and me. This was unacceptable. I feverishly dialed Trent. He answered in a very pissed off manner.

"I really do not want to talk to you right now, Alexandria," he huffed, then hung up the phone.

I then dialed Tyler, but it went to voicemail.

"Come on! What the fuck? I give this guy the ultimate hook-up, and Tyler is not picking up his phone!" I started to panic. I rolled myself into the fetal position on the floor, holding my cell, rocking back and forth just stewing. It was starting to get dark in the loft as I slowly pulled my aching body off of the floor.

So much for the new lease on life—that lease has just expired. I was distraught. I turned on the floor lamp, then headed over to the kitchen table and flipped open my laptop, typing in my search for 'cheap tickets.' I was going to St. Louis to straighten this whole damn mess out.

After booking a ticket, I texted Tyler:

I assume you are at rehearsal. You better not be ignoring me, asshole. I'm going to fly into St. Louis Lambert Airport and should arrive before Thursday's show. Leave me a fucking ticket at the venue. Trent won't talk to me. You better fucking call me tonight. I hit send.

CHAPTER 14

ST. LOUIS

"After I bought this ticket, I sent Gage Heston a dozen roses saying that I was sorry. You know that's how that man apologizes for almost everything!" I laughed as I waved my ticket in the air as Nova threw my suitcase in her trunk.

"This thing with G-Man has been a very dangerous game between the two of you since day one!" Nova shook her head.

"I was just looking for revenge. I know that's not the answer, but hitting him where it hurts, like his wallet, is a good start. I know it doesn't solve anything. But..." I paused.

"I feel better. Plus, Tyler and the guys from WHIP really deserve this. They dumped Gage's record label for the way he mistreated me in the past, so now I landed this soundtrack contract for them while mistreating him right back." Nova made a *tisk-tisk* sound as she started her car.

"I do want to thank you for helping me that evening at Vanity, girl. I did, however, have his attorney William add a few things into the contract while Gage was distracted by your kiss, you know?"

I tisk-tisked her right back. She laughed.

"They get full rights, and all the dough the production company makes off the soundtrack." I was proud of myself as I patted myself on the back.

"You sneaky little devil, you!" Nova howled.

"Well, good for WHIP and good for Tyler. I swear I still don't get this relationship between the two of y'all. I think you secretly love Tyler." Nova glanced over at me as I just inverted my lips while batting my lashes. She laughed as we made our way to the DFW airport.

Hugging Nova at the terminal drop off, I said, "Here we go, wish me luck!" I pulled away from our embrace as I bent down and picked up my suitcase.

"Honestly, Nova." I paused for a breath.

"Yeah?" She rubbed my shoulder.

"I hope I really didn't lose Trent over this bullshit. Tyler texted me that he's a torn up mess, that his heart is shattered. They all think I slept with Gage." I pouted. Nova then took my suitcase and handed it to the airport personnel and turned to me and said, "He'll come around, girl. You just wait and see. These boys can be so dramatic." Nova rolled her eyes as I flipped through my cell hoping for a text message from Trent or Tyler, but nothing was there.

Suddenly, a car honked its horn, startling me as I shut off my phone.

"I gotta go. I'll call you later, girl." I waved to Nova as I ran into the airport to catch my flight.

Arriving in St. Louis, I knew I was cutting it short as I shuffled my way off the airplane and began sprinting through the terminal, searching for the taxi stand. I nervously tapped my foot as I stood in line waiting for a cab, just staring at my watch. *WHIP's live concert will be starting pretty soon.*

I panicked as I slipped into the backseat of a yellow cab with strawberry air fresheners hanging from the mirror. The smell made me want to puke as I rolled down the window.

I was quickly dropped off at the venue's will-call window just as they were about to pull the shade. "Hey! I'm here!" I tapped on the glass.

"Umm, Tyler Black from WHIP left me a ticket and a pass."

I flashed my identification card as the woman wearing 'The Lou' blue t-shirt shook her head.

"I think the show has started, hun. Shall I hold on to that suitcase till after?" She pointed at my suitcase while flashing me a sincere smile.

"Oh, please and thank you. It was a rocky flight from Dallas," I said as I wiped the sweat off of my upper lip.

"Texas, huh? Okay then, here's your ticket. You just head straight that way." She pointed to a set of doors leading to an executive box as I grabbed the ticket and fled to the VIP boxes.

I could hear the crowd roaring as I slipped into my seat. No one was around me. I had the row to myself as I set my purse down on the floor and gave WHIP my fullest attention.

The crowd were on their feet below waving lighters and flashing cell phones as they swayed to WHIP's music. My heart melted as I watched Tyler sing from behind the microphone stand. His swagger was Bowie but his vocal range was Ann Wilson. He looked strong, still rockin' the dress scarves, tight tee, messy hair and sunglasses.

Wait, sunglasses? He must be hiding the bruised eye. I tensed my shoulders up just picturing Trent sucker punching Tyler the other day after Trent heard from Gage's mouth that I fucked him real good. "Ugh," I sighed as I stared at Tyler. While the drum solo played on, Tyler turned and grabbed a second microphone stand and set it up right beside his microphone stand.

As the song came to a close, the crowd whistled and clapped while Tyler just stood there flashing them a beautiful smile. When the audience finally settled, the stage lights turned blue, lighting up just the two microphone stands. Trent walked up next to Tyler on stage. I bit my lip as I was trying to figure out what the hell he was doing. His hair had grown past his shoulders as he rocked a five o'clock shadow. He was still wearing his eyeliner with a deep V-neck black shirt, exposing a hint of chest ink where multiple necklaces dangled. I was turned on. He looked pretty fucking sexy.

Suddenly, the guitarist started a new song. *I kind of liked this medley of ballads; it was a welcoming change as WHIP developed musically*, I thought to myself as Trent then stepped towards the microphone, gripped it and began to sing. Wait. Trent was singing now? I stood up as my eyes dilated three sizes while I intensely listened.

Where were you? I was all alone. It's not the same when it's over the phone. He paused.

Listening to the empty silence, I already knew. The distance meant we were through. My body stayed tense. His soul just spilled out onto the stage with his raspy voice flowing as he sang an old WHIP song that he wrote a while ago when I was dating Gage physically and dating Trent emotionally. I was stunned as he poured his shattered heart all over the stage.

Then Tyler joined in singing,
I loathe here in pain, someone attend to me before I act insane. My knees weakened as I sat back down in my seat as tears began to stream down my face. My lover and my best friend were singing together so beautifully that I couldn't handle much more of the suffering.

Tyler repeated, *I loathe here in pain, someone attend to me before I act insane.* Which must have been directed towards either me or Olivia—either way it was agonizing.

I wiped my endless stream of tears on my sleeve as the guitarist went into a solo. Trent stood there holding the microphone as I couldn't take my eyes off of him.

He kept singing, *I used to think without you, I'm no longer me. Now, there's so much more I could be. But, still your absence haunts me.*

Then it finally hit me. Did my absence haunt him? Wait, is our relationship absent? Are we really over?

When the band ended their set, I just stayed seated in the balcony seat staring straight ahead. I was pondering if I should stay at the venue or if I should go back to Dallas. I grabbed my purse, pulled out a mirror and quickly fixed my face. I decided I was going to pull up my britches and face the music as I got to my feet, put my shoulders back and headed backstage.

I walked straight past Zack, past the band, past Tyler, and stopped right in front of Trent. He was wiping his face with a towel as I grabbed it and tossed it aside, huffing. Trent glared at me without saying a word. Neither one of us had the courage to speak first until Trent suddenly broke the silence.

Looking straight into my eyes he said, "I don't think I'm going to love you anymore." I just blinked in shock as my heart dropped to the floor. I saw it in his painful eyes... our last goodbye. Turning his back on me, he walked straight out the exit door to the concert venue's loading dock and got onto WHIP's tour bus.

As I was standing at the gate to catch my red-eye flight back to Dallas, I noticed that I forgot my suitcase. I flew out of the venue in such a huff that I never grabbed my bag or even stopped to speak with Tyler... the only thing I got was dumped. I had two bites on my ass cheek that night, one from karma and one from Gage Heston. I couldn't believe I got dumped by Trent. I must have been in shock as I kept repeating that line over and over in my head, *I don't think I'm going to love you anymore*, as I boarded the plane like a zombie.

Arriving back home, I was still stunned. I didn't even remember the flight, the cab ride home... nothing. I only remembered his deeply wounded eyes staring back into mine. In shock, I went straight upstairs, shut off my cell phone, and collapsed on the bed.

The next morning, I opened my eyes and immediately the tears were there to greet me. It wasn't a bad dream, it was reality. If Trent would only allow me to explain, but when it came to Gage Heston, there was never an explanation. There was no good excuse. I had to give Trent his space.

Maybe Tyler could fix this, but with that sucker punch Trent gave him, I didn't think he was in the mood to hear any of Tyler's bullshit right now. I couldn't process anything else. My brain was just going to explode all over my comforter. I then decided to get up, get out of my bed and go downstairs to the balcony.

Opening the door, the fresh morning air began to soothe me as I stood there letting the wind brush past my face. I took a deep breath in then let it out.

"It'll be alright," I told myself as the tears began to slowly subside. My phone was off a full twelve hours when I elected to turn it back on. Nothing from Trent. I then dialed Tyler.

"There you are, baby girl. What the fuck happened to you last night?" he asked while yawning into the phone.

"What the fuck was with the tune, dude?" I snapped.

"Tune? Oh, that old song? That was Trent's lame idea. Every fucking emotion of his comes out into his music. He's still hurting, so he had to belt it out during a melodramatic ballad. It sounded pretty fucking good though, huh?" I interrupted Tyler.

"Yeah, but not in an arena full of people. He just sounded so deeply wounded." I paused.

"Have you guys talked at all?" I asked as I was feeling a bit hopeful.

"Nah, we only had that rehearsal and after he put his fist through my eye, I didn't want to fuck with him. Give him some space, girl," Tyler sighed on the phone.

"I, on the other hand, appreciate you, girl. You faced Gage Heston on my behalf and scored me the movie deal. I am forever indebted to you." I could hear him light up his cigarette.

"Tyler, yes that was for you, but also for the entire band. Have y'all even read over the contract yet?"

I was getting pushy.

"Nah, we have a meeting with Zack when we get back to Dallas about the bullshit details. Then I believe I'm heading to Los Angeles to record my part." He blew out his smoke and coughed.

"Hum?" I said. "When are y'all coming home?" I swiftly changed the subject.

"In a few weeks or so. It'll be just me, though, Alex." Tyler paused.

"I heard Trent say he was heading back to Louisiana for a mental break of some sort." I fell silent.

"Alex? Listen girl, you have me. I know this rejection pill is hard for you to swallow. Olivia fed me the same fucking dose. I'll be back soon, and we'll head back over to that *Broken Hearts Club* where our broken-hearted asses can sit and have a fucking drink." He laughed.

"It's just me and you again, baby girl."

I let out a subtle laugh. "Me and you, Ty," I said softly as I clicked off the line.

CHAPTER 15

A few weeks had crawled on by since the drama went down in St. Louis. My nights were still sleepless and my days were a silent distraction. I never heard from Trent after I found out that I was blocked from his cell phone. I barely even spoke to Tyler. My heart ached. I lost faith, dignity and five pounds. I then picked up the phone and dialed my mother.

"Hi Mama," I said sadly over the line.

"My, what made you call me today, Alexandria?" My mother was a little snobby towards me.

"I'm sorry I haven't called. My heart has been tangled in a ball, Mama. Men can be so draining," I said as I moaned on the line.

"Honey, dating is agonizing. Fix your hair, put on your face and handle your mistake, whatever it may be." I huffed at her. How'd she guess this was my mistake?

"I think I really messed up this time with my boyfriend," I confessed, as I knew she thought my breakup with Gage Heston was all my fault and now Trent as well. I sensed she still wanted me to work it out with Mr. Fancy Pants Gage, if she had her pick of the two for me.

"Well, whatever you did, you just ask for forgiveness,

hun, and if he doesn't forgive you, then you move on and take this as another life lesson in your constant hunt for the perfect relationship." She paused on the line.

"I mean, there really is no perfect relationship out there, Alexandria. There will always be ups and downs. Do you think there's always another chance and another? Just fix it already, hun." I sighed.

"You're right, Mama. I'll be honest, and I'll ask for forgiveness."

I pouted as she said, "Well, I have company arriving soon. You pull up your britches, Alexandria, and get yourself together and fix this. I'm sure your boyfriend will understand. And, go get some exercise while you're at it. Don't lose your figure over this!" she sassed me.

I paused for a moment, reflecting on my mother's advice.

"Alexandria?" she asked.

"I'm here. I'll go fix this, Mama. I'll talk to you later," I promised as I clicked off the line and rubbed my eyes.

A few hours later, I knew my mother was right about the exercise part, so I decided to grab my tennis shoes and head back over to the Santa Fe trail and go for a much needed run. I had to clear out the confusion that was swirling in my brain over Trent.

"I can't believe he fucking blocked my call!" I blurted out as I startled another jogger passing by.

I picked up my pace as I wanted to try and outrun the agony I was feeling inside, but I couldn't outrun it. I continued jogging as I made my way back over to the pedestrian bridge of locks as I stopped and tried to catch my breath.

"Whew!" I blew out a long hot breath. My lungs were burning from the run, and my heart was burning from Trent. I just moved at a slow pace as I lingered on the bridge, looking at all the locks.

I stopped in front of the black one Trent and I locked on the bridge and just kicked it.

"Love locked forever, my foot!" I said as I pouted. I put my hands on my head and breathed out as I watched another couple attach their locks in the same manner as Trent and I did. *Did they even know what they were getting themselves into?* I thought as the familiar tears started to surface as I turned around and ran back to my truck feeling completely lost.

The loneliness continued to antagonize me until the day finally arrived where I had to pick up Tyler over at *Head Rush* after the guys returned from their ten city tour. I had squirrels fighting amongst themselves in my abdominal wall as I drove slowly over to the studio. I was so nervous that I would have to face Trent when I picked up Tyler that my heart and mind just wouldn't stop racing.

I made a right onto Dragon street and saw the familiar tour bus parked in the parking lot. Pulling in, I noticed everyone was gone except Tyler, who was standing alone, leaning against the bus. I honked my horn as I put my truck in park then jumped out to greet him. Tyler ran over to me and wrapped his arms around me so tightly that I couldn't breathe.

"I missed you, Alex!" He held me for another second

longer. I stepped back and took a good look at him.

"You smell a little funky, but you look real good, Mr. Black." I smiled as I leaned down to grab his backpack.

"Throw your shit in the back. You're finally home!" I hollered.

"Yeehaw! I'm finally home, baby girl!" Tyler shouted.

"I was a lonely mother fucker out on this leg of the tour. No sluuuts to warm me!" Tyler complained as he grabbed another bag. Distracted, I stood there for a moment looking around as Tyler set the bag into the back of my pickup truck.

"He's gone Alex. He rolled out his motorcycle from the studio and took off after we unloaded the bus. I'm really sorry," Tyler said, as I turned around and shrugged my shoulders.

"It is what it is, I guess," I huffed as we both hopped in the truck and made our way home.

Later that evening, Tyler settled back in as I was cooking us a light dinner. I lit some candles and put some Coltrane on the record player. Tyler, my 'partner in rejection,' sat at the table across from me as we quietly chewed. He then put down his fork and ran his finger through the candle's flame a few times.

I set my fork down as I just watched him tease the fire.

"Burn the memories... Burn the love... Burn what made us, us," he sang softly, reciting his lyrics from his song, "Betrayal."

"What?" I swallowed my food.

"Let's burn the memories of Trent and Olivia," he said softly as he glared at the candle. My eyes widened as I watched him flicker the flame with his finger once more.

"Neither one of them is fighting for us, Alex. They turned their backs on us. I say let's grab their shit, their sappy letters, fucking CDs of love songs and fucking burn it all. We played with fire and we got burned." Tyler looked directly at me as I nodded my head in agreement.

"Okay," I said as the two of us pushed our chairs out from the table and headed to gather up shit from our exes to burn.

With our exes' shit in our hands, we made our way outside to a rusted barrel in the back of the loft's parking lot against the garage wall, tossing in all of our relationship mementos. Tyler anxiously fished his jean pockets for his cigarette lighter. An evening thundercloud announced it was nearby, so I wasn't too concerned about setting the building on fire, just the burning barrel of wasted love. He started to light a few letters then stepped back as the flame took over. Tyler began to sing the lyrics from his song "Betrayal." "*Burn the memories... Burn the love... Burn what made us, us.*" I stared back at the flame, feeling a sense of freedom as we both knew we needed to do this.

A few raindrops started to fall from the sky as I remained still just listening to the fire crackle. My white braless tank top started to cling to me as the rain thickened and began to pour down. I didn't care.

Tyler then grabbed a hold of my hand and said, "I've been so lonely." I squeezed his hand and shook my head in agreement as I watched the fire burn. "Ugh. Me too, Ty. Me too," I said in a depressing manner.

The pouring rain was so cathartic; it was like it was washing away both of our lingering pain as we stood underneath it, never minding our wet clothes.

Tyler looked at me with his sad eyes and hair dripping as he leaned over towards me, pushing me against the garage brick wall and started kissing me. I couldn't resist. I needed to feel something other than pain at that moment, as I kissed him back heavier than I ever had before.

I began to run my fingers through his wet strands as I thrusted my tongue against his tongue ring as he moaned for more.

"Oh, Alex!" he cried out. His tongue felt so warm as I kept circling it with my tongue as the cool rain continued to pour down on us.

Tyler ran his fingers up under my tank top and scratched my back with his nails. I let out a sigh as I withdrew my tongue and began feverishly sucking on his neck. I wanted to feel anything else but abandonment at that very moment as I looked up at him and said, "I want you to fuck me, Tyler."

Tyler, just as lonely as me, stepped back and paused. He then grabbed my hand and pulled me towards the elevator for the loft.

When we reached his room, I grabbed his jeans and started quickly unbuttoning them as I licked his neck once more, noticing the sucker bite I left in the throes of passion. Tyler moaned for more as he heatedly unbuttoned my jeans and pulled them off of me as I stepped out of them, kicking them aside.

In a hurry, he then pulled off his clingy wet t-shirt as

he leaned back in towards me and bit my lower lip. I was turned on as I wanted to sleep with my best friend. I pulled his wet jeans down as he cried out, "I want you, Alex, I need you!"

Tyler then pushed me onto his bed as I threw my arms up over my head. His shadow was hovering above me as he grabbed a hold of my panties and pulled them off.

"Oh, Tyler!" I called out as he then pulled my soaking wet tank top off with one fell swoop, pulling it over my arms and throwing it onto the floor. He started to lick my breasts one at a time as I called out, "Oh, Tyler!"

The rain continuously beat against the window as my rapid breathing continued to turn Tyler on. He quickly spread my legs and entered me with his aching cock. I closed my eyes and accepted his fullness as I ran my nails down his back in return. Tyler was so turned on by my nail scratching as I dug them deeper into his back that he began to thrust harder and faster. *He fucked differently than Trent*, I thought, as I didn't care. I needed to feel anything other than Trent at that moment. I was still crushed from being dumped in St. Louis.

I started to feel an intense orgasm arise as I began releasing a plethora of emotions.

"Oh Tyler, you're going to make me come so hard!" I hollered out as Tyler kept fucking me. I licked his lips once more as he opened his mouth, accepting my tongue, kissing me with so much passion that my knees gave way as I started to have an orgasm. I couldn't catch my breath. This void needed to be filled.

"Alex, oh Alex!" he cried out as he started to come.

We both needed this climax to relieve any pain we were feeling at that particular moment.

Tyler then fell onto my chest as I kissed his shoulder and closed my eyes.

"I needed that, Tyler," I whispered as Tyler rolled off of me and onto his back, reaching for his marijuana. "Me too, Alex. You have no idea, baby girl. Thank you." He smiled as he fired up his joint.

As we both laid there naked and content, not one more minute was consumed with thinking about Trent or Olivia.

"Do you want a hit?" Tyler passed me his burning joint as I grabbed it with my two fingers and inhaled.

Handing it back to him, I just stared at the yellow and green tinted remains of a bruised eye that he received because of me. I started to feel bad. My wounded friend had a bruised eye, scars on his inner arm, a crushed ego and a broken heart.

"What are you staring at?" Tyler asked me as he set the joint down into an ashtray on the bedside table. "I know I always say this... but you are truly so beautiful, Tyler." I trailed my fingernails down the cut marks on his severed porcelain skin. He let out a breath.

"If you think so." He rolled his eyes as he looked towards the window, watching the rain continue to fall.

The pot was giving me a calming high as I looked over at Tyler and blurted out, "I did not sleep with Gage." Tyler looked back over at me with surprise.

"Are you telling me the truth?" he asked.

"I always tell you the truth, and the truth is I never slept with that asshole Gage. I'll tell you all about it some other time. I just don't want to invite thoughts of him into this bedroom tonight." Tyler shook his head in agreement but still registered surprise as he took another hit from his joint.

I don't know what overcame me at that moment, but I sat up and crawled back onto Tyler's lap. Smiling at him, I pushed his hair behind his ears, kissed his bruised eye then slid my tongue back in his warm mouth. Tyler happily accepted it as I could feel him get hard again. I then lifted my hips up and let him enter me slowly for a second time.

I didn't just want sex now; I was begging for a connection. I began to moan as I slid up and down Tyler's hardened cock.

"Oh, you're killing me, Alex. This feels so amazing," he said softly as I slowly rocked him while Tyler closed his eyes and ached with emotion.

"I need you, Tyler," I whispered in his ear as he turned his head to kiss me. He tasted differently, he touched me differently. I wanted everything to feel different from Trent as I continued to have sex with him once more. We both let ourselves go and started to climax again for the second time that evening.

The next morning I sat up, grabbed Tyler's Twisted Sister t-shirt, pulled it on and slid down to the edge of the bed. Tyler was still sleeping as I glanced over my shoulder and shook my head. He was even more beautiful when he slept.

I smiled as I stood up and made my way to the kitchen to brew us some coffee.

As I sipped my drink, I heard, "That smells amazing." I laughed as I retrieved a second mug out of the cupboard and poured Tyler his coffee. He walked into the kitchen with messy hair, smeared eyeliner and wearing last night's jeans.

"How'd ya sleep?" I asked him as I handed him a mug as he took a seat at the kitchen counter.

"Never better. I can't seem to ever sleep in hotel rooms, though. It's when I'm home I get the most rest."

I nodded my head.

"That makes sense." I smiled as I took another sip. Tyler reached out his hand and pulled me over into his personal space between his legs. I smiled as I looked at him.

"I like you in my clothes." He lightly laughed as he tugged on his concert t-shirt. "Actually, I prefer you out of your clothes." I rolled my eyes.

"Last night..." He paused, getting serious. "We both needed that. Any regrets?" he asked while holding a breath. I shook my head no.

"No regrets," I said, comforting him.

"I'm always going to need you, Alex." I looked down at the floor as I blushed.

"Do you miss him?" he asked.

I swallowed hard then said, "Yeah, that's how it works, right?" He just touched my face as he leaned in to kiss me softly on my lips. My toes curled as I kissed him back.

CHAPTER 16

Tyler and I were inseparable over the next six weeks. We cooked, watched movies and made sure we curled up with each other every night, comforting one another. We were too frightened to be left alone our entire lives after Trent and Olivia walked away from the two of us.

Nearing the weekend, I kept myself distracted with a deadline I was on to design a band's website when I suddenly had trouble logging into their account.

"What the fuck?" I said out loud as I nervously tapped in passwords.

"I'm locked out." I sat back and tried to figure out what was going on.

I then scanned my inbox and noticed an unopened email in there from Gage Heston's record label. I scanned through it and couldn't believe what I was reading. That asshole blacklisted me from his client list! I was fired! All my projects were turned over to another freelancer, and I was no longer the lead designer for any project pertaining to the label.

"Fuck!" I screamed again.

That was a huge percentage of my earnings. It was one thing he never took away from me after our breakup because it was business and not personal. Now, that asshole was getting personal. *I'll have to do double the design work to make up for what his company paid me quarterly.* I was distraught.

Tyler walked out into the living room asking, "What's up baby girl? What's all the 'F' bombs for?" He laughed as I stared at my computer in disbelief. "Dude, Gage blacklisted me from the company. I can no longer work on any of his clients' designs. I'm so fucking screwed!" I yelled as Tyler ran his hands through his hair.

"If you need money, baby girl, I'll give you money," he offered sincerely.

"I need my fucking job! That dirty bastard! He screwed me over like I screwed him over on y'all's movie soundtrack contract. Fucking karma!" I screamed as Tyler took a step back.

"I still have a few clients on the side, but this was the majority of my work! I'm in the process of building my own roster of clients, I'm just not there yet!" I let out an 'ahh' as I pouted and slammed my laptop closed. Once again, I was bitten twice on the butt, once by karma and once by Gage Heston. I sat there shaking my head in disbelief.

"I'm so sorry, baby girl. It's all my fault," Tyler apologized.

"No, it's not your fault. Stop that. I needed to eventually pull away from Gage's label sooner or later; I was just hoping for a little later, that's all," I said as I bit my lip, watching Tyler pace the living room.

He continued pacing around the loft, counting down the hours until WHIP's much awaited meeting about this contract for the rock and roll film project. I knew he was amped and ready to dive into this project. I could just sense his tension and anxiety.

"Is the meeting finally tonight?" I asked to shift the focus off of Gage and me and put it back on the band.

"It is scheduled for seven o'clock. Oh, can I take your truck to the studio?" Tyler asked while nervously scratching his head.

"Sure," I agreed. I did not want to tag along tonight. This was WHIP's moment to hear all about the contract details, as I wanted nothing more to do with this stupid film contract that seemed to turn around and bite me right in the ass.

"Can you do me a huge favor, though?" I asked as I stood up and stretched my arms while Tyler stood there with his hands on his hips staring at me.

"What?" he asked.

"Can you please tell Trent that I did not sleep with Gage?"

Tyler huffed. "What's the fucking point of that?" he asked.

"I..." I stuttered. "I really want him to know the truth. I actually want everyone in WHIP to know the truth. They can do what they want with it, but I feel like they see me as nothing but a damn whore." I pouted.

"*Whores*!" Tyler hollered out, referencing one of WHIP's tunes "Whore's Gone Astray."

"Very funny, Ty. I'm serious. Just wait till you hear all the details of the contract, Mr. Rock Star. You're going to be very pleased."

I stuck out my tongue as Tyler returned the gesture then started to head back into his room, stopping mid-stride he turned towards me and asked shyly, "Will you go to the meet-and-greet dinner with me? It is some 'get together' for film executives, producers and the director. Will you be my date, baby girl?" He blew me a kiss as he flirted.

I tapped my fingers on my hips, wondering if this was a good idea or not.

"Sure," I said, caving into Tyler's beautiful smile.

"I need you there," he said as he went into his bedroom.

"I know. I'll be there," I whispered back.

Later that night, I put away my computer for the second time as I rubbed my eyes and made my way to the shower.

Afterwards, I had wet hair and comfortable clothes on as I crawled into Tyler's bed and curled into a ball. I just couldn't keep myself from stewing about my contract loss and WHIP's contract gain and just the whole meeting in general. Every bad scenario swirled in my head and tortured me when suddenly I heard the front door slam.

"Where ya at, baby girl?" Tyler hollered.

"I'm in here, Ty," I called out as I stretched myself out over his comforter.

"I love that you're lying in my bed." Tyler paused, standing in the door frame long and lean, admiring me.

"How was the meeting with Zack? Did you finally get a moment to talk to Trent?" I rubbed my eyes as Tyler sighed while he crawled into bed next to me and rolled onto his back. I couldn't hold out, I had to get straight to the point. Tyler stretched his arms as he released a breath.

"Trent didn't care," he said with a pouty voice. My eyelashes just batted about a dozen times as Tyler looked over at me.

"Fuck him," he said as he dodged the Trent conversation and flipped the script to focus on him.

"However, you goddess, you fucking hooked us up, girl!" Tyler smacked and rubbed his palms together. "We have full rights to fucking everything! We get all the damn money! You are so amazing, Alex! Again, how did you do this without using your fine pussy?" Tyler laughed as he elbowed me.

"Fuck you, Tyler, not cool." I play-punched his arm as I pouted.

"You really look out for me huh, Alex?" Tyler whispered seriously as I rolled my head back in his direction.

"I do." I smiled as I softly brushed his cheek with my fingertips. "I do," I repeated.

He then rolled over on top of me, pinned me down on the bed, and gently started kissing my neck. "Thank you, Alex," he whispered his gratitude again in my ear. "Thank you," he repeated.

I parted my lips and stuck out my tongue as Tyler licked it with his as he continued to push his way into my mouth. My knees seemed to weaken every time this pretty band boy kissed me. I eagerly begged for more.

"I love how your tongue feels in my mouth. Kiss me more!" I pleaded as I allowed him to lick my lower lip with his barbelled tongue and then up to my upper lip and slide his tongue in once more. Chills just flushed down my spine. I then closed my eyes and began to relax while he continued to softly kiss my lips.

Tyler grabbed a hold of the side of my jogging pants and pulled it down slowly past my hips. I moaned, knowing just right where we were headed.

He began to slowly dry hump me while grabbing each of my hands and folding them into his. His hard cock felt amazing rubbing against my pussy as I started to become wet.

"Oh, you're such a tease, Mr. Black," I whispered as I began to breathe heavier. He was quickly becoming aroused as he let go of one of my hands and slid his two fingers into me, feeling my wetness. "Oh, Tyler!" I moaned as he slowly slid his fingers inside and out. I gently scratched my nails up and down his hard cock that was waiting inside his jeans with anticipation to be released.

"I need to be inside you right now, Alex," Tyler panted in my ear.

"I need to feel you. I need to fuck you." I then unbuttoned his tight jeans and pushed them down slowly with my foot as he squeezed my one palm tighter into his. He moaned as I swiftly pulled off his black ribbed tank top, letting my hand go free as he then pulled my jogging pants completely off and opened my legs.

My nipples hardened under my tank as I traced the tattoos on his arm, watching him pull out his endowed cock. He then rubbed his saliva on the tip and entered me slowly.

"Tell me you want only me, Alex," he demanded as he began to thrust.

"I only want you, Tyler!" I answered him breathlessly, knowing his insecurity was shining through.

"I only want you, Tyler," I repeated as I threw my head back in ecstasy.

"Oh Tyler. I want only you!" I called out again as I slapped his ass and pushed him deeper inside of me. "Make me come like you do, Tyler. I want to come for you again tonight," I panted as he slowly fucked me.

"Oh, Alex!" he moaned, as I continued to push him inside of me until we both climaxed.

Who was the real rock star here? I smiled to myself. Once again, I had amazing sex with the lead singer.

The day of the meet-and-greet dinner with the film executives was upon us. I stood in Tyler's closet, pulling out articles of clothing to create the perfect outfit for him as he laid back on his bed watching me.

"Put this black button up dress shirt with this black jacket and these black jeans." I grabbed a few maroon and black colored scarves off the closet door.

"And definitely these scarves, layer them," I said as I wrapped the scarves around the dress shirt hanger, slipping it over the bathroom door.

"Still rock your eyeliner, Ty, but please let me fix your hair." I turned around to check if Tyler was listening to me as he just smiled while admiring my choice of clothing.

"I'm going to look so good that I just might want to fuck myself," Tyler said, laughing as he leaned up on his elbow.

"Johnny Cash might be the only one proud of all this black you're rockin' tonight, but either way you'll give off that sexy rock god vibe to these film douchebags," I laughed as I boosted his confidence, knowing he was a nervous wreck about meeting everyone tonight.

"And..." I sat on the edge of the bed.

"I'll be dressed in black, too." I blew him a kiss.

"Thank you, Alex. I mean, thank you for going with me. I know I have the guys and all, but I really need you there with me." I leaned into him as I brushed his layered hair out of his eyes.

"You're going to look like a fucking star. Don't get yourself so worked up. These executive douchebags want you,

Ty. You pleaded to me that you wanted this gig, so don't puss out on me! Again, this is an amazing opportunity. I'm still really, really proud of you." I kissed his head and lightly tapped on his butt.

"Now, get your skinny ass up off that bed and into the shower!" I ordered.

"I need to put my face on and get myself all gussied up. Plus, Nova and Zack will be here in one hour, so chop chop, Mr. Black!" I patted his ass once more while he moaned, rolled out of bed and headed straight to the shower.

"Tyler, can you please get the door? I think Zack and Nova are here. I'm still getting ready!" I hollered over the loft down towards Tyler's room. I could smell a hint of marijuana as I hollered for a second time.

"Ty?" I heard a huff and ignored it. I stood in the mirror adjusting my form-fitted black lace cocktail dress while slipping on my other black high heel. I wanted to look good on Tyler's arm tonight. This evening was about him and the band, not me.

"Hey hooker." Nova peeked her head into my bathroom.

"You look real pretty, Alex," Nova complimented me as I began to collect makeup for my purse.

"Yeah? Thank you. I don't know why I feel so nervous. I just have to sit there and politely chew." Nova laughed.

"You're nervous about seeing Trent, that's all." She called me out. I didn't respond to her as I just kept fidgeting. Nova then stopped my hand and squeezed it.

"I'll set those WHIP boys straight tonight. I'll take all

the heat, girl. Listen, I distracted Mr. Heston while you handled the attorney. And fuck Trent if he doesn't believe you. Y'all have been through so much that he should have just asked you straight out if you slept with Gage or not." Nova released my hand then tapped it once more, trying to comfort me.

"He straight out punched Tyler in the face is what he did. Tyler told him the other night at the meeting that I didn't sleep with Gage, but I got nothing. I'm just confused. I do know that Trent just wants me to have nothing to do with Mr. Gage Heston, nothing girl. Hey, but I do appreciate the offer to confess our ploy, but what's done is done." I shrugged my shoulders as I peeked my head out the bathroom door, listening for Tyler.

He and Zack were chatting on the balcony when I leaned back in towards Nova and quietly whispered, "I slept with Tyler twice." Nova put her hand over her mouth.

"Say what? How was that?" she asked sweetly, sensing my emotional load was getting pretty heavy.

"It was really good, girl. I mean, he's a mess, I'm a mess. We're just two birds licking each other's wounds." I paused.

"Tyler needs me. Trent doesn't." I glanced to the floor.

"It's okay, Alex. It's not like you had a one-night stand with some stranger. It was Tyler." I shook my head.

"You're right, it was Tyler, and who am I closest to in this whole world?... Tyler." I reached out and hugged Nova, feeling like a small weight had just been lifted.

"Well, let's get this show on the road. I'm going to need a drink after that lil confession." I laughed, knowing Nova loved me and would not pass any judgment.

CHAPTER 17

The four of us pulled into the valet at the newest, hottest hotel that was just built in Victory Park.

"This place is stunning!" Nova squealed as Zack helped her out of the car then reached for my hand.

I stepped out and just stared while admiring the grand statues posing in tranquility gardens all along the trim of the building.

"Stunning," I repeated. Tyler shut the car door behind me as he placed his hand in mine. I gave it a light squeeze, letting him know that it was okay.

The four of us walked into the hotel restaurant as Zack confirmed our reservation. The hostess politely smiled as she directed us towards a private dining room reserved for WHIP and the production company. Everyone from WHIP was already seated as we entered the dimly lit room.

"Girl, this ambiance is so romantic," Nova whispered over her shoulder to me as Tyler and I followed her to our assigned seats. A large wooden table was fully set with dinnerware, white linens, fresh flowers and candles glowing. A soft sound from a piano drifted from the bar as I panned the room secretly hoping I wasn't seated next to Trent.

Just then six executives in business attire pushed out

their chairs and stood up in unison, as one said,

"There he is. This must be the famous Tyler Black." Tyler smiled as he reached out his free hand to shake each one of their hands. I just held on to the other hand, letting Tyler dictate this event.

"Oh, gentleman this is Alexandria Rae." Tyler introduced me, and I just smiled as Zack gestured for all of us to take our seats. Tyler pulled out a chair so I could be seated, then he sat down right next to me. Nova took her seat on the opposite side, which made me feel like I had some sort of friend barrier around me to protect me tonight.

I nodded to the other guys from WHIP, then quickly glanced away. I could see Trent out of the corner of my eye, but did not make contact. He was in a black velvet jacket with his infamous low V-neck shirt and half a dozen necklaces hanging. The hair was still past his shoulders and loosely hanging from a man-bun. He looked quite sexy. Dismissing my attraction for him, I just let out a quiet breath as I shook my leg in nervous frustration. Just then Tyler slid his hand onto my leg to soothe my nerves as he rubbed it softly up and down all while he kept talking with the film executives.

Finally, a few black tie waiters arrived with wine in hand and began pouring our glasses.

"Now that's what I'm talking about!" Nova said, as she held up her glass to receive some wine. The waiter turned towards me as I nodded yes for him to fill my glass. I then grabbed Tyler's glass and had the waiter fill his as well.

"You're so cute. Look how you take such good care of him," Nova whispered as I glanced over at Trent then set

Tyler's glass down in front of him. Tyler turned towards me, picked up the glass and lightly tapped my glass with his.

"To you," he whispered as I batted my lashes and returned the gesture.

Some of the band members held up their glasses and saluted me as well with asshole smirks on their faces. I just sunk down into my seat. I felt like everyone was judging me, that everyone thought I was a whore who sold myself out for Tyler Black. But it just wasn't true.

The drinks turned into dinner. I didn't have much of an appetite as I pushed my steak around my plate. Tyler picked off his plate from time to time as he continued to chat as everyone just fawned all over him.

The film executives began handing out schedules while discussing their timeline. I only heard that Tyler would record vocals, including their new song "Betrayal" in L.A., the band would record in Dallas and everything would be mastered in Nashville as I zoned out. All the boys seemed to be in agreement as they kept toasting one another.

As the dinner came to a close, the executives stood up, once again shaking Zack's hand, nodding to all the guys as they signed the bill and left the hotel restaurant. WHIP just all leaned back in silence, processing everything until Nova who was feeling a bit tipsy broke their silence.

"Okay, gentlemen, I want all of your attention!" She stood up and set her wineglass down on the table.

"I'm setting something straight right now. I've never

fucked any of you. I've always been just a fan of your music. I've always supported you, so I believe I deserve a moment of your time." Zack hushed the boys down as they all looked up at Nova. I squeezed Tyler's hand, feeling a flush of embarrassment pass through me.

"I flirted with Gage Heston. I distracted Gage Heston. I slipped Gage Heston a valium." The boys let out a subtle laugh at that little tidbit.

"I, I, I," Nova stressed her I's as she continued to go on.

"Now, knowing her history with Heston, my girl Alex here put herself into an uncomfortable position to deal with him on y'all's behalf." She slurred her words a bit.

"Alex handled the attorney, William, single-handedly. She made sure Tyler was the only vocalist on the film, that WHIP were the only musicians, and that y'allllll got all the fucking rights and money." She pointed to everyone as she stressed y'all.

"So no one fucked Gage literally; we just fucked him out of his own record label's contract." The guys began to laugh as they all looked at one another and started nodding their heads.

"I'm really sorry, Alex. I shouldn't have assumed." The drummer initiated the first apology.

"Yeah, we're very sorry, girl," the guitarist said as Trent leaned back in his chair and didn't say anything as he shook his head in disbelief.

"I thought you told Trent?" I whispered in Tyler's ear.

"No, he didn't, Alex." Trent took a sip of his wine then slammed the glass down as he pushed out his chair and got to his feet.

He looked straight at Tyler and yelled, "Parasite! Man, you're nothing but a fucking parasite."

149

The room grew silent once more as Trent turned around and walked out of the dining room. WHIP all got to their feet in unison and started apologizing once again to me. I just waved it off as I scooted my chair out and followed Trent out of the hotel.

I caught him standing at the valet station. "I'm not a fucking whore like in one of your songs, Trent. I really loved you." I hollered at him as he turned around to face me.

"Why did you put yourself in that position? After everything I did for you in Louisiana, that was a very dangerous position to be in, Alex. I warned you that I would not have it if you interacted with Gage in any way after I saw the two of you together at the radio station," he shamed me.

"It was for..." He interrupted me.

"It was for fucking Tyler, Alex. Everything is always for fucking Tyler. It's exhausting competing for your attention all the time. I can't play these games anymore." He shook his head as he handed a tip to the valet.

I choked up and couldn't find my words as I stood there watching Trent hop on his motorcycle and take off. I couldn't believe he just left. I felt his emotional punch to the gut as he disappeared.

"Well, at least he knows the truth now," I whispered as I felt the warmth from a body standing behind me, assuming it was Nova.

"Why didn't Tyler just explain everything?" I ran my fingers through my hair in frustration while I tapped my heel.

"Because I'm in love with you, Alex," Tyler confessed

as my eyes widened as I just continued to stare straight ahead. I could feel Tyler's breath on the back of my neck as he wrapped himself around me.

"I love you, Alex," he whispered once more. *Holy shit*, I thought. I was trying to process those three fucking words that continuously get tossed around like confetti.

"Oh, Tyler." I shook my head as I turned around and faced him.

"Are you ready for me to feel this way?" he questioned me.

"I don't want to lose you, Alex." I said nothing. I could not hurt my best friend right now. I was confused.

Nova approached us asking, "Are y'all ready to go yet?" Tyler stepped back away from me and climbed into Zack's car.

I looked at Nova and with a sudden epiphany I said, "I think I'm in love with Tyler? Trent doesn't want me anymore." I pouted as Nova put her arm around me.

"You two wounded birds are a hot mess. Now you're lovebirds?" Nova laughed as she opened the back door for me.

"Go back to the nest with Tyler, girl. He's just a rebound. Don't get yourself so tangled up in love. This mess will play out. Don't push it so hard," Nova reprimanded me.

She was right. I had to give Trent his space. Was it so bad if I took comfort in Tyler while he figured out what the hell he wanted? I released a breath as Nova reached over and patted my butt as I slid in next to Tyler, intertwining my hand in with his and squeezing it tightly. Nova shut the car door and Zack drove us back to my place.

❦

Walking into the loft, it was dark with only my nightlights guiding the way. I heard my radio playing power ballads that I always leave on for Ernie when I'm out. I set my purse down as Tyler locked the door. I paused in the corridor as Tyler walked up behind me and slid his hand around my waist.

We said nothing to each other as he leaned in and kissed my ear. With heated passion, I turned around and pulled him in towards me to kiss me.

"Alex," Tyler moaned softly as we kissed one another.

I stepped back on my heel, pausing for a moment to think about Trent. I was hurt. *Why didn't he forgive me tonight after he found out that I didn't sleep with Gage?*

"Hey, where's your head, baby girl?" Tyler asked sincerely as he held my chin and looked into my eyes.

I shook my head.

"I don't know. I just hate how all these fucking feelings are confusing me," I said as I looked down at the floor.

"The only feeling I want you to fixate on tonight is pleasure. I want to please you, Alex. Take your mind off everything, from all the bullshit, and just relax." I let out a subtle laugh.

"And, thank you for coming with me tonight. I needed you there with me. Thank you," he said as I looked up into his dark eyes.

"You're right. Fuck tonight. I'm over this constant anxiety. I'm all yours tonight, Tyler. Do with me what you will." I nodded my head yes as I pulled off his jacket and tossed it on the floor.

He laughed and said, "Umm, relax. I got this."

Tyler then pulled one of his scarves off from around his neck and with a smile he blindfolded me with it. I was breathless as I trusted him, knowing he knew what he was doing. He pushed me up against the wall as he slowly unzipped my black dress.

"Oh, Tyler," I panted as the dress dropped to the floor. I stood there blindfolded in my black lace panties and bra, aching for his touch.

I reached out for Tyler as I slowly traced my hands along his shirt, searching for its buttons. Feeling one button at a time, I unbuttoned his shirt and felt the warmth of his skin underneath as I removed it. From this new heightened sense of touch, I ached for more. I ran my nails slowly up his chest, then up into his hair as Tyler moaned. Gently tugging on his hair, I pulled him in for another wet kiss.

He paused, whispering to me, "Breathe out so I could breathe you in." As I released a breath, he slowly slid his barbell tongue into my mouth and encircled my tongue once more.

I could feel the heat penetrating between our bodies as he passionately kissed me.

"Oh, Tyler!" I moaned, egging him on. I was hell bound on not fixating on Trent tonight as Tyler took my hand in his as he guided me to his bed. He gently sat me down on the edge and knelt on the floor between my trembling legs.

I tried to untie the scarf as Tyler reached up for my wrists, grabbing them and whispered, "Don't take it off. Feel what I'm doing to you." I gasped as he pulled on my black lacy panties and Trent flashed through my mind. *This is how tender Trent treated me.* I suddenly stiffened up. Tyler could feel my body tense as he squeezed my leg. "It's okay, baby girl. I want to be gentle with you. Relax," he whispered as he slowly slid the panties over my knees and onto the floor. He then spread my legs open and slowly licked my lips up one side and down the other. He then flickered his barbell over my clit a few times as I tossed my head back, letting the wetness of my pussy arouse me from his mouth-watering oral sex. Tyler slowly slid one finger in as I squeezed my hands, gripping the bedspread. This felt like heaven.

"You feel so warm, so wet, Alex," he said as he began licking my neck, then slid his tongue in my mouth while continuously pleasuring me.

I broke free from the kiss and reached my hands out for his jeans, feeling for the sharp zipper as I pulled it down to unveil his hardened cock. It felt like velvet as I rubbed my hands up and down on it while licking the sweat off his chest.

"You taste so good, Tyler," I moaned. Everything was heightened: his smell, his touch, his taste as I begged for more.

"I love how you touch me!" I whispered breathlessly as Tyler slid his soft fingers once again along my pussy.

"I now want you to feel how much I want you," he whispered back into my ear. I felt goosebumps flush over my body from the heat of his mouth as he kissed my neck. My last breath lingered on the word 'want' as I felt this emerging connection.

"I want you tonight, Tyler. Make me feel anything but pain," I pleaded as Tyler leaned me back and crawled on top of me. He opened me and slowly entered as I cried out, "Tyler!" as he pushed himself inside of me. I could feel his hair brush against my neck as his warm mouth kissed my ear as he slowly pushed deeper.

"Tell me you only want me," he panted as I held on

to his hips as he found the right spot to slowly rock my world.

"I want you, Tyler! Right there, you're pleasuring me right there!" I cried out as I couldn't hold out any longer as I started to release all my pent-up feelings onto Tyler. He pushed his tongue into my mouth and kissed me as I released every draining emotion that surfaced from this evening.

Pulling out his tongue, Tyler then whispered. "You're going to make me come so hard, Alex," he said tenderly, thrusting once more.

"I can't hold out, Tyler. I want to come with you! I want you!" I cried out as he thrusted harder and harder until we both climaxed. All I could sense at that moment was that sex with Tyler just kept getting better and better.

Gently un-tying the scarf around my eyes, I could feel him giving me butterfly kisses with his long black eyelashes. I smiled as I blinked a few times, trying to focus as I looked back into those endless dark makeup-lined eyes. *This lost soul loves me.*

Tyler rolled off me as he searched for a cigarette in the bedside drawer. After lighting one up, I noticed that from behind the cigarette I could sense a peace of mind.

CHAPTER 18

The production company had Tyler's flight, hotel and recording studio all booked. I stood in his closet once again as I pulled out items for him to pack.

"How many t-shirts do you want?" I hollered towards him as I sifted through a bin of concert tees. Tyler was in the kitchen brewing himself some afternoon coffee.

After grabbing his suitcase and tossing it up onto the bed, I looked out the closet and noticed that a few papers flew out onto the floor. I walked out and gathered up all the loose notes as I sat on the floor and began to organize them. One was the set list, another was the band's rider, and then I noticed my letter I wrote to him before the last ten city tour. I picked it up, and to my surprise it was unopened.

"Hum?" I muttered out loud. Why didn't he read my letter? Trent thanked me for the one I slipped into his suitcase, but Tyler never even opened his. I was hurt.

Tyler then walked back into the room with his coffee mug in hand.

"What's all that?" he asked as I was shoving the papers in the nightstand drawer.

"Nothing, just shit that fell out of your suitcase. I think

I got enough t-shirts," I laughed as I pointed to the pile of swag on the floor.

Tyler sat down on the bed next to the suitcase, sipping his coffee as he watched me pack for the L.A. trip.

"Are you nervous?" I asked while I folded his Rage Against The Machine t-shirt, setting it into the suitcase.

"I'm excited. I can do this, right Alex?" He looked over at me for confirmation.

"Of course you can do this. Oh, I also bought your throat more tea and honey." Tyler laughed.

"You have a refill of your medication. You have a tight schedule, so really, Ty, there's no time to fuck around. Plus, you wanted this chance to reboot your image, remember? You landed this cool-ass soundtrack gig. Now go and kick some fucking ass." I smiled as I folded his jeans and stuffed them into the suitcase next to the t-shirts.

"I wish you would go with me." He pouted while tapping his fingers on the coffee mug.

"You need to do this alone, Tyler. No WHIP, no drugs, no alcohol, and especially no me. Anyway, I have to line up another design gig for myself." I blew him a kiss.

"Okay," he said as he pouted once more.

"Look, knock out a few vocal recording sessions, then maybe I'll fly out there and we'll hit up Las Vegas or something to celebrate. Deal?"

He smiled and said, "Deal." *Man, I get weak in the knees when this beautiful disaster flashes me a smile. I'm going to miss him but I could use the much needed space. I feel like I'm drowning in his insecurities.*

Later that evening, I made us some dinner as we listened to chilled music. Tyler's burdens and suitcases were packed and parked by the front door ready for tomorrow. Glancing over at them, I was actually starting to feel relief. I needed to let this lil bird fly free. He'd come so far with the medication, no hard drugs, just a glass of wine or two—so much more control on his end—I had to hand it to him.

He was also taking his vocal career much more seriously, as he was with his relationship with me. My heart fluttered for a second as I thought, *Is this a relationship between Tyler and me?* I stood there washing the dishes, stewing on 'us.' *We've never declared ourselves an item. And with the latest emotional storm, I know he said he loves me, but do I love him in that way? I know I love him, but am I... IN LOVE WITH HIM?* I blew out a breath as I rinsed a dish.

Startling me, I felt Tyler's hand slip around my waist and hold on to me.

"I'm going to crash out, baby girl. I want to be fresh for the morning flight. Are you feeling tired?" He kissed the back of my neck as I reached for a dish towel and dried my hands.

"I'll join you, boo," I said as I clicked off the kitchen light and followed Tyler into his room.

He pulled off his t-shirt and crawled into the bed, making an "ahhh" sound as he tapped on the bed, gesturing for me to join him. I flipped off my Dallas Cowboy slippers and crawled into the bed beside him. He wrapped his arms around me, nestled his nose in my hair, and while spooning with each other we fell asleep.

The next morning I waved goodbye to the taxicab that picked up Tyler for the airport from my balcony. I then sat down on the wicker chair and just breathed in my nose and out my mouth a few times as I released the anxiety. *I finally have the place to myself. No Trent. No Tyler.*

I decided to go into the house, turn up the volume on my music, and go for the cleaning supplies. I wanted to clean and organize my space as a way of getting some sort of control back. I opened the windows, letting the season of autumn's breeze slip in and clear out the summer dust. I felt energized as I scrubbed, swept, changed the bedding until I reached my upstairs closet.

As I emptied my laundry basket, I looked up and saw Trent's clothing still hanging from the rack. I immediately leaned into them and inhaled a deep breath. His lingering scent made my eyes water as I slid down to the floor, pulling a t-shirt off the hanger with me. I began to cry as I rubbed my face into the shirt. *What happened to us?* I couldn't stop sobbing. I was just too busy comforting Tyler that I put my own needs on the back burner and did not fight hard enough for Trent. But, did he fight hard enough for me? I was aware Tyler was in the middle as I struggled to find the answer.

Immediately, anger began to overcome me as I stood up, grabbed all Trent's belongings and shoved them into a box.

"Fuck it!" I screamed as I tossed the box over the railing, letting it crash onto my kitchen floor. I then ran downstairs, pulled the box out the door and loaded it into the back of my truck.

Heading back into the loft, I went straight into Tyler's room and grabbed the unopened letter out of his bedside table drawer, set it on fire, then tossed it into the kitchen sink. I then collected all his belongings and shoved them into a box as well. I felt so alive again!

"I'm no longer insecure or fucking naive!" I let out a liberating scream as Ernie ran upstairs and hid under my bed.

"If Trent doesn't want me, then to hell with him. Or if I just want to fuck Tyler, then so be it—I'm in control! I have my own wings to spread and fly above all this bullshit!" I let out another "ahhhh" after my temper tantrum.

Suddenly, I got an idea as I ran over to my art table, grabbed my charcoal pencil, and began feverishly sketching out a pair of angel wings. This new air of confidence was refreshing as I stood there drawing, trying to calm myself down. When I was finished, I cleaned myself up and got dressed. I made the decision that there was somewhere important that I had to be.

As I walked into the familiar tattoo shop, I looked around, letting it fuel my desire for ink. Yes, I wanted ink. A man with a shaved head, a pierced nose, and tattoos clear up to his neck asked, "Can I help you, lil darling?" I smiled as I walked straight up to him and handed him my drawing. He turned it around and said, "That's pretty fucking good. Did you draw this, hun?"

I nodded my head yes. "I'd love to have this inked on

my back, please." I blushed, starting to feel a bit nervous about the rash decision I just made to get a tattoo.

"I can do this no problem. The shop is pretty quiet today... shall we start now?" he asked me.

I swallowed hard, then answered, "Yes, please." He laughed, as he could sense my intimidation. I then followed the tattoo artist into his private room where all his essentials were laid out on a metal surgical tray next to a red leather chair. He had heavy metal music playing in the background as he gestured for me to take a seat.

"I'm going to upload this design into my computer." I nodded yes as I set my bag down on the seat and fished for my headphones.

Within a few minutes, he returned and asked me to remove my shirt so he could place the paper on my back and trace it as a reference. I giggled as I pulled off my racer-back tank top. The man just looked away as he fiddled with his tattoo gun, remaining professional. I then turned around for him as he began pressing the paper against my back, making an imprint of my angel wings.

"Now go take a look, darling." He pointed over to a mirror as I stood there covering my exposed boobs and blinked.

"Go take a look," he directed me for a second time. I walked over to the mirror to look at my reflection, then I gasped.

"The wings look so beautiful!" He smiled as he gestured for me to come back to the tattoo chair as he finished adjusting it for me.

"Sit down right here, pretty lady, and let me get started." He tapped the leather seat a few times.

"Do you need a drink? Or do you need to throw up?" He started to laugh as he teased, sensing my anxiety.

"I'm ready, sir," I said as I put my earbuds in to listen to music to soothe me as I laid down on my stomach in the cool red leather chair. If I could handle the physical pain of Gage and the emotional pain of Trent, I sure as hell could handle the pain of a tattoo. I then let out a much needed deep breath as I let the artist get to work on my angel wings.

A few hours into the session, I shifted my neck, noticing everything felt numb.

"I'm almost there, darling. I'm so proud of you," he complimented me as he poked and wiped, poked and wiped.

I laid there listening to tunes when all of a sudden I heard the all-too-familiar song by WHIP start.

Just perfect, I thought as I laughed to myself. *I can't do anything without those two, can I?* I shook my head as I turned up the volume and pictured Tyler in L.A. singing in the recording studio right about now.

When the session was over, I stood up, walked to the mirror for a second time and looked at the pair of black angel wings that spread across my shoulder blades and down to my mid back.

"Ooo." I switched positions and took another look.

"I love them!" I shouted as he just smiled and removed his black latex gloves. He then ran through all the after-care instructions, handed me a jar of tattoo-goo and patted my butt with the bill. I laughed as I reached into my purse and paid him with cash.

"Thank you, darling. You come back and see me again

now." He smiled at me as I walked out of the tattoo shop and headed for my truck.

Once I reached Axl, I noticed Trent's box sitting in the back as I paused for a moment, contemplating.

Should I swing by *Head Rush*, or should I just go home? I kicked the tire of my truck, trying to make a decision then said, "Fuck it! My new angel wings are giving me the freedom to do whatever I want, and if I want to drop his shit off, then I'm on it!" I laughed as I hopped into my truck and drove straight over to *Head Rush*.

CHAPTER 19

I knocked on the studio door a few times, but no one answered. I set Trent's box down on the ground as I looked around. The lot was empty, but his motorcycle and one car were still parked out back.

"Hum?" I waited a minute more, then decided to try the handle.

The studio was open. I picked up the box, went inside and set it down on the floor. Tonya, one of the girlfriends from the band the REVENUE, ran right into me as she was leaving the studio in a hurry.

I blinked at her as I moved the box away from the door so she could get through.

"Hi," I said as she smiled with her chestnut hair and tight daisy duke shorts, grabbing her car keys out of her purse, and quickly walked out the door. *Well, that was a little suspicious*, I thought as I closed the door and walked in, quietly looking around the studio for Trent.

I could hear a soft melody flow towards me as I listened to Trent play on his piano. I walked over to the band's rehearsal room and stood in the doorway, watching him play.

"That sounds sad," I said.

Trent immediately stopped playing and lifted his head.

"It is. His lover left him for another," Trent said quietly as he put the cover to the keys down.

"Hum." I paused.

"You shouldn't leave your door unlocked like that." I looked over my shoulder at the front door.

"I just saw Tonya leave." Trent dismissed my comment.

"Well, I have a box for you," I huffed as I kept my head up high as I looked directly at him.

"The dumpster is out back. Just toss it in there," he said, turning away from me as he took a sip from his water bottle while pretending to fuss with his sheet music.

"Okay." I was disappointed with his attitude as I went to turn towards the exit then paused when he spoke.

"We got so close, Alex. I have frequently wished that he wasn't in the middle," Trent said softly.

"Who are you talking about? Gage Heston again?" I put my hands on my hips and stood there sternly.

"Tyler. Alex, I'm talking about Tyler." *Oh Lord, I hope he doesn't know what went on between us.*

But, by the looks of Tonya rushing out of here, I had no idea what was going on with him, as all the confusion made my brain start to swirl. He released a breath then spoke softly once again.

"Gage is an asshole. We all know that. I'm sorry I didn't have enough faith in you. I always had this lingering fear that he would surface and hurt you somehow, Alex." I continued to glare at him as I stood there listening.

"I'm relieved you didn't sleep with him. I just wished that prick Tyler would have told me so. Misery just loves company, and that selfish prick just wanted you all to himself, Alex." Trent paused.

"And you are always there to fix him. It's just so cliché, Alex." Hearing him say my name multiple times made a butterfly flap in my stomach. I shook my head and remained silent as he went on.

"Thank you for including the band in the film contract. That surprised me. I assumed it was only to fulfill Tyler's needs until our band meeting." He stood up and straightened out his tee while running his hand through his silky hair.

"Your hair got so long." I tried to change the subject as I longed to run my fingers through his hair. He flashed me a half grin.

I then blurted out, "Tyler is my best friend. We needed each other to heal from his addiction, from Olivia to Gage..." I paused. "To you." I rubbed my shoulders from the chilled look he just flashed me.

"Me?" he asked.

"You dumped me in St. Louis!" I let out a sigh.

"It kind of sounds like a good title for a song, 'You Dumped Me in St. Louis.'" I repeated jokingly as I looked to the floor. Then the tears started to surface as I looked back up at Trent. "I was so easily discarded, you just stopped loving me," I said as my glare burned a hole right through him.

"I can't stop loving you, Alexandria Leigh Rae." He used my full name as I just blushed while a few tears began to run down my cheek.

"I'm just unsure if I can ever trust you again," he said as I looked back down to the floor.

"I feel so smothered with emotions lately that I just need to break free," I said as I paused and wiped my nose with my hand.

"Tyler is in L.A., and I just need a fucking break. I guess you and I need a break as well. Yes, my intentions were not to hurt you, Trent, but to help Tyler. I made a promise to him. I wanted him to stay focused on this tour. The cutting was one thing... I just feel so responsible for him." I started to cry as Trent interjected.

"He's not your responsibility. We..." He stressed the word 'we' as he pointed to the pictures of WHIP on the wall. "We were all trying to focus Tyler professionally to help him with his burdens. How did all this get so fucked up?" He was standing in my personal space now.

"I don't know." I shook my head as Trent wrapped his arms around me. I shuddered as I pulled away from him.

"What's wrong?" He registered surprise.

"Can't I even hug you anymore?" he asked as I reached for his hand and squeezed it lovingly.

"Of course you can hug me. I'm just a little sensitive at the moment." I wiped my eyes, then turned around so he could see the new black angel wing tattoo poking out from my racer-back tank.

"Oh, my god!" Trent gasped.

"It's like the Deftones song we spoke about how you grew wings and left Heston. Let me see them!" He gently lifted my tank and looked at my new angel wings tattoo.

Nodding his head in appreciation, he asked, "Did you just do this? It's still bleeding." I laughed as I pulled my tank top down and turned back around to face him.

"Yes, not only is my heart bleeding, but so is my back," I huffed.

"Look, I need a break from Tyler, and you need a break from me," I said as Trent gave me a sympathetic look.

"I'm sorry, Alex, I'm really sorry."

I sighed and said, "Me too, Trent. Where do we go from here?" I asked as he answered:

"Give it time. I just need some time." I nodded my head and elected to leave it at that.

Feeling relieved that Trent was no longer cross with me, I returned to the loft exhausted. I poured myself a glass of wine as I set out Ernie's kibble.

"Hey Ernie, it's time for your dinner," I called out, but the cat was nowhere to be found. I shrugged my shoulders, grabbed my glass of wine and headed up the stairs to my bedroom. I tossed my cell on the bed and my bag into the closet as I walked over to the bathroom mirror.

Setting my wine glass down, I pulled off my tank top and stood there reflecting on my fresh set of black inked angel wings. My cell startled me as it started to buzz on the bed. I quickly grabbed a t-shirt off the floor and threw it on as I answered my phone in a hurry.

"Hello?" I huffed.

"You sound out of breath? Are you alright, baby girl?" Tyler asked.

"Hi sugar, I'm fine. How's the session going?" I walked over to grab my wine back off the bathroom counter and then sat back down on the bed to listen to Tyler.

"I'm stretching my vocal cords like a mother fucker, girl!" he hollered out. I laughed, knowing that no range was too high for Tyler.

"Tea and honey," I replied.

"I know, I'm drinking it right now," he laughed on the line.

"Well, I'm drinking wine." I sipped as Tyler laughed at me.

"Well cheers, baby girl! I do miss you," he said.

I paused.

"I miss you too, Ty. Umm, guess what crazy shit I did today?" My mood began to perk up.

"You cleaned," he said as I just rolled my eyes and laughed.

"Yes I did. But I also got a tattoo!" I started yelling into the phone, celebrating as the wine was making me feel a bit giddy.

"Say wha?!" Tyler hollered on the line.

"Of what? Is it a tramp stamp, baby girl? Now you'll really look like a fucking *Whip-ette* with a tramp stamp!" Tyler laughed.

"No tramp stamp, asshole. It's a set of black angel wings on my back." I took another sip of wine as I smiled, proud of what I went through today.

"Girl, that sounds so amazing. You're my new hero." I smiled.

"I wouldn't say that, but I'm spreading my wings now, Tyler! I feel so liberated!" I hollered out.

"You go girl!" Tyler cheered me on. He seemed so happy in L.A. that I didn't even want to mention the little fact that I just saw Trent.

"Hey, these guys are taking me out to dinner, then I'm crashing out. Can I check on you tomorrow?" Tyler asked.

"You better, and Ty..." I paused. "I'm proud of you." I could hear him smile on the other line.

"I'm proud of you too, blondie. My girl got a fucking tattoo!" he hollered as I giggled.

"Good night," I said.

"Night, baby girl." Tyler clicked off the line. I felt like all things were right in my universe tonight.

A few weeks had passed, and I was settling into having the place all to myself. I kept busy as I worked endlessly on my new clients' design projects while Tyler was still recording in Los Angeles. I felt content now that my focus had shifted back onto me and off Tyler for the moment. I still hadn't heard from Trent since I dropped his box off at *Head Rush*. Nevertheless, I was doing okay with the much needed space.

I decided to heat up my leftovers and possibly sketch something out tonight. I went into the kitchen and searched the fridge while taking out foiled covered dishes. I then looked at Ernie's full feeding bowl and noticed that he wasn't eating any of the kibble.

"Ern?" I closed the refrigerator and called out in search of my cat. I heard nothing. I went upstairs and looked under my bed.

"There you are. Why are you hiding?" I pulled him out from underneath my bed and set him onto my lap. I began petting him as he just laid there.

"What's the matter, little buddy?" I asked as I continuously stroked his fur.

"You haven't been eating." I stood up and carried him down to the kitchen and set him in front of his food bowl. He just stood there, looking uninterested.

"Shit," I muttered.

I picked up my cell phone and called our veterinarian. The vet office made me an immediate appointment as I went in search of Ernie's carrier. I threw on a flannel shirt, grabbed my bag and my keys. I then grabbed the cat and quickly headed to the elevator.

When we arrived at the animal hospital, I turned off the truck, grabbed the carrier and ran inside.

The veterinary technician escorted me immediately into an exam room, then scurried away to fetch the doctor. I pulled Ernie out of his carrier and set him on the exam table. Usually he made a fuss about the carrier, but today he was quiet. Dr. Nickels walked right in and asked, "How's Ernie today?" as he started petting him.

"He's not eating, and he's been hiding under my bed," I answered with concern for my cat's welfare.

"Let's take a look at him." The doctor picked up Ernie, listened to him with his stethoscope, then weighed him.

"It looks like he's lost some weight." My eyes widened. *How could I have missed that?*

"Let me draw some blood and let's see if that tells us anything." I nodded yes as the doctor scooped up Ernie and took him to their treatment room.

I paced the exam room back and forth until my cell phone ring startled me.

"Hello?" I answered all flustered.

"Are you alone, Alex?" I heard Trent ask on the line.

"I'm at the vet hospital with Ernie." I was short with him.

"How's my little buddy holdin' up?" he asked with sincerity.

"He's not eating. They are running some sort of blood work," I snapped as I sat down in the exam room chair just as the doctor knocked on the door.

"Hold on, Trent." I put the phone down as he set Ernie on the exam table.

"It looks like our little friend is in acute renal failure." My eyes dilated two sizes.

"What?" I asked nervously.

"Kidney failure," the doctor answered.

"What do I do, Doctor?" Dr. Nickels looked at Ernie as he softly petted him.

"He's suffering, Alex. Do you want my advice?" he asked, looking at Ernie with sympathy.

"We really should compassionately say our goodbyes and let him go." I shook my head in disbelief. "Why don't I give you a few minutes to make a decision." The doctor tapped my hand and then stepped out of the room as I put the phone back up to my ear.

"Trent, are you still there?" I asked.

"Yes," he answered.

"Ernie's dying," I said to Trent as I shook my head as the tears began to stream down my face.

"I'm on my way." Trent hung up as I turned off my phone and just stared at my cat.

"Jesus wants you back, Ern." I wiped my tears as I began petting him again.

"You've been an amazing pet to me. The biggest favor I can do for you is to end your suffering. Why is there so much damn suffering in my world right now? Huh Ernie?" I pouted as I put my head on my dying pet.

"You've been my main man for as long as I can remember, before any of the other boys. How can I just let you go?" I paused as I reflected on how my cat saw me through everything. *All my boys seemed to be slipping away from me*, I thought as I sadly continued to pet Ernie.

There was another knock on the door as Dr. Nickels peeked his head in.

"Let's say goodbye, Doctor," I said as he nodded.

"I'll give you some more time. Please take a minute with Ernie. I'll collect everything I need and I'll be back." He squeezed my hand as I pulled away and wiped my dripping nose.

Just as he stepped out of the room, Trent stepped in. I looked up at him and tears just continued to stream down my face.

"I'm so sorry, Alex." He handed me a few tissues, then put his arm around me, rubbing my arm as he started petting Ernie.

"This little man has been a constant comfort to you." Trent said as I shook my head yes as I released a breath, wiping my nose.

The doctor tapped on the door and walked back in and gently closed the door behind him. He quietly walked over to Ernie and gave him a shot for light sedation. I continued to pet his head as we waited patiently for Ernie to fall asleep. The doctor then injected euthasol slowly into his vein, and soon after my Ernie had passed.

Taking the stethoscope out of his ears, the doctor said, "He's gone, Alex." I nodded my head as I turned towards Trent and buried my head into his chest. Trent stroked my hair as I wiped my eyes. The doctor then wrapped Ernie in a blanket and left the exam room.

I let out a deep breath, then grabbed Ernie's carrier and solemnly walked out the room and straight out the front door. Trent followed me to my truck and stood there quietly, keeping an eye on me to make sure I was alright.

"I can't believe he's gone, Trent," I said as I placed the empty carrier in the bed of my truck then leaned against it. Tears started to surface again as Trent leaned in and lovingly wrapped his arms around me as I started to cry hysterically once more. Trent held me so tightly to his chest, never saying a word as he gently patted my head, allowing me to sob tears all over his t-shirt.

After a few moments, I looked up at him as he just stared back into my sad eyes and began to wipe them with his soft fingers. I sniffled as he said, "I'll follow you home, Alex." I said nothing in return as I just nodded my head yes.

CHAPTER 20

Exhausted, I walked into the loft with the empty carrier, setting it down by the door as I kicked off my shoes. Trent locked the door behind me.

"Come on, Alex, let's get you upstairs and into bed." I said nothing as I made my way up the stairs and stood in my bedroom in disbelief. Trent went to the bathroom cabinet and grabbed a valium then filled a glass of water. He stood in front of me and said, "Here, take this. It'll help you rest." I grabbed the little pill from his palm as he handed me the glass of water.

"Now, you should crawl into bed." I just stood there looking at him.

"Come on," he said as he started to unbutton my flannel shirt and my jeans. He removed them then slipped a t-shirt over my head. I just remained frozen. He pulled the comforter down, then walked over and reached for my hand so he could guide me into the bed. I laid down as he covered me. He sat on the edge of the bed and ran his fingers through my hair to soothe me.

"Get some sleep. You'll feel better tomorrow." I reached for his hand.

"Stay with me till I fall asleep." I blinked my drowsy

eyes. He nodded okay as he crawled on top of the comforter and laid next to me, scratching my head as I slowly drifted off to sleep.

The next morning I awoke to the sun shining through my window.

"Ugh," I said as I sat up and looked around. No Ernie. No Trent. My stomach hurt as I put my feet on the floor and looked over the railing towards my kitchen.

There on the counter was the most beautiful arrangement of colorful flowers along with English muffins, mixed fruit and sweet tea. I smiled. *Did Trent do all this for me?* I grabbed my hair and twisted it up into a bun and headed downstairs to the kitchen.

Inhaling the scent of flowers, I stood there and smiled. I poured a glass of sweet tea. While sipping it, I reached for my cell phone and texted Trent, *Thank you.* That was all I needed to say. He texted back,

Anytime. I let out a breath, closed my phone and stood there poking at the fruit.

A few hours later I was lying on the couch, still only in my t-shirt from last night, mourning the loss of my pet. Suddenly, my cell phone rang, startling me.

"Hi rockstar," I answered pathetically.

"Hi baby girl," Tyler greeted me.

"Guess what?" he asked.

"What?" I huffed as Tyler whistled into the phone.

"I'm hanging out here for another week!" he hollered as I rolled my eyes.

"Y'all aren't finished with the vocal parts yet?" Honestly, I didn't give a shit if they were recorded or not.

"Yeah, we wrapped, but I met up with the REVENUE, and I'm going to sing backup vocals for one of their songs on their new album." I let out a slight smile.

"You're on a roll, rockstar." I pouted into the phone.

"Hey?" Tyler questioned me.

"Yeah?" I responded.

"Are you okay? You sound like shit, and usually my news gets you all amped up?" I could hear Tyler lighting up a cigarette.

"Got one of those for me?" I asked as I paused.

"Look, Ernie was sick, Ty. I had to let him go yesterday." Tyler was silent for a few seconds.

"Bummer dude," he said as he blew his smoke out. I just waited patiently to hear a little more empathy on the line other than 'bummer dude,' but nothing came. *Tyler is such a narcissist.*

"So," Tyler paused. "I'll be in the studio tonight. I'll let you know how it goes. I'm totally stoked," Tyler said.

"Good luck," I whispered as Tyler let out a breath on the other end.

"Rock and roll," he said as he clicked off the line.

I just threw my phone down on the coffee table, slid back into the couch cushion, and stared at the empty cat tree. As my eyes grew heavy, I cried one last time and fell asleep on the couch.

A few hours later I opened my eyes to a darkened living room. I rolled over onto my side and reached for my phone off the coffee table. No call from Tyler. Then I noticed a missed call from Trent. I clicked my voicemail button and heard his deep voice leaving me a message:

"Hi Alex. I wanted to call and see how you're holdin' up. Losing a friend is never an easy thing. I'm here at the studio with the rest of the guys just taking a break from our recording session. The songs are pretty kick-ass for this soundtrack I must say." He had a contagious laugh.

"It's all coming together. Your Tyler has done well."

My Tyler? I thought as I rolled my eyes.

"Well, anyway, aside from how you were feeling, I wanted to see if you would like to go to a concert this weekend? One of the guys couldn't make it to the Deftones, so he hooked me up with a couple of tickets. Interested? Ummm, It's not a date or anything, it's just a kind gesture to cheer you up. Hit me back if you want to go. Bye." The voicemail ended.

I sat there pondering for a minute on the invitation. It was a sweet gesture, more than Tyler's 'bummer dude' response. I decided I wanted to go as I texted Trent, *I'd love to go. Thank you.*

And I left it at that.

Saturday evening arrived as I stood in the mirror adjusting my backless black form-fitted dress. *I love how wearing this dress puts my new angel wings tattoo on display and not my boobs for once.* I laughed to myself as a sudden knock at the door startled me.

"Here we go, girl!" I was giving myself a pep talk before the concert as I smoothed out my dress. I knew Trent said that it wasn't a date per se, but I still had butterflies doing numerous somersaults in my stomach as I slipped on my ankle boots and headed for the door.

Opening the door, I stepped back on to my heel as Trent stood there holding his motorcycle helmet, flashing a grin.

"Good evening, Alex. Wow! You look beautiful!" he said. *I love that he always compliments me. It gives me such a boost of confidence.*

"Are you ready to go?" he asked.

"Just one sec. I need to grab my purse." I turned around to grab my clutch off the entry table when I heard, "Wow!" for the second time as I laughed.

"Didn't you just say that?"

Trent laughed. "I mean, wow, that tattoo looks incredible! It's healing so nicely now." He stepped towards me, and as he went to touch my exposed back, he quickly withdrew his hand.

"May I?" I nodded my head yes as I turned around to show my back to him. Trent slowly traced his finger along the lines of my feathers.

"This has to be your design." He retracted his finger as chills just flushed down my spine.

"Yes, it is my design. I'm glad you like it. I'm really happy with the way it turned out." I turned back around to face Trent.

"You look good too," I complimented him as I gave a quick once over to his skinny jeans, V-neck shirt which I loved that showed off his ink, and a black scarf around his neck. *What is with these guys and their stage-gear dress scarves?* He took a bow as I just giggled.

"Let me lock up and we can hit the road."

Arriving at the *Turn it up!* concert hall, we were directed to park in the VIP lot.

"Ooo nice," I said to Trent as he put my truck in park.

"I have VIP box tickets too!" He fanned me with two tickets as I laughed.

"Nice hook up, rockstar," I said as Trent hopped out of the truck and walked around to the passenger side to open the door for me. He held out his hand and guided me out of the vehicle. *That was sweet*, I thought to myself as I adjusted my dress. *It's nice having a man around that still believes in chivalry and not some pretty fragile boy that doesn't pay any mind to it like Tyler.* I then promised myself that I would not fixate on Tyler any more tonight; I was going to enjoy this concert.

Trent handed the security guard our tickets at the entry as the man fist-bumped him saying, "How's it going dude?" recognizing him from past rock shows that WHIP performed as he just gave us a goofy smile. I just giggled. With his hand placed on the small of my back, Trent guided me to our private box.

Sitting in the balcony box reminded me of St. Louis as I squirmed in the maroon velvet auditorium seat, scanning the room. Trent sat down next to me.

"Hey, I had this view in St. Louis." I nervously tapped my hand on my leg. Trent looked over at me and gently patted my hand so I could settle down.

"I never had a chance to tell you how good you sing. I mean I loved the old WHIP song you resurrected so beautifully." Trent blushed, smiling at the compliment.

"I'm glad you got to hear me sing. I don't have the range of Tyler or anything..." I put my hand up to stop him.

"Just take the compliment." I tapped his hand in return just as the house lights were dimming.

"Wow, we're just on time!" I sat up straight in my chair,

watching the opening band step out onto stage and start their set.

"It's nice to have the pressure off from performing for just one night," Trent said, leaning back as he started to relax and enjoy the show.

By the time the headliner came on, we were having such a good time. We sang every song. I clapped my hands and danced around while Trent whistled.

Finally, the band played their encore, which was my favorite song "Change (In the house of flies)." Trent leaned in and whispered, "Here's your song, Alex." I lit up as I turned towards him and began to run my hands through his hair. I was dying to do that ever since I returned his box to the studio.

Allowing me to touch him, I gently pulled his scarf towards me as I leaned my lips in and kissed him softly on the lips. I could hear him let out a slight moan as he opened his mouth as I slid my tongue in. His mouth was warm as I slowly circled his tongue with mine.

Pulling my tongue back out, I whispered, "I've been wanting to do that all night." Trent shifted in his seat.

"I need to take this slow, Alex. I wasn't looking to hook up tonight. I just wanted you to feel better after losing your little buddy." I pecked his lips one more time as I looked up at him, batting my lashes.

"Do you want me to stop?" I questioned him. Trent then grabbed both my hands and set them into my lap.

"I just can't jump back into anything just yet. I've missed you, Alex, but..." he whispered as I nodded my head, feeling so shunned.

"Thank you Dallas, and good night!" I looked away from Trent and back to the stage as I focused on the band as they all stepped up and took their bows while waving to the crowd.

"I guess it's over," I said as I pouted, wondering if I truly meant the Deftones concert or me and Trent.

After the concert, Trent drove me home as the two of us did not say much to one another. He parked my truck, then walked me to my door like a gentleman. He handed me my truck keys as I said, "Thank you. I really mean thank you for tonight. I needed this." I opened the door as Trent reached down to retrieve his helmet from my doorway then looked back, giving me a smile and said, "I'll see you soon Alex." I nodded my head yes as I closed the door.

Later that week I was futzing around aimlessly on social media. *I'm bored and lonely*, I thought to myself. My extended workload I took on after Gage Heston blacklisted me was now complete. WHIP were wrapping up their film soundtrack project in the studio in Dallas and Tyler was still in L.A. doing god knows what. I decided I needed to hit up my girl Nova and see what trouble she was getting into.

"Hey girl," the sultry voice answered on the other line.

"I'm bored!" I shouted into the phone as Nova laughed.

"I really miss you, girl. What are your plans this weekend? I've been imprisoned in my own loft!" I shouted once more as she just let out a long throaty laugh.

"I was just going to call you. Zack and the boys are heading out to Las Vegas to celebrate their finished soundtrack project. I thought Tyler would have called you about this?" Nova paused on the line.

"No," I said as I let out a breath.

"I'm taking much needed space from those WHIP boys. By no fault of his own, Tyler confessed his love while Trent pulled away his love. It's exhausting. I feel I really screwed things up by getting involved in WHIP's affairs by dragging in Gage Heston. No good deed goes unpunished, I guess." I pouted.

"I just wanted to keep my focus on Tyler because we promised to look out for one another, but that seems to upset Trent. Tyler was my 'partner in rejection' through-out this whole drama with Trent. It's all a big mess girl," I groaned to Nova on the line.

"Girl, you don't owe either one of them a damn thing. You gave them the ultimate hook up with the soundtrack deal. They should be kissing the ground you walk on. I know Trent gets queasy when you have to deal with Gage, but he's a big boy. You didn't sleep with Gage. And as for Tyler, he was just a rebound because of this rejection from Trent. You guys were two lonely birds," she huffed.

"Well, since the movie soundtrack project is now com-plete, y'all can all move on from this damn mess. Don't you miss Tyler? He's finished recording with the REVENUE, and we're all hitting Las Vegas to celebrate!" Nova shifted the conversation to partying as she dismissed giving out any more relationship advice about the usual drama with the leather twins.

"The new single sounds pretty kick-ass per Zack, so we're about to hook up in Vegas, baby. Why don't you join us?" she pleaded as I stayed quiet on the line. *The REVENUE, huh?* I thought to myself. The last time I saw the REVENUE was at the lake party where I snorted cocaine in their RV.

"Are you still there?" Nova asked, as I snapped my attention back to her offer.

"I need to get out of Dallas for a bit. I guess I'm game, girl. I could use a little cheering up," I said, releasing a breath.

"Text me your flight details, and I'll try to get on a stand-by," I said.

"Whoo-hoo! That's my girl!" Nova hollered.

"It'll be fun, girl! Let your damn hair down already!" Nova cheered as I laughed.

"Let me book my ticket," I said as Nova and I clicked off the line. I then bolted upstairs in a hurry to pack a bag and change into my party dress. I guess I was heading to Las Vegas.

CHAPTER
21

LAS VEGAS

I finished sweeping another coat of mascara on my lashes when the pilot startled me as he began his descent announcements. Nova elbowed me.

"Vegas, baby!" she squealed as Zack took out his cell phone and started making plans with WHIP. Some of the guys were on board and some were coming in an hour, so we should all be together for the party tonight.

"Where is this party?" I asked Nova.

"I think it's just in the REVENUE's hotel suite. They got a two floor suite that has a panoramic view of Vegas." She shrugged her shoulders.

"Zack booked a room for the two of us. Are you going to crash with me, or are you staying with Tyler tonight?" I looked out the window, just staring at the bright lights below as we were coming in for a landing.

"Hello?" she asked.

"Umm, I'm not sure yet. I'll just put my bag with you, and we'll figure it out later," I said as Nova shook her head as she turned back to talk to Zack.

Nova, Zack, two members of Whip, their girls and me

all hailed a taxi van to drive us to the REVENUE's suite. Nova and I stopped by her room first, dropped off our bags, then adjusted our party dresses in the mirror.

"I love that white backless dress, girl!" Nova's compliment made me smile.

"You have to let me borrow it." I nodded okay as I pulled my hair over one shoulder so my back tattoo could be exposed.

"It's been so long since I've seen Tyler!" I said to Nova excitedly. I never brought up the 'not-a-date' I had with Trent the other night. It was just all too confusing to me right now. I stared into the mirror as my thoughts shifted to Trent.

"Just have fun, girl. We're here to party. It's all about fun, mama!" Nova jerked me back to reality with her excitement. I laughed as I adjusted her black mini dress in the back and tapped her on the butt.

"Let's go!" she squealed as I followed her out of the hotel room.

We stepped into the elevator as I watched Nova hit the Penthouse button and purr. I giggled. *Fun, just like Nova said, I'm definitely going to have some fun tonight*, I thought to myself.

As we stepped off the elevator, Zack was standing there talking to the REVENUE's tour manager.

"Hi girls," he greeted us as he kissed Nova.

"Everything's inside." He pointed towards the door as I could hear the music and laughter seep out into the hallway.

Nova led the way into the suite hand in hand with me. Musicians, groupies, tour managers, studio engineers, hookers... I mean everyone was at this party. I looked around in awe as I stared at the cathedral ceilings. The suite had two floors. The bedrooms were upstairs. The DJ was set up in the corner. White leather couches and several ottomans occupied by guests scattered the room. Lights were dim. Cigarette and marijuana smoke clouded my vision as I stared at the wraparound balcony that was open to the view of the Vegas strip below.

"Wow," I said as Nova laughed with how easily I got impressed.

"Thank the lord, there's the bar!" Nova pointed to a kitchen-ette that housed all the liquor you could dream of. I squeezed her hand as she led the way to the young, energetic bartender who was pouring guests their drinks. Nova ordered herself a champagne cocktail as I declined having anything to drink at the moment. I waved to the guys from the REVENUE as I stood next to Nova just people watching.

"I want to dance!" Nova hollered over to me as she sipped her champagne, pointing to a group of people dancing in front of a mirrored wall.

"Girl, this music is so sexy!" she said as she toasted the DJ for his choice of music that oozed sex. Nova pulled me into the intimate crowd of people who were dancing and gyrating on one another.

"These people are so gorgeous!" I yelled in Nova's ear as I looked around at all the party guests dressed to the nines.

"You're gorgeous!" she laughed as she stepped up to me and started swaying her hips.

A remix of the band Great White's "House of Broken Love" started to play as the dancing crowd woo'd with excitement. I began swaying my hips in tune with Nova. Zack secretly slid up behind her and slowly pulled her away as he began grinding his hips on hers while kissing her passionately. I stood there gawking. *I loved how the two of them were becoming an item*, I thought to myself as I continued to watch them.

Startling me, I felt something wet touch my back. Tyler's warm tongue started to lick me from the bottom of my spine very slowly as he made his way up to my neck. I purred as I leaned against him.

"You look fucking incredible," he whispered in my ear as he swayed with me on the dance floor. I smiled, feeling a sense of relief that he was here. I turned myself around and for the first time in months I saw my best friend.

My heart fluttered as my pulse started to race. I reached up and lightly touched his face as he kissed my hand. I just stood there blinking while looking into his eyes as I appreciated how pretty he was.

"You look so good, Ty," I whispered as he pulled me in and started kissing me. With the comfort of his kiss, I was now in my happy place. I returned his kiss as I flickered his barbell tongue with my tongue a few times as he gripped on to my hips, starting to dance with me.

"I'm giving myself a cheat day," he whispered as he leaned in towards my ear. I paused our dancing and sternly glared up at him.

"What's that supposed to mean?" I snapped quickly.

"Settle down, baby girl." He kissed my head.

"Okay listen, it just means dieters get a cheat day to eat anything they want without the guilt, right?" I nodded.

"So, I want to party tonight without all the damn guilt. I've been really good, Alex. You'd be surprisingly proud of me. My session with the film soundtrack is done and recorded. The REVENUE's song is done and recorded. So, now I have you here with me in fucking Las Vegas to celebrate, so come on baby, let's party!" I stood there contemplating his bullshit reasoning for abusing drugs until Nova came up behind me and disrupted my focus on Tyler.

Nova pushed me into Tyler as I became sandwiched as the three of us started a slow erotic dance with one another.

"Do you want to party?" Impatiently, Tyler asked the stupid question as he looked at the two of us trying to persuade us to leave the dance floor.

Nova yelled, "Hell yeah I do!" Tyler howled then grabbed a hold of both of our hands and dragged us down a hallway until we reached the bathroom.

He pulled us inside as Nova quickly shut the door behind us. I took a deep breath in, wondering if this was such a hot idea or not.

"You're fun, Nova," Tyler said, as he sprinkled a line of cocaine on the bathroom sink.

"See girl, fun. I told you to have some fun tonight." Nova looked at me, then bent down and snorted the line of powder off the bathroom counter.

"Whew! That was good!" she laughed as she wiped her nose.

"Well, gang, that's all the skiing I'm partaking in. I'm going to go hunt down Zack and pounce! I sooo need to enjoy this high with him." She then kissed my forehead and walked out of the bathroom.

Tyler ignored her as he focused on setting up another few lines on the counter for the two of us as I looked him over. Tonight he had on his black leather pants, a tight gray t-shirt, his gray dress scarf and heavy black eyeliner. I licked my lips, knowing damn well this man in the band was very dangerous and I couldn't let this get too out of hand.

"Here, baby girl." He handed me a short plastic straw.

As I grabbed a hold of it I said, "Fuck it," then bent down and snorted a line of blow for the second time in my life.

"Man, you're fucking turning me on, Alex," he said as he lightly scratched my angel wings tattoo with his finger-nails as I was bent over the bathroom counter wiping my gums.

"Here." I turned around and handed him the straw.

"Rock and roll." Tyler smiled as he bent down and snort-ed a line. He flipped his head back, letting out an "ahhh" as he wiped his burning nose. I just laughed as I shook my head. *God, he's sexy*! I thought to myself as I watched him stupidly do drugs again.

He then said, "Really Alex, I do fucking love this gothic angel wing tattoo." And, with a devilish grin, he slowly turned me around to face the mirror as he began to swiftly lick my wings on my back, the left one first, then the right. I gasped as he simultaneously started to trace his fingers up my dress slowly then brushed my thigh and continued to run them along my pussy. I moaned as the rush of co-caine began to flush through me.

"Oh Tyler, that feels like heaven! I've missed your touch!" I cried out as I bent over the cold tiled counter as Tyler unzipped his tight leather pants.

Quickly, he pulled out his hardened cock, spread my legs wide then inserted himself as he started to fuck me. I was breathless as I watched him in the mirror. His layered black hair fell in his face as he closed his eyes, and I just creamed staring at him. *He is such a bad-boy that I succumb to every time he flirts with me,* I thought as I stared at the reflection.

He thrusted a little rougher than usual, being that he was on drugs in Las Vegas and not softly pleasuring me like at home.

"You feel so amazing, Alex," he said as he panted as he was pushing himself deeper into me.

"Oh my god, Tyler!" I said as I wiped my dripping nose.

Pausing sex, he began to pour more cocaine on my back as he snorted a second line while he was still inside of me. He then slapped my ass and rubbed his gums.

"I want to turn around and face you," I pleaded as he pulled out, turned me around and sat me up on the sink counter.

"Here," he said as he put more cocaine on his hand and held it up to my nose. I snorted the line then leaned back against the mirror as euphoria continued to wash over me. Tyler stood there running his hands through my hair as he leaned towards me and began licking my lips then inserting his wet tongue into my mouth while feverishly kissing me once more. I was hot, I was horny, and I was starting to feel out of control.

Panting, I returned his kiss.

"I want you back inside of me, Tyler!" I pleaded once more as I pulled on his hard dick, grabbing a hold of it then quickly sliding it back into me.

"Ahhh," he moaned as I sucked on his neck.

"I haven't had an orgasm since the last time you fucked me, Tyler! It's been too long. Fuck me!" I cried out as he laughed as he thrusted harder.

It was rough, and it was fast, but the desire for his

touch just overcame me as I started to experience an intense high orgasm.

"Oh my god, Tyler!" I said as I pulled his hair.

Tyler laughed and fucked me harder as he began to come. "Fuck Alex! Fuck, I needed this!" he cried out as he came hard.

My eyes began to dilate as I stared back into his endless dark eyes and long black lashes.

"Kiss me again," I demanded as I pulled his scarf in towards me for another kiss.

"Wow," I said as Tyler stepped back and ran his hand through his own hair.

I then slid off the counter and straightened out my dress as Tyler wiped the snow off of my nose. I just giggled.

"I love to fuck on cocaine, girl," Tyler said as he zipped his leather pants back up.

"I love fucking you on cocaine," I said, as he began to set up two additional lines.

We were snorting a lot of blow in a short amount of time.

"Just a little bit more, Ty. I'm feeling a little bit crazy." He laughed.

"*A crazy little thing called love!*" he sang out as he snorted his line.

"Man, this shit burns." He rubbed his nose, dusting off the powder as he leaned in towards me and licked my lips. I fixed my dress and shook out my hair as I laughed, looking into the mirror.

I then grabbed his hand and said, "I have so much energy, let's go back out there and dance!" Tyler smiled. He wiped the remaining residue off the counter, checked himself in the mirror then allowed me to take the lead as we left the bathroom and headed for the dance floor.

When we walked out of the room, there was a line forming down the hall impatiently waiting for the bathroom as we both laughed. A ballad began to ooze out of the speakers as the party guests hollered their approval. I pulled Tyler into my embrace, and we began to slowly dance. I held him so tightly that on cocaine I felt like I never wanted to release him. His body heat penetrated through my dress as he held me so close, a dime couldn't squeeze between us.

Crazed, I looked up at him as I swayed and ran my hands through his hair as he scratched his nails up my back. We were on an intense high and we were happy.

Nova poked my arm, trying to gain my attention, as I couldn't pull my stare away from Tyler.

"Hey girl." She poked for a second time. I just gave her a smile as she laughed.

"Fun right?" I nodded as the drugs made me feel anything but myself.

Suddenly, the DJ interrupted the song as he was announcing that Roger from the band the REVENUE was about to marry his long-time girlfriend Tonya at the chapel down the block. Everyone cheered as waiters began to walk around with trays of champagne.

Tyler grabbed two glasses for us as we began to toast one another. He took a sip, then opened my mouth and shared his sip with me. I swallowed the drink as I pulled him in closer. He kept feeding me champagne as the love song continued to play.

While everyone was cheering, Tyler bent down and whispered in my ear, "Fuck Roger and Tonya, I want to marry you." My legs almost gave out beneath me. The last time I heard that was from Gage and I wanted to vomit, but when Tyler whispered those words in my ear, my heart just pounded. *I deserved to be loved.* I pouted as I swayed with Tyler.

"Let's join them!" Tyler shouted, all amped up as he pulled my hand, making our way over to Nova and Zack.

"Let's go to the chapel with the REVENUE. I want to marry Alex tonight!" he shouted. They both laughed and drunkenly agreed as we all followed the herd out of the suite and onto the Vegas strip heading for the little white chapel.

All the drunken friends started to sing *"Going to the chapel and we're going to get married!"* I just laughed at them as I tightly held on to Tyler's waist.

"You're in white after all," he pointed out as he wrapped his arm around my shoulders and hugged me closer.

"I want nothing more than to marry you, Alex. You are the only one who ever fucking gets me. Olivia wanted to change me, then she left me. Trent left you. No one is in our way now. It's just me and you, baby girl." He squeezed my arm as he kissed the top of my head as I just listened to the crowd singing, not saying a word.

We reached a small white chapel on the strip with red neon hearts blinking in the window as I just laughed and thought, *If my mother could see me now.* High on champagne and blow, nothing seemed more romantic or more rock and roll at that very moment than for two lonely birds such as me and Tyler to get married.

The crowd packed into the little chapel as both Roger and Tonya made their way through the crowd as they passed me and Tyler. Tonya gave me a little shove as she gripped Roger's hand and followed him to the front to exchange their vows. I stood there shifting my weight in my heels, ignoring her as I knew she wanted her and Roger to have the center stage and not me and Tyler.

"After Roger and Tonya, we're getting married next!" Tyler shouted as the crowd cheered as Nova pinched my side.

"Hell yeah, girl. Are you and Tyler really doing it?" I laughed as I tried to focus my blurry eyes on Roger and Tonya, the main reason we all shuffled down to the chapel in the first place.

"It's Vegas, Nova, anything can happen!" I cheered as Nova grabbed a piece of white lace that was thrown over a table lamp in the entryway and placed it on my head as a veil. I laughed as the room began to spin a little off kilter. The crowd was singing as Roger and Tonya were reciting their vows while Tyler rubbed his nose then squeezed me in to stand in front of him.

"I can get you to do just about anything for me, huh baby girl?" he bent down and whispered in my ear as I stood there not saying a word.

"I knew I could get you to fuck me." He leaned in my ear once more laughing as I began to fume.

"I used you to get back at that asshole Gage Heston, and for him to give me that soundtrack contract. I wanted to take you away from Trent, and when you marry me tonight, I will have. I can get you to do just about anything," he repeated as I turned around, lifted my hand up and slapped his face hard.

"What the fuck, baby girl? I'm just teasing! We're supposed to be in this together, right?!" He rubbed his cheek as he noticed me intensely staring over at the entrance.

I had recognized Trent over Tyler's shoulder as he was standing in the doorway of the chapel with the other members of WHIP.

At that very moment, the veil of illusion that was covering up my heart had just been lifted. I pushed the lace out of my face as I just kept staring at Trent. Tyler stood there watching me.

"You never look at me the way you look at him, Alex." I looked back up at Tyler as I listened to his sad words.

"You always look at me with self-pity, but you always seem to look at Trent with fucking adoration and love." He shook his head. "The beautiful ones hurt you every fucking time," he sighed as he reached up to rub his bruised cheek again.

I pushed Tyler out of my way, started shoving myself through the small crowd, until I reached Trent. Trent opened his arms and received me lovingly. "I don't want to marry Tyler!" I cried out as I was enveloped in Trent's arms. I was delirious. I had no idea what I was doing or how I even got to the wedding chapel.

"What are you talking about, Alex? Roger and Tonya are the ones getting married!" He stepped back and looked at me with concern.

"I was in line to marry Tyler next because you don't want me anymore, Trent." I pouted as I slurred my words as I looked up at Trent.

"I want to marry you!" I blurted out as I gave him a light push of frustration.

Tyler then walked up to us with his pissed attitude.

"You discarded her so easily, you bastard!" Tyler shouted as he pushed Trent out the doorway.

"That's between me and Alex, Tyler. You get the fuck out of here!" He urged Tyler to leave.

"I love her, Trent. And you can't stand that! She was my 'partner in rejection,' she was my best friend before you ever knew her, before you ever even joined the band! What gives you the right to have her? You fucking bailed on her! Over what? Pathetic Gage Heston? Or, because I'm too much of a threat to you? Where's your balls dude?" He tried to pull me away from Trent's arms.

"Don't touch her, Tyler! You're all fucked up again, Mr. Rockstar. You can't even handle a little stardom, let alone Alexandria. You're a fucking disaster, man! Get a goddamn grip!" Trent furiously pushed Tyler aside as he fell to the ground.

Nova ran out yelling, "What the fuck is going on here!" She bent down to check on Tyler.

"What are you doing here, Trent?!" she hollered as Zack came over and pulled Tyler to his feet. Tyler tried to go after Trent once more as Zack held him back.

"Get that asshole out of here before I hurt him. Get him fucking sober!" Trent hollered as he looked back at me.

Suddenly, blood began to run out of my nose and started to drip down my face and all over my white dress.

"What the hell, Alex? Are you okay?" Trent quickly grabbed my head, tilted it back as he feverishly started wiping the blood with his hands. I began to feel dizzy and then I fainted.

❧

The next morning I tried to focus my eyes as I heard rustling around the hotel room.

I started to cough, rubbed my sore nose, and rolled over. Trent stood there holding a cup of hot coffee and some aspirin.

"What the hell are you doing here?" I asked as I propped myself up into a sitting position.

"Ugh," I said as I held my head.

"Here, take these." Trent handed me the pills and the warm mug. He sat on the edge of the bed and watched me intensely as I sipped the coffee.

"Why are you looking at me like I'm a zoo animal?" I asked as I set the mug on the nightstand beside me.

"Your dress is ruined." He pointed to my bloody dress rolled into a ball on the floor. I looked down at myself and noticed I was wearing only his t-shirt.

"What happened last night, Alex?" he asked with sincerity. I chewed my nail as I looked at him.

"I don't know. I was at the REVENUE's hotel suite, I was dancing and drinking champagne and..." I paused.

"Tell me, Alex," Trent demanded.

"I snorted cocaine with Tyler." Trent cracked his knuckles.

"Did you fuck him?" I shifted my feet under the comforter, hesitating to answer a question that he already knew the answer to.

"We aren't dating any longer. You broke up with me, remember? Why are you here with me?" I sounded snotty as I snapped at him, trying to change the subject.

"I don't remember what happened, Trent. I snorted way too much coke and mixed it with alcohol. I..." I paused.

"I was at a party having fun." I pulled my legs into my

chest and began rocking back and forth like I was six years old.

"Imagine what could have happened to you if I didn't show up?" Trent chastised me.

"Tyler was wasted, and it took two guys from WHIP and one from the REVENUE to get him back to his room and sober him up. I looked after you because that no good girlfriend of yours was way too hysterical to care for you. My only concern was you. Honey, things got way out of hand. You almost married Tyler." Trent glared at me.

"Whaaat?" I put my hand over my mouth in disbelief. *That pretty boy sure is trouble.*

"Come on, now that can't be true." I folded my arms as I tried to recollect last night's events.

"I don't remember you there, Trent?" I was ashamed.

"Well, I showed up with the other guys at the REVENUE's suite, and we heard that half the party were on their way to the chapel for Roger and Tonya. So, I went down to check it out, and then I saw you standing there with a lacy doily on your head, gripping Tyler's hand and blood running down your nose." He shook his head.

"Oh my god," I mouthed.

"I then put you into a cab with me, took you to this hotel room, stripped you out of your bloody dress and sat with you on the bathroom floor while you vomited champagne," he huffed.

"Ew," I said as I was embarrassed by my behavior.

"You started to come down as I was wiping your face with a cool wet cloth, leaning against me on the floor confessing to me. You spilled your beans about everything, Alex. I mean everything. You just kept apologizing to me over and over telling me how much you loved me and how everything else was just a distraction from me." Trent paused as he looked straight into my eyes.

"Do you want Tyler, or do you want me, Alex? I believe I deserve an answer now that you're sober." He paused.

"Last night you pleaded that you really loved me. Do you still love me?" I shook my head yes.

"I never stopped."

CHAPTER
22

DALLAS

"Oh Lord, I'm so happy to be home!" I shouted as I walked into the loft, dragging my feet.

"Hey, I'm going to take off. I'll let you get some rest," Trent said as he set my bag down on the kitchen floor. He then glanced over at Tyler's room and noticed the packed up box sitting in the doorway.

"Yes, I'm giving Tyler the boot. I had his skinny ass all packed up before the Vegas trip. I packed your box and then I packed his box. We all just need our space right now," I laughed as I poured myself a glass of iced tea from the fridge.

"He needs his own crash pad until you figure out what you really want, Alex," Trent said as he walked over and took a sip of my tea, still glaring at the box in the doorway.

"Well, Tyler's flight is landing later today, so I'll get this all worked out with him. And, as for you, I'm here when you're ready to talk more. Take all the time you need. Ever since the contract was signed, my life has been turned upside down with you two. I'll always love Tyler; he is my best friend. But I'm in love with you, Trent. You digest that, and I'll respect whatever decision you make," I said confidently as Trent nodded his head and rubbed his tired eyes.

"It takes time, baby. Settle back in and call me later when Tyler is all done and over with. You really need to confront Tyler before I even entertain the idea of us getting back together. I do miss you, but I was in this relationship with you, not you and Tyler." I nodded my head, understanding just what he was getting at.

"I'll be at the recording studio working." He gave me a hug. I felt a sense of relief that Trent and I weren't completely done and over with just yet. There seemed to be a sense of hope reflecting back at me as he looked into my eyes. I smiled up at him as I then watched him turn and walk out the door.

He had listened to everything I confessed to him in Las Vegas, but didn't completely walk out of my life. I guess what happened in Vegas was going to stay in Vegas. *I'm one lucky bitch if I get another chance to love him again*, I thought to myself.

A few hours later, I was feeling refreshed from my shower when I turned on my record player and started a load of laundry. I then heard a key turn as I walked over to my front door.

"Hello?" I called out.

"Hi baby girl," Tyler said as he walked in and closed the door behind him. I stood there speechless as I watched him walk towards me then wrap his arms around me.

"I'm so sorry I'm such a fuck up. Vegas got way too out of hand. You know I would never hurt you, right?" He pulled back as he looked into my eyes.

"Yeah, but somehow you always do, Tyler. The drug abuse has crept back into our lives, and you are not that nice on drugs. I'm just as guilty for allowing both of us to take part in it. Plus, the rebound sex, it's not right. That will not heal either one of our broken hearts. It was a mistake."

He ran his hand through his hair, then snapped at me. "A mistake?" he huffed. "Yes, abusing once again was my mistake, but to me you were never a mistake. I truly love you, Alex." Tyler glanced to the floor.

"You need to love yourself first, Tyler. Not me, not the band, just yourself," I said as I rubbed on his arm. "I need you to find your own place. Trent isn't staying here either. I need to be alone," I reassured him.

"Well, don't worry, I'll be out of your hair very soon, girl!" He pushed past me with his attitude and headed for his room.

Stopping in the doorway, he huffed as he kicked the packed up box.

"Looks like sooner than later. You already packed me up," he sadly pouted as I walked over towards him.

"It's for the better." I grabbed his hand and pulled him in towards me.

"I'll always be here for you, Tyler, but right now I need space. We both just need space from each other. You just need to get your act together without any favors from me." I looked up into his dark eyes that were glossed over with tears.

"You love me, but not in that way, huh?" I said nothing as I pulled on his t-shirt and shook my head. "It's okay, baby girl. I get it." He bent down, grabbed the box then said, "Will you give me a ride at least?" I nodded yes as I followed him to my truck.

A few weeks passed and I hadn't really put any more energy into Trent or Tyler. I was just letting the whole mess die down and dry up on its own. My cell phone began to ring as I flipped on the living room light in search of it. Grabbing it, I answered, "Hey girl," as I greeted Nova.

"Hi Alex!" Nova said as I smiled.

"Wow girl, it's been like a month or so since Vegas. How are you?" she asked.

"I'm holdin' up alright, girl," I said, letting out a breath.

"Whatever ever happened to the leather twins?" Nova laughed into the phone.

"Tyler is in his own place. Trent is in his, and I'm just letting the whole thing play out," I huffed.

"Well, good for you, girl. Say, are you up for the *Broken Hearts Club* tonight since you're still kind of nursing a broken heart?" she laughed as she invited me to join her.

"Me and Zack are heading there in a little bit. They are having their infamous acoustic jam again tonight. You remember, they play covers and people sing acoustically?" I rolled my eyes as I recalled Tyler singing Prince before his meltdown.

"Sure, I remember," I said.

"Well, pick you up in, say, an hour?" she asked with excitement.

"Yeah, that sounds good," I agreed as Nova said:

"Good. See you in one hour." I then clicked off the line and headed upstairs to get changed.

"I need to get out of my mind and out of this damn house!" I muttered to myself as I sifted through my closet, searching for a rock tee and my faux leather leggings.

"I can't believe I'm heading back over to this club." I shook my head and laughed as I got dressed.

Walking into the *Broken Hearts Club* once again, I smiled as Nova grabbed my hand and pulled me into a booth beside her and Zack.

"I do really like you with Zack, girl!" I said, as she grinned from ear to ear.

"I know. We're getting pretty hot and heavy, girl." I laughed as I missed a little hot and heaviness myself, but I was actually happy for Nova who finally found it.

A server then approached the table and took our drink orders as I leaned back in the booth and listened to a cover of The Cure's "Lovesong" as a crowd began to pack in the joint.

Nova and Zack sat there whispering into one another's ear as I began to feel like a third wheel as a little sadness washed over me. I felt like Tyler pouting in the booth as I longed to whisper in Trent's ear once again.

I sipped my second glass of wine and said, "Fuck it, I want to sing!" as I slammed the wine glass down. Zack looked over at me and started to laugh.

"Where's that confidence coming from?" he asked as I laughed and saluted my wine glass to him.

"Oh, okay. Well, let me go over to the guitarist there and introduce you two." He pointed to a man with dreadlocks playing his acoustic guitar.

"He can play just about anything. Just tell him what

tune you want to sing, and he'll play it." I nodded my head as I wiped my sweaty palms on the black linen tablecloth covering our table.

Zack slid out of the booth and walked over to talk to the guitarist as Nova tapped my hand.

"I've only heard you singing drunk at karaoke, girl." She laughed.

"Well, it's no different. I mean it's live musicians, not a cheesy television screen that you follow the lyrics to. I can do it." I shrugged my shoulders as I stood up confidently, smoothed out my faux leather leggings, and walked over to Zack to meet the guitarist.

"Ray, this is Alexandria. Go ahead, tell Ray what you want to sing." I blushed as I asked.

"Can you play Jewel, 'Foolish Games'?" He nodded his head.

"Yeah, I like those lyrics, girl. I can play that tune. No problem." He smiled as Zack tapped my shoulder.

"Okay, I'm heading back over to Nova. Good luck," he said as I took Ray's hand and stepped onto the small, dimly lit stage and stood behind the microphone stand. *This must be the view Tyler always had. Wow, it sure takes guts*, I thought to myself as the guitarist started strumming his guitar softly. I took in a breath, held the microphone lightly, and started to sing.

Nova cheered as Zack whistled through his fingers. I closed my eyes, envisioned Trent, and just let the lyrics slip out from my lips. I had this pulsing ache that wouldn't subside within my body as I continued to sing, complimenting the artist Jewel.

A few lighters flickered as my voice sadly sang the ballad as I directed my attention back towards the crowd. I was the one hurting this time around inside this lonely *Broken Hearts Club.* I was nearing the end of the song as I glanced over at Ray, and he just smiled as he harmonized with me and continued to play his acoustic guitar.

After I finished the song, I shyly said, "Thank you," as the small crowd clapped with appreciation as I nodded my head in gratitude. I then kissed Ray on the cheek and stepped off the stage as I started to make my way back over to our booth.

"Are we finally done with these foolish games?" I heard someone ask as I laughed and turned around to see who asked the corny question.

Trent was standing there in his tight black V-neck sweater and black jeans and hair thrown back in a messy man-bun. He had watched me perform the entire song from the back of the room. My eyes widened as I just put my hand over my mouth in surprise.

"You sounded..." Trent paused.

"You sounded really beautiful up there. I never knew you could sing like that?" I laughed as I recalled singing "I Got Friends In Low Places" with a group of friends wasted for a few nights at the karaoke bar, but never quite this good.

"You tell me. Are we tired of these games?" I asked Trent, as he placed his hands in mine and pulled me into his embrace.

"I miss you, Alex," he said, as he kissed my head a few times.

"I've missed you too, Trent." Tears started to surface as I closed my eyes and just swayed with Trent as we held each other so tightly.

"You're not cross with me any longer?" I whispered.

"No," he said.

"Any connection with Gage Heston still has to go." I nodded my head in agreement.

"Believe me, he has cut the last tie." I was referring to my lead designer position being dissolved. Trent furrowed his brow with concern as I didn't want to expand on the Gage subject.

"Oh, and as for Tyler, you guys need to take a back seat on your friendship for now. I made an agreement with the band tonight at practice to be civil with him for the music's sake, but not for personal pleasure, understand me?" I pouted a little bit, but I knew he was right.

"I took care of that, too. I haven't spoken to either one of you since Las Vegas," I said.

"Do you want to join us over at the booth?" I asked Trent as I tried to change the subject as he scratched his head glancing over at Nova and Zack.

"Nah, can I pick you up, say tomorrow? I don't want to intrude on you and Nova tonight," he asked sweetly as I nodded my head yes. He bent down, softly kissed my lips then turned and headed out the front door of the club. I just blinked my eyes a few times as I watched him leave, trying to slow my pulse down.

"Alex, come over here, I'm so proud of you!" Nova waved to have me rejoin her as I released a breath of relief and went back to our booth.

November's chill was starting to set in as I rubbed my shoulders, looking over the balcony waiting for Trent to come over as promised. I could hear Trent's motorcycle pulling in the parking garage as I smiled. He parked then walked out of the garage and looked up at the balcony towards me. Shielding his eyes from the sun, he asked, "Want to go for a ride? It's so beautiful outside!" I nodded my head yes as I turned to go inside to grab my riding boots and leather jacket.

I met him downstairs as he revved up the bike once more and waited until I slid in the seat behind him. I wrapped my arms tightly around his waist.

"Ready cowgirl?" he asked as I replied:

"Ready!"

Trent took off riding through the streets of Dallas. I welcomed the breeze as it blew back Trent's silky hair, tickling my face. He was muscular to the touch as I gripped him a little tighter as we turned up Greenville Avenue. We passed all the bars as everyone was out and about on a beautiful day like today. Trent just kept on riding until we reached a secluded park.

We pulled in and hopped off the bike.

"Look at all the trees!" I said as I spun around. Trent walked over to me and grabbed my hand, squeezing it.

"Let's sit under one," he said as I chose my favorite, kicked off my boots and sat down between Trent's legs, leaning against his chest. He nestled his nose into my hair and lightly kissed my head.

"I really love you, Alex," he whispered into my ear. I smiled as I glanced around the peaceful setting.

"I know you do." I paused.

"Thank you for coming back for me once again. Thank

you for forgiving me after Las Vegas, for forgiving me after the Gage debacle. Just everything..." I released a breath as he rubbed my arms up and down. I felt like we were getting back on track after our slight derailment.

I then sat up and turned around to face him. Brushing his long hair out of his eyes, I leaned in and kissed him with heated passion. Trent was taken aback by the moment as he accepted my kiss by pulling my body in towards him.

"I want you to make love to me so bad, baby," I whispered as the all too familiar ache set in.

"We haven't been intimate since our phone sex in St. Louis! Can you believe that?" I pouted as I continued to pepper his soft lips with kisses. I then felt his cock harden within his jeans as I ran my hand over it and bit his lower lip. He let out a deep laugh.

"You're killing me, Alex. You know how hard it is to control myself around you." He panted slowly as I stood up and removed my jeans. Trent laughed as he looked around to an empty park, then shrugged his shoulders. No one was in sight, it was only the two of us hidden amongst the trees.

"Baby, I want to make love to you so bad," he groaned as I straddled him and slowly unfastened his jeans as I passionately kissed him once more. I tugged on his jeans as I slid them down just enough to where he was able to hold himself and slowly enter me.

"Oh my god," I quietly panted in his ear as his cock pushed itself in deeper.

"Oh god, how I've missed you," I said again as he slowly thrusted inside of me. I pushed his hair out of his face as I slid my tongue back into his warm mouth, flickering it softly with his tongue as he moaned for more.

"You feel so tight, Alex." He allowed me to push myself deeper down onto his cock.

"You feel so good, baby. I have missed you." He moaned once more. I was breathless as he grew harder for me while I slowly rocked back and forth, fueling my desire for him.

"I like sliding back and forth on your hard cock, Trent," I whispered as Trent's breathing picked up as my words began to turn him on.

"I want you to come with me, baby. I've waited so long to feel you inside of me again. I missed this," I whispered in his ear.

"Oh, how I longed to be inside of you, Alexandria. I've really missed you so much baby," he whispered as he kissed me affectionately once more as my heart began to melt.

I couldn't hold out much longer as I rocked back and forth on his lap in the grass. Trent grabbed a hold of my hips and moaned as he pushed deeper.

"That's it, Trent. God, I've missed this." I couldn't control how much the word 'miss' just kept slipping out of my mouth. I started sliding my hips up and down on him.

"Baby, if you're going to do just that, I'm going to come," Trent whispered in my ear as I licked his neck.

"I want to feel you coming. I can't wait much longer." I let out a breath, trying to control myself.

"Ahh," he moaned into my ear.

"Oh Trent, you're making me come!" I cried out as we both climaxed together.

After making love, I stood up and pulled my jeans back up over my hips as I laughed, jumping around, trying to zip up the zipper.

"Look at you, you Mexican jumping bean!" Trent laughed at me as he buttoned his jeans.

"Here's your boots, cowgirl." He tossed my boots at me as I sat back down on the ground and pulled them on.

"The sun is setting. It's so lovely out," I said as he smiled over at me.

"Say, are you up for a movie by any chance?" he asked me.

"A movie? That's inside. I'm enjoying the outside way too much," I said as I stood up and spun around, enjoying the fall weather.

"It is outside. Come here, let's go get on the bike," he said as I took his hand as we walked back to the motorcycle and hopped on.

Trent rode over to the Dallas Museum of Art and parked. He took my hand and walked me over to the lawn out front of the building.

"I love this place!" I said as he smiled at me.

"I know you do. Look!" He pointed over to a movie screen set up on the museum's lawn.

"It's an outdoor movie!" I squealed as he laughed.

"How cool is this!" I said as I watched all the people gather on the lawn, setting up blankets and chairs underneath the stars.

"Let's pop a squat and we'll watch the film, then I'll take you home." I smiled as I watched Trent remove his leather motorcycle jacket and lay it down on the ground for us to sit on. He sat down on it first then reached for my hand so I could sit between his legs and lean back on his chest.

"Didn't this just get us into trouble at the park?" I teased as he kissed my head, laughing. The movie started to play as all the guests started clapping their approval.

"What are we going to watch?" I whispered.

"Citizen Kane," he said as I smiled.

"I love old movies!" I cheered.

He kissed my head again and said, "I know you do, baby. I know you do."

After the movie ended, we returned to my loft all happy. I kicked off my riding boots as Trent sat down on the entry-way bench and removed his.

"Wine?" I asked him as I headed towards the kitchen.

"Yes, please." I had an extra giddy-up in my step now that Trent and I made love once again. Trent's cell began to buzz as I stood there opening the wine.

"Who's bugging you now?" I groaned as I stuck out my tongue at him. He leaned back on the bench and answered it.

"Hey Zack." I rolled my eyes. *It's my day with Trent, not the band's*, I quietly pouted to myself as I poured two glasses of red.

"You're kidding me, right? That's so fucking cool. I'll be there, dude." Trent hung up the phone and let out an "Ahhh!" as I just laughed asking:

"What's the happy grin for?" I handed him his glass of wine as he stood up and toasted me.

"First, to you, my love. Thank you for today." I blushed.

"And, second, Zack is totally kicking ass. He is having our single 'Betrayal' dropping soon with the soundtrack, and we're going to shoot a music video for it this week before the holiday break." My eyes widened.

"This week? I love that song!" I raised my glass to Trent. And to think that asshole Tyler almost threw that song away.

"Yeah babe, it'll be shot in this abandoned house that the city is going to tear down soon. The production company is trying to score the location, squaring away permits and such, then it's game on!" he said with excitement.

"*Burn the memories...*" I sang as he kissed me.

At that very moment all I could think of was me and Tyler's burning our exes' shit outside in the barrel of wasted love in the rain then having incredible sex afterwards. *I missed him.* Trent broke my train of thought when he whistled.

"Whew, good luck lugging a fucking piano out to the ghetto," I laughed as I toasted him and WHIP once more to their new music video.

CHAPTER 23

In the early hours of the day of the shoot, I rolled over in bed and looked at Trent. He was still in a deep slumber, lying on his back as I fluttered his long black eyelashes with my fingertips. He didn't budge. I traced the cross tattoo on his chest as he just kept sleeping. *God, he's gorgeous*, I thought as I smiled and quietly rolled over to reach under my bed for my sketch pad and charcoal pencil.

I sat upright and began quietly sketching Trent while he continued to sleep. His black hair was flopped over his eye, his five o'clock shadow was rough and his bare inked chest was defined as I stared while blending my charcoal. Trent's eyes slowly opened as he tried to focus on me.

"Baby, what are you doing?" he groaned.

"Don't move, I'm almost done. You, my sexy rockstar, are my favorite thing to sketch," I laughed as I blew on the drawing and brushed away the residue.

"How many sketches do you have of me now?" he teased as he poked my side with his finger.

My art laundry line hanging downstairs above my art table had nothing but Trent drawings clipped to them.

"You're my muse. You inspire me," I said as he laughed.

"If you say so, babe." He then rolled over and sat up in

bed naked with only a sheet hanging from his waist down.

"Big day today." I smiled as I waved the drawing around so he could appreciate it.

"Yep, I better get a move on. I'll hit the shower if you could please start the coffee." He leaned back and snatched the sketch out of my hand.

"Hey!" I laughed.

"This is really good, babe," he said as I smiled and snatched it back.

"I know." Laughing, I crawled out of bed, went downstairs and hung up my new addition to the line then started our morning coffee.

*

Arriving on set, I could feel the butterflies barrel rolling inside my stomach for WHIP. How exciting, they were shooting a music video! I stood on the sidewalk and just stared at the old, abandoned home that was about to be torn down. *How many memories will dissipate into thin air when the wrecking ball arrives?* I pondered.

The small house was white with paint peeling down both the front and sides. It had rotted wooden steps that led to an open porch and some of the window panels were busted out. I took out my camera and snapped a few pics. *I would love to draw this house*, I thought as I shoved my camera back in my bag.

Spotting the crafts services trailer parked to the left of the house and the band's trailer behind it, I made my way over to security. I stepped over a rope that lined the premises so none of the fans or homeless vagrants could disrupt shooting as I walked up to the officer and gave him my name. He checked the guest list, then motioned for me to get out of the way as the crew pushed past us with the band's equipment. I caught my breath, then skipped through the overgrown grass as I made my way to the band's trailer.

Tyler was standing outside, smoking his cigarette.

"Hi Ty," I greeted him as he stepped on his cigarette bud.

"Hi baby girl," he said quietly. He seemed lost as he looked around at all the chaos swirling around him. Both Trent and Tyler agreed to be professional and work with one another for the sake of the band. And true to word, they still kept it at just that for the time being.

"Don't be nervous." I blinked my lashes as I stared at him.

"You always get me, don't you?" He blew out a breath.

"Hey Ty, where are all the hot music video models?" I laughed as I looked around and saw nothing but a dude-fest.

"Yeah, really? What the fuck? Where's my 'Cherry Pie' girl?" I smiled as Tyler made a reference to one of my favorite hair bands.

"Well, you look really fucking good, Mr. Black," I complimented him as I bit my lip, shaming myself for always being Tyler's ego-feeder.

The trailer's door suddenly opened up as Trent stepped out.

"Hey, you made it." He smiled as he stepped towards me and gave me a hug. I stepped back and fussed with his jacket.

"Why so much eyeliner?" I blended his eyeliner with my fingertip. Laughing, he said, "The video is in black and white, and the makeup artist went a little heavier on the makeup today." I rolled my eyes as I looked over my shoulders and noticed Tyler walking away. I could sense this uncomfortableness between us at the moment, and I didn't like it one bit.

Trying to distract me, Trent grabbed my hand and asked, "Do you want to see the set before we start?" I nodded my head yes.

My eyes lit up like stars as he walked me towards the front of the house. The crew scurried past us as they set up cameras. A few fans were hanging on a rusted chain-linked fence, hollering for Trent's attention as he grinned and gave them a slight wave.

I squeezed his hand a little tighter as I followed him into the abandoned little house.

"Wow," was all I could muster as I looked around the set. To the left was a vintage black upright grand piano placed under an antique chandelier with numerous candles scattered along the top. The room on the right had the drum kit set up in front of the old fireplace with the guitars leaning on the adjacent wall. Candles littered the original wooden floor.

Trent then pulled me up the creaking staircase that was also lined with candles leading to a bedroom that had only a mattress on the floor with a plethora of polaroids scattered about of an emotional woman either crying, laughing or sleeping in them. I looked around in amazement.

"I totally get this! Wow, you guys nailed it. *Burn the memories*," I whispered as Trent nodded his head yes as we turned around to head back out of the house just as the director called out for the band on his megaphone.

"Hey, I'll hang for a few takes, then I'll split. I don't want to hover." I looked up at Trent as he leaned down to kiss me.

"I like you hovering." He kissed me once more as he brushed his fingertips along my cheek. I let go of his hand then pranced over behind the director's chair so I could stand next to Zack to watch as the art director gathered the band.

The guys were all in place as the film crew started rolling while Trent began playing the haunting opening melody to "Betrayal." I got the chills as I watched him play.

He had on his usual black velvet jacket, black low cut t-shirt exposing his inked chest, multiple chains around the neck and his black jeans. His eyes were both lined in black, and his long hair was shining under the chandelier as he played the piano with so much passion. My chest pounded as I just listened to him play note for note as the candles flickered, hence *burn the memories*.

The director shot a few takes of Trent, then sent a crew inside the second room to shoot the drummer while the fireplace crackled behind him. The rest of the guys all followed suit as they all wore their best black threads, looking like a bad-ass prog-industrial band. *This is going to look so bad-ass in black and white film.* I relished the thought as they filmed a few more takes of WHIP playing their music.

Startling me, the director turned around and hollered, "Hey blondie!" I looked around oblivious as Zack brushed my arm with his.

"I think he means you, Alex." I laughed.

"Yeah?" I yelled back at the director.

"Interested in helping me out with a scene?" I shrugged my shoulders as he approached me.

"I need a woman to lie face down under the white sheet

on the mattress upstairs, exposing just her hair and back. We want a shot of a woman sleeping. The model from the polaroids got the flu, so I need a body." I gulped, as I didn't want to intrude. *How do I always get dragged into WHIP's crazy world?* I nodded my head yes as the art director grabbed a hold of my hand and led me into the house.

Tyler hollered out, "Go get 'em, cherry pie!" as I just laughed and flipped him the bird.

Trent grabbed my arm in passing. "Hey, are you okay, babe?" I nodded my head yes.

"Is it okay if I'm in a scene? I guess I just need to lie down on the bed for a shot." Trent laughed.

"Of course it's okay, but the bastard better be paying you." I blew him a kiss as I continued to follow the art director up the stairs.

"Can you lie down topless on your stomach? We just need to see your hair over your shoulder and your back exposed, giving off the illusion that you're naked in bed." I laughed.

"I can handle that." I closed the door, pulled off my tight sweater, unsnapped my bra and crawled under the sheet feeling like I was about to receive a massage.

"I'm in!" I called out as the crew stepped back into the room with their camera.

"Holy shit, I love that tattoo. It's so gothic!" the art director shouted as he stared at my exposed back. "That's perfect with the black angel wings and platinum hair. This is going to look so killer in black and white!" I giggled as I laid in bed while the crew began to film a few takes.

"Okay, blondie, that's a wrap." The art director smiled as he pushed the guys out of the room and closed the door.

While I was getting dressed, I overheard the director

call out, "Set up the porch scene next!" I hurried down the stairs and ran outside back over towards Zack as he fist bumped me while I stood there staring at the porch.

The director focused on Tyler. He was in his black button-up dress shirt with the sleeves rolled up, exposing his ink on his forearms. He had various bracelets dangling from both his wrists as he rocked his notorious black dress scarf, messy hair, and black skinny jeans. *Yum. The girls will love this tall drink of water.* I smiled as I watched him nervously pace the front porch.

"Hey Tyler. I need you to lean against the front door as we shoot you singing a few verses. Then we'll film a few shots of you singing on the porch step. Dig?" the director called out as Tyler nodded his head yes as the song began to ooze through the speakers.

He leaned his body against the rickety old door and started to dramatically sing the song as if every lyric he was belting out was crushing him emotionally. I couldn't take my watery eyes off of him. As always, he was just so painfully beautiful to watch. I stood there biting my lip as he sang the final verse directly towards me: *"Can't believe the truth. Can't believe I've failed. You ripped my heart out. The final sign of betrayal."*

He glared right through me as I swallowed hard, then wiped my eyes.

Did I betray him by promising to always be there and then pushing him out first thing after Las Vegas when he needed me the most? I let him in emotionally and physically as we just used one another to stave off the loneliness. Ugh, we both got so hurt in the end. But, I needed to keep my promise to Trent and set this wounded bird free to fend for himself.

The buzzsaw going off in my head was starting to make me dizzy as I grabbed a hold of Zack's arm to steady myself.

"Hey look, I'm going to split," I said as I kissed his cheek. "Good luck with the rest of the music video." I turned around and walked off the set.

CHAPTER
24

"Hey my video vixen, I'm here!" Trent hollered up towards the loft, searching for me as I was sitting in my bed working on my laptop.

"I'm up here!" I hollered at him as he ran up the staircase.

"I've missed you." He threw himself on the bed, bouncing the mattress, making my computer slide off my lap.

"Yeah, I thought the edit suite swallowed you up? Man, it's been a week. Are they still not done editing that music video yet?" I laughed as I readjusted my computer on my lap as Trent crawled towards me, softly kissing my lips.

"YouTube," he said as he pulled away from my lips.

"What?" I wiped my mouth as I typed in the search box, YouTube.

"Okay, now what?" I glanced over at him as he rolled onto his back, smiling.

"Search for WHIP's 'Betrayal.'" My eyes widened as I quickly typed. WHIP's video popped up, and I squealed.

"Holy shit!" I pushed play as the video opened up with Trent playing on the upright grand piano.

"God, you look sexy!" I smiled as I watched intensely. He just laughed. The camera then slowly rolled over to me as I laid in the bed, panning from my hair, down my back, and off to the floor scattered with the polaroids.

"Hey, they used that shot!" I giggled. The video slowly focused on the guitarist sitting on the stairs, the candle-lit staircase, then the rest of the band playing their instruments until Tyler appeared on the porch. I gasped.

Trent leaned up on his elbow and kissed my arm as I ignored it while I continued to intensely watch the video all the way through. When it ended, I turned my head towards him and said, "Oh... My... God. It's fucking amazing!" Trent nodded.

"I love that it was filmed in black and white!" Trent agreed.

"You color my black and white world, baby." I smiled as I bit my lower lip. I was beaming as I leaned in and kissed him.

The video was out. The song was on the radio. The tour was being planned. And... the movie was coming out Thanksgiving weekend.

"What a roll you guys are on!" I pushed play to watch the video once more all the way through.

"Talk about a band image reboot! Gage Heston couldn't have pulled all this shit off." I laughed as Trent didn't respond.

"It's everything you've ever wanted..." I held my breath as I glanced over at Trent.

"What?" he asked.

"Fame," I said.

The next morning, I sat on the balcony wrapped up in my southwestern printed blanket and sipping my coffee as my cell phone rang. I took a deep breath in then answered it.

"Hi Mama," I greeted her on the line.

"You've been hiding out, Miss Alexandria. Your father is very worried about you." I pouted.

"I'm fine, Mama. Just busy, that's all," I said as I took another swig of my coffee.

"Thanksgiving Day is tomorrow, dear. Are you planning on joining your family for dinner?" I paused as I thought about it.

"Alexandria?" my mother called out.

"Do not disappoint your father now. Austin will be in town as well." I huffed, wondering if I was in the mood for turkey and a side of family bullshit.

I asked, "Will it be 'just the family,' or are you throwing another infamous dinner party for the entire city of Dallas?" I laughed to myself.

"Do not sass me, Miss Alexandria!" Mother shouted.

"Yes Ma'am. I'm sorry," I apologized, then sweetly asked, "Can I please bring someone who is very important to me?"

Pausing, my mother answered, "Of course you can, dear. Is it that boyfriend that gives you trouble with matters of the heart?" she asked sarcastically as I let out a breath.

"Everything is fine with Trent, Mama." I started to contemplate right then and there if I should introduce Trent to my parents or not.

"Bring him along, dear. Your father is the one that needs to meet him," she demanded.

"Yes Ma'am. I'll be there tomorrow with Trent," I huffed.

"Okay hun, see you and Trent at four o'clock sharp." She then hung up the phone as I got up and walked into the kitchen for a refill of coffee.

Trent was standing there in only a pair of unbuttoned jeans as he sifted through the cupboard in search of sugar. I squeezed his butt and laughed.

"Want to do me a solid?" I asked as I reached for the coffee pot.

"What?" he laughed as he poured sugar into his coffee.

"Do you want to go with me to my family's Thanksgiving family dinner?" I blew on my mug as he flashed his intoxicating grin.

"I'd love to, babe. My mum's not home this holiday, and I really dig your brother Austin, so sure, why not?" Trent shook his shoulders as he leaned in towards me and kissed my head. I felt a sudden wave of nerves flush through me as I began to worry about my parents accepting Trent.

The next day I stood in the mirror fussing over my tight cream sweater and tapered jeans as Trent walked up to me and wrapped his arms around me, swaying.

"Baby, what's going on in that head of yours?" I grimaced as I swayed with Trent for a minute.

"Are you sure you want to meet my family today? I mean, are we there yet?" Trent kissed my cheek and sat down on the bed as he began lacing up his boots.

"I hope we're heading in that direction." He paused.

"I'd love to meet the rest of your family. I vividly remember you saying in Las Vegas that you wanted to marry me, so I hope that one day your family becomes mine." I blushed with embarrassment as I sat down next to him, recalling myself in my white dress, doily on my head, and blood running down my nose.

"That train wreck? You'd marry that train wreck? What's wrong with you?" I laughed as I stood back up, grabbed Trent's hand, and pulled him up off the bed.

"Come on, let's go. My mother does not like tardiness." I tisk-tisked him as he laughed.

We pulled into my parents' driveway as I parked my truck over by Daddy's familiar workshop. Trent hopped out and blew out a breath as he looked around the property. He then looked over at me as he shut the passenger door and said, "This house is really amazing, Alex." I looked around and shrugged my shoulders.

"I guess. D-towns elite," I snickered as Trent smacked my hand then squeezed it.

Suddenly, Austin ran out of the house to greet us.

"Alex!" He hollered out as I let go of Trent's hand and ran up to hug my brother. He stepped back, took one look at me and said, "You look so good sis!" I smiled as I leaned in for one more additional hug. Trent walked up behind us and asked,

"How do I look, bro?" Austin blurted out laughing.

"Hey man, it's so nice to see you again." He held out his hand and shook Trent's hand.

I glanced around the driveway asking, "Are we the only ones here? Please tell me it's just the family." Austin laughed as we turned towards the house and headed in.

"It's just us," he confirmed as I let out a sigh of relief.

Austin opened the front door and called out that we were here. Mother ran out from the kitchen first, removing her apron while fidgeting with her pearls.

"Oh, I'm so glad y'all are here! So Alex, who is this fine

gentleman joining us today?" She stood there extending her hand to shake Trent's hand as she looked him up and down.

"Mother, this is Trent Van Zant." He shook her hand softly then went back to holding mine.

"Austin, go drag your father away from that football game and get him in here at once," Mother ordered my brother as he turned to go fetch Daddy.

"Well, it's nice of you to join us, Trent. You'll have to excuse me. I need to make sure the rolls don't burn." Mother gave us a fake smile as Trent nodded his head.

She turned and walked past Daddy, stopping him by gripping his arm and whispering, "He has on more makeup than our daughter." I rolled my eyes as I knew Trent only had a smidge of guyliner on. But, he was still gorgeous to me.

"There's my girl! How you holdin' up, sugar?" My father came over and gave me a hug.

"Hi Daddy! I didn't mean to pull you away from our Cowboys, but I really want you to meet Trent." I stepped back as Trent shook my father's hand.

"Nice to meet you, sir." My father smiled as he returned the stern handshake. He then said, "So Austin tells me you're a musician? A real good one at that."

Trent smiled, responding, "Yes, sir, I am."

I rubbed Trent's arm as Austin interrupted us by asking, "Does anyone want some wine?" I nodded an exaggerated yes as Austin laughed and directed us towards the dining room table.

Trent pulled out my chair, then slid into the one next to me. My father seated himself at the head of the table as Austin sat across from me and Trent.

"So, Austin, where's your dinner date?" I laughed as he smiled.

"Which one?"

Trent let out an "ooo" as we both just laughed. "Come on, there's got to be at least one?" I pushed the question as Austin lifted the wine bottle, asking "Wine anyone?" as he dismissed the question. I lifted my glass so he could pour the wine as I dropped the prodding.

I then turned towards Trent and toasted him whispering, "Thank you for being here with us." He nodded as he returned the toast, sipping his wine, cool as a cucumber.

When my mother joined us in the dining room, she sat at the other end of the table and gestured for all of us to hold hands and pray before the meal. I giggled as I took Trent's hand in mine. I was so elated and relieved at how easily Trent talked with my family. He was gracious, he laughed at the family stories, and he even collected the dishes after dinner, which pleased my mother to no end. Tyler was right, I always looked at Trent with adoration and love.

"Well kiddos," my father interrupted us, "I'm going to finish watching the football game and probably nap." My mother rolled her eyes as he pushed out his chair and stood up.

"Do you want to take dessert home with you, dear?" she kindly asked.

"We're good. I have something sweet at home." I nudged Trent.

"Well, we're going to take off then. We both have a lot of projects on our plates, and I really do need a good night's rest," I said graciously. My father walked over to us, shook Trent's hand then hugged me goodbye.

"I like that kid," he whispered in my ear as I smiled.

Then the two of us walked back to the truck.

"Whew, we did it!" I shouted as I slammed the door and started up the truck.

"Sorry we didn't stay for dessert, but..."

Trent leaned over and kissed me softly on my neck, whispering, "You're my dessert." I licked my lips as I quickly put my truck in reverse.

Pulling into the loft, I shut off the engine and dodged out of my truck, racing for the elevator.

"Baby, what's the hurry?" Laughing, Trent picked up his pace and met me in the elevator.

"Dessert! I want dessert, and I want it right now!" I pushed Trent against the cold elevator wall as he let out a sigh. I slipped my heated tongue into his mouth and licked his tongue a few times as I ached for him.

"We were so good at dinner, but tonight I want us to be so bad!" I said as I licked his neck up to his ears, panting as I grabbed his jeans and unbuttoned them. The elevator dinged as I kept kissing him, pushing him towards the front door. Trent shuffled around in his pockets for the key, unlocked the door all the while he had his hot tongue in my mouth. He pushed me through the door, kicked it shut with his boot and kept kissing me. My cell phone then started to ring.

"Ignore it baby," Trent begged as he kept kissing me. He pulled my sweater off over my head as my breathing grew ragged. Again, the cell phone started to ding with text messages over and over.

"Wait." I paused our foreplay as I pulled my cell phone

out of my pocket.

"It's fucking Tyler. Oh my god, look how many messages! I'm fucking so irritated with him, I could smack him!" I stomped my foot.

"Fucking lying to you about Gage, not reading my letter, the cocaine, and all that damn Vegas drama. The list is endless." I shook my head as anger flushed through me. *He was ruining my moment with Trent.* I pouted as I tossed the phone on the floor.

"Let's not rehash it, Alex," he said as I stared at the floor.

"I already talked to him when he returned from Las Vegas. I've just kept him at arm's length ever since then to give him his much needed space to work his own shit out. What do you think he fucking wants now?" I asked furiously as Trent shook his head, saying nothing.

"Hit me then." Trent finally spoke.

"What?" I looked up at him, thrown off by the request.

"You have all this pent up anger and aggression towards Tyler. You need to let it out. I can handle it." Trent stepped towards me and pushed me against the door.

"Hit me," he repeated. I gave him a slight slap across the cheek as I huffed.

"There you go, baby!" He then grabbed my arm as I slapped his cheek harder this time and gave him a good push forward. He leaned right back into me as I really pushed him harder the second time.

"There, there's a good push to release my frustration!" I yelled as Trent smiled.

"That's it, baby, I can handle it!" he reminded me.

I then reached up and grabbed his hair as I yanked him back in towards me, letting the sexual desire overcome me. In a fever, I ripped his dress shirt open as the buttons flew out, bouncing off the wall. Trent laughed as I bent over and began licking his V up the right side and kept going till I reached his nipples, giving them a twisted pinch.

He cried out, "Oh, Alex!" I then pushed my tongue forcefully into his mouth as he moaned while kissing me a little bit rougher.

We wanted each other, and we wanted each other bad. He quickly turned me around and pushed me against the door as he licked the end of my spine all the way up to my neck. I gasped as he pulled at the clasp of my bra and set my breasts free. Grabbing them both, he tugged on my erect nipples as I pushed my ass against him.

"Oh god!" I cried out in ecstasy. He reached around to my waist and unbuttoned my jeans, pulling them to the floor. I took all that pent up anger towards Tyler, and I was going to use it sexually on Trent tonight. *My, how the tables have turned.* I took my pain out on Tyler, and now I was taking my frustration out on Trent.

Standing there naked in the entryway, I turned to face him as I ripped his jeans off swiftly and tossed them onto the floor as well. I let his hard cock spring up and greet me with excitement. I grabbed a hold of it, got down on my knees and pushed it into my mouth.

"Fuck! Alex!" he groaned as he pulled my hair. I glanced up, watching him get off as I blinked my lashes up at him while sucking on his cock.

"Alex, baby. You're going to make me come if you keep that up!" he warned me as he pulled back as I wiped my mouth while standing up and pushing him down on the entryway bench.

He submitted to me as I straddled him, reaching for my scarf hanging on a hook above our head. I feverishly blindfolded him as he moaned.

"You're a bad girl, Alex."

I laughed as I whispered in his ear, saying, "I want you to feel the sensation of me opening up my slit and slowly lowering it down on your big, hard cock." He threw his head back, panting for more as I began to slowly slide down him as I began to work him up and down.

"Oh Alex. Take it out on me, baby!" he moaned as I thrusted harder and harder as I was releasing all the built up angst.

"Oh, Trent!" I cried out again as I ran my tongue across his bottom lip as I kept fucking him.

"Come for me!" I ordered as I gave another hard slap to his face. He moaned as he stuck out his tongue, licking my neck then sliding it into my mouth.

I was getting so turned on as he grabbed my hips and pushed deeper inside of me. I felt a tension-releasing orgasm as he panted and kept fucking me. I trembled on his lap as I tried to release a breath. As I slowed my pace down, I ordered him, "Pull out your cock and get ready to come for me." I then stood up, slid off his lap, got back down on my knees between his legs, and stroked him hard as I watched him orgasm all over his abdomen.

"Oh, Alex!" He cried out once again, leaning back on the bench. I began licking him from his V, up his abdomen, all the way up his body till I reached his ear and whispered, "Now, that's dessert." He laughed as he wiped the sweat off of his upper lip and I untied his blindfold.

CHAPTER 25

Late the next morning, I quietly tip-toed to the kitchen to start brewing our morning coffee. Trent was sound asleep up in the loft area as I smiled, looking at all our clothes scattered all over the floor from last night's romp. That was fucking hot sex. I wiggled my hips in my robe, replaying the act in my head. I then walked over to my laptop and started it up as I patiently waited for my coffee.

I had left open the *Revolver* Magazine website window and immediately saw an article posted about the rock and roll film that WHIP recorded the soundtrack for premiering tonight.

"Holy shit," I whispered, as I completely forgot about it. *Why didn't Trent go to the premiere?* I furrowed my brows, thinking about it as Trent walked into the kitchen.

"Why the face?" he asked, startling me as I laughed. I stood up and walked into the kitchen to grab my mug of coffee.

"Why are you up so soon?" I asked as he looked over at me, handing me my mug.

"Why the face?" he asked for a second time.

"The movie comes out tonight. It's Thanksgiving weekend, one of the hottest movie premiere weekends of the year." He smiled as he retrieved the milk from the refrigerator.

"And?" he asked.

"Why didn't you attend the premiere?" I curiously asked.

"Baby, I didn't want to go. That's a gig for all the actors and film geeks. Tweedle Dee and Tweedle Dumb went, though." He laughed as he stirred his coffee.

"Who's Tweedle Dee?" I asked as I sipped my coffee.

"It's Roger from the REVENUE," he said, flashing me a smirk.

"And, Tweedle Dumb?" He paused then looked at me, knowing I should know that fucking answer. "Tyler," he said.

"You're so mean!" I pouted as I sipped my coffee once more.

"Me? Mean? Let me remind you that you slapped me a few times last night during our tension-releasing sex." I laughed, feeling a little embarrassed by my behavior as I slapped his butt, then walked back to the computer.

"Well, we'll know by the end of the weekend if the movie was a hit or if it bombed out." Trent shrugged his shoulders, brushing me off.

"We'll see," he said as he walked out of the kitchen and headed straight upstairs to shower.

I kept surfing the internet until my cell phone rang. Not recognizing the number, I picked it up anyway.

"Hello?" I answered.

"Hey Alex, it's Roger." I scratched my head just thinking how strange it was that we were just talking about Tweedle Dee.

"Yes, hi sugar. How's married life treating you?" He let out a deep laugh on the other end of the line. "Oh, my

Tonya, she treats me right." I smiled and rolled my eyes, knowing that bitch didn't like me one bit.

"That's good. What can I do for you, sir?" I asked.

"Listen, your buddy Tyler here gave me your number, so I hope you don't mind the call, but I wanted to see if I can hire you for something?" He let out a low smoker's cough. *If this has anything to do with drugs, I'm so going to strangle Tyler's neck.*

"The guys from the band want to see if you can help design our new album cover? We just finished recording, Tyler sang some vocal melodies on a few of the tracks, and I wanted to get your opinion on a design. WHIP's logo is the bomb, girl," he complimented me as I just blushed. *Wow, Tyler remembered that Gage's record label had fired me, so he hooked me up with another rock band to help generate some income—kind of sweet of him, actually,* I thought to myself.

"I'd love to. Why don't you email me some of the band's ideas, and I'll sketch a few things out for y'all. We can put our heads together and come up with something cool." Roger agreed as I gave him my contact information.

"Get in touch with me when you get back to Dallas, and I'll have some preliminaries drawn up and ready for you." I smiled with glee.

"I'll be sure to do that, Alex. Again, thank you." I clicked off the line, then squealed.

"How fucking cool is that!" I hollered.

"What's up, babe?" Trent called out from the bathroom as he was shaving.

I closed my laptop and skipped up the staircase to the bathroom to share my good news. Trent was standing in nothing but a towel. *God, I love when he is half naked.*

"What's up, babe?" he asked again as he turned around to give me his full attention.

"The REVENUE. They want me to design their new album cover!" I threw my arms up in the air and shook my hands like I was shaking pom-poms.

"Bad-ass babe. I'm so proud of you," he said as he leaned over to kiss me.

"Tyler pulled through for me. That was a nice hook up. He scored me a much cooler gig! The REVENUE is a way better project than working on the local bank designs," I laughed as I wiped the shaving cream off my chin.

"It was thoughtful of him. I'll give him that." Trent nodded his head in agreement, cutting Tyler some slack.

"Look out though," he said as I frowned.

"What?" I asked.

"Fame." He laughed.

Later that evening, Trent was still hibernating at *Head Rush* when I laid down on my couch and started channel surfing. My cell phone rang, startling me as I just selected something to binge watch.

"Hello?" I answered.

"Hey baby girl." Tyler was on the other end of the line. I quickly grabbed the remote, shut off the television, and sat upright on the couch.

"Ty? Where are you at?" He let out a subtle laugh.

"I'm in my hotel room." He sounded a little tipsy.

"Were you drinking tonight? Were you celebrating? How was the movie premiere? And what were the hundred text messages about last night?" I had so many questions as I sat there impatiently waiting for Tyler to answer just one of them.

"I really needed to talk to you. Just hush and listen, baby girl," he ordered as I shut my mouth.

"You got me this gig, Alex. The rock and roll movie was so fucking awesome." He paused as I heard him light up a cigarette on the line then blow it out.

"I got to do this soundtrack because of you. Hell, I get to do everything because of you." I sat there listening just thinking that when Tyler has too much to drink he tends to get verbal diarrhea.

"I didn't mean anything I said in Las Vegas, aside from wanting to marry you. I can be so fucking cruel at times when I'm feeling pain. Do you forgive me?" I stayed silent on the phone as he continued.

"Look, I want to go back in time. I really miss our friendship, Alex," he sniffled on the line.

"I'm keeping every one of my promises I made to you, whether Trent likes it or not. Granted, I had some wine tonight, but no more drugs, no more cutting, no more strange pussy, no more bullshit. You saw me through the worst, and you still fucking loved me. You helped me through detox in Louisiana. You helped me build back my confidence to play this rock god again. And..." He paused.

"My selfish ass just took advantage of your broken heart, and I'm sorry. I just miss you. I miss our friendship and want you back in my life. It's been too long." Tyler started to cry.

"I'm sorry, Alex, I'm sorry. I'm such a fuck up." He sniffled once more, then continued with his apology.

"Listen, Trent is an amazing guy, and I knew exactly what was going to happen the very night you laid your eyes on him at the Steel Door a few years ago. Somewhere deep inside of me I was secretly jealous," Tyler confessed as I smiled as I recalled the very night I met Trent.

"Trent aside, I really miss you, Alex. I have no one else but you. My mother is out of the picture, and my father is an asshole. You are my only family." Tyler then became silent on the line.

I started to cry at his apology, then opened my mouth.

"I've never lied to you, Tyler. Even if it would hurt you, I was always open and honest with you. I miss you so much it hurts. I just miss us—you're my best friend. I don't regret you being my 'partner in rejection.' If I had the choice for anyone to go through the heartache with again, it would be you. I just kissed you with my eyes closed so tight." I wiped the tears that were pouring down my face.

"If I'm going to make this work with Trent, I need to earn his respect back." I paused.

"It's just not fair to Trent. I disrespected him when I used you as a rebound. I disrespected him when I strung Mr. Heston along. And, I definitely shouldn't have meddled in the band's business. My heart was in the right place, but it ruined all of our relationships." I paused as I released a breath.

"But, I still need you, Tyler. You are my best friend and will always be my best friend. Look, Trent has forgiven you. I have forgiven you. Hell, WHIP has forgiven you." I laughed as Tyler continued to stay silent on the line.

"Come on home, Tyler," I pleaded.

He blew out a breath of relief and said, "Okay then, thank you baby girl."

"Thank you," he whispered as I released another breath of relief as well.

As he hung up the phone, I clicked off the line, staring straight ahead, processing our conversation.

Trent startled me as he stood there sympathetically, watching me. I had never heard him come over.

"What was that all about, Alex?" he asked with concern, as I wiped my teary eyes. I tossed my phone on the end table and looked up at Trent.

"Closure," I said, feeling the same sense of relief wash over me.

"Gage Heston has left the building. Tyler Black has asked for forgiveness. You, Mr. Van Zant are my only last concern. Are we okay again? I do not want to rehash this over and over every time you and I have a disagreement. No more meddling in the band's business either. I promise. Can we just put it to bed and move on?" I asked as he leaned down and kissed me softly on the lips as he wiped my eyes. "We're okay, baby. I promise." I let out a breath and finally let the anxiety go.

CHAPTER
26

It was a few weeks until Christmas, and every one of my new clients were on a holiday until after the New Year. I had some down time to myself that I actually wanted to use to start sketching out something for the REVENUE's new album cover. I pranced over to my art table and grabbed a sketch pad and a pack of charcoal pencils.

Sitting back on the living room couch, I started to draw. I was so relieved that this crazy-ass year was finally coming to an end. I felt I was back on track with both loves of my life.

Suddenly, my cell phone rang, which startled me as I slid my drawing pencil behind my ear and answered it.

"Hi Tyler. How you holdin' up, hun?" I asked my best friend.

"Hi baby girl. I'm back in the big D again." I smiled, feeling relieved now knowing that he was back in Texas safe and sound.

"I wanted to pick up where I left off on our last phone conversation," he said as I pushed my sketch pad aside.

"You have my attention, Mr. Black," I said as I listened attentively.

"Alex, I'm going to head back to Louisiana over our holiday break and take part in this retreat the detox clinic is offering. It's just a few weeks away from all the noise to get my affairs back in order." He paused, awaiting my response.

"Thank you, Tyler. I'm so glad you are taking the reins on this one. You need to shut down and reboot. I'm very proud of you." I grinned from ear to ear, listening to his plan as I could hear him smile on the other end of the line.

"Thank you for the endless support. I'm going to list you as my contact person in case of an emergency, but I'll be unable to call you any time during the retreat. It's clinic rules." I pouted for a second.

"Not even for Christmas? Boo," I pouted once more.

"That's okay, Tyler. The New Year is approaching us, so it'll be a fresh start for all of us. A new chapter." He let out a subtle laugh.

"New chapter," he repeated.

"Look, Trent offered to drive me to the detox clinic. I feel it's the better option because if you drive me there, I'm afraid I'll fall apart on you." I smiled thinking, *What doesn't that man do for me? God, I really do love Trent.*

"Okay, but if you need me at any one moment, you call me. Why don't you take your journal and write? Who knows? You just might write another hit song from all this mess." I suggested as I blew him a kiss on the line as he just laughed.

"I'll check in when I need you, baby girl. You take time for you as well, and we'll plan on seeing each other after the New Year." His voice cracked as I sensed he was trying to keep it together. I so wanted to wrap my arms around him at that very moment to comfort him, but Tyler needed to do this alone.

We said our goodbyes as I clicked off the line, letting out an exaggerated long breath. *I do need time for myself.* I wasn't going to spend any of my down time fixing Tyler; I was going to enjoy my holiday with Trent. I paused as I thought it was good for the two of them to drive to Louisiana without me. *Who knows? Maybe they will strengthen that bond between them once more, a little holiday forgiveness.*

"Holiday?" I then shouted out loud.

"That's right!" I laughed to myself. *I'm going to head downstairs to the storage locker and lug up that damn Christmas tree! How perfect, a quiet Christmas alone with Trent.* I smiled to myself.

One hour later I had the Christmas tree all set up in the corner of the living room with its lights on as I sifted through a box of ornaments listening to Elvis Presley's Christmas album. Trent walked in through the front door, whistling.

"Hi babe. Whatcha up to?" He paused in the corridor, kicking off his boots.

"Is that Elvis you're listening to?" I laughed.

"Do you like the Christmas tree?" I asked as I held up an ornament shaped like a guitar.

"It looks good, babe. What can I do to help?" he asked as I smiled over at him.

"You can pour yourself a glass of wine then come sit down over here and hand me my ornaments." Trent laughed as he flipped on the kitchen light.

"I can handle that." Trent poured a glass of wine for himself and one for me as well, then he walked over to the living room area.

"To the tree!" he toasted as I took the glass from his hand and toasted him back.

"To our tree!" I said as he smiled, leaned down, kissed my lips then sat on the couch.

"I wanted to thank you for offering to drive Tyler to his retreat in Louisiana," I said as I sipped my wine, looking over at him.

"It's no problem. He needs this retreat, and I'm giving him all the credit on this one. No one is pushing and dragging him there. He's going on his own merit, and I respect that." I blinked my lashes as I couldn't believe how Trent was complimenting Tyler as I set the glass down on the coffee table and hung the guitar ornament on the tree.

"They're all musical instruments!" Trent laughed as he unwrapped another guitar.

"You are definitely my girl, Alex," he laughed.

"You are definitely my girl," he repeated as we quietly decorated our tree.

It was Christmas Eve, and I was cooking dinner for just me and Trent. WHIP were all on holiday with their families. Zack was spending Christmas with Nova, and Tyler was on retreat in Louisiana. I never felt so relaxed as I fussed with the potatoes wearing my paw print apron.

"I could get used to this." Trent came up behind me and wrapped his arms around me and swayed. I laughed as I purred.

"Aw, you have a paw print pattern on your apron. I miss our lil buddy." I stopped my mixer and paused, thinking about Ernie.

"It seems awfully quiet here at times, I must admit. I do miss Ernie's motor running in my ear every morning," I pouted as I went to the refrigerator and grabbed the butter. Trent gave me another kiss on the cheek, then purred in my ear. I just laughed as I scooped a piece of potato out of the bowl and fed it to him.

"Are you hungry, babe?" I asked.

"I am. Everything smells so incredible." I smiled at the compliment.

"Can you help me set the table, and I'll set up our plates," I asked sweetly as Trent walked over to our table, lit a few candles and set down the rest of the dinnerware.

Holiday tunes were quietly playing in the background as I filled two plates with food. I walked over to the table and set them down as Trent pulled out my chair.

"Thank you, Mr. Van Zant," I replied, appreciating the kind gesture as I removed my apron and sat down. He then took his seat across from me as he set his napkin onto his lap. I just took a moment as I reflected on my feelings towards Trent.

"I never stopped loving you," I whispered as Trent looked up at me. I stared straight into his honest eyes as I repeated, "I never stopped loving you. I really love you Trent." He blushed as he blinked his long black lashes back at me.

"I know you do, Alex," he whispered.

"Now, you only get two small presents tonight after dinner." He pierced the potatoes with his fork as I laughed.

"Two? I thought we agreed on one!" I lifted my glass of

iced tea to toast him.

"Merry Christmas." I smiled.

"Merry Christmas, beautiful." He returned the toast.

After dinner, Trent helped me clean up the dishes while we sang cheesy Christmas songs out loud. I then turned off the kitchen light and went over to the lit Christmas tree. I retrieved a present from underneath it and sat on the couch, tapping the cushion next to me.

"Here, come open mine first!" I giggled with excitement. Trent smiled as he sat down next to me as I handed him a box wrapped in silver paper and a green holiday bow. He slowly untied the bow then admired it for a minute.

"Can I use this on you later?" He asked jokingly.

"Just open it, you pervert," I laughed as I was getting impatient as Trent unwrapped the paper and opened the gift box.

"It's sheet music paper. How beautiful!" He paused with surprise as he read the inscription.

"It has music and lyrics by Trent Van Zant. This is such a thoughtful gift, baby." I smiled at him happily, and I was pleased with the gift I chose for him.

"You compose so many beautiful pieces of music, and that folder with bits of loose paper with music notes scribbled on it is not good enough for a real professional. So, here are professional music sheets!"

I was elated with his reaction as he gently placed them back into the box.

"How thoughtful. You never cease to amaze me, Alex." He leaned towards me and kissed my lips softly as he said, "Thank you."

I then bounced up and down on the cushion and said.

"Your turn!" I felt like I was eight years old again, waiting for my Malibu Barbie doll as I rubbed my jeans with excitement. Trent laughed as he watched me get all giddy with excitement. He stood up and said, "I'll be right back." I watched him walk out the front door and knock on the neighbor's door.

"What the hell is he doing?" I asked myself as I slapped my leg, waiting impatiently.

Trent then walked back inside, kicked the door closed behind him and headed back to the couch, setting a box with holes in it on the coffee table.

"This isn't wrapped very pretty, but I'll take it!" I laughed as I stared at the box.

"Open it, babe." He nudged my arm. I leaned towards the box, opened it up, and two sets of eyes blinked back at me.

"Oh, my god! They're two black kittens!" I squealed.

"Beatle and Beethoven!" he hollered out.

"I just adopted them from the SPCA downtown for you. I know how much you miss Ernie, so I thought they would help heal your heart after losing your main man." I picked them both up and squeezed them into my chest as one let out a meow.

"I love them!" I said as I swayed with them.

"This is the perfect gift!" I smiled.

"My cup runneth over," I whispered.

"I love my Beatle and Beethoven." Trent laughed as I then set them both on his warm chest as they both crawled into a ball and started purring.

CHAPTER 27

LOUISIANA

The phone was vibrating on the nightstand next to my bed as I moaned, "Who now? What the fuck time is it?" I wrestled my hand around, searching for the phone, grabbing it. I read the name flashing across the screen and tossed it over to Trent.

"Dude, it's Zack."

I rolled my head over on the pillow as Trent said, "Hey man, what's up?" He was rubbing his eyes as he listened.

"Really? That's fucking awesome, dude. I'll tell Tyler later. Thanks for the call, Zack." He set down the phone and stretched his arms over his head.

"What's fucking awesome?" I asked as I kicked my leg out from under the cool sheet, huffing.

"Zack just spoke to one of the executive producers from the film, and he told him that the rock and roll film had broken box office numbers over the holiday." He rolled over and gave me a sleepy smile. "You're kidding right? It only took them like two months to get back to y'all about its success!" I immediately perked up.

"How amazing is this!" I let out a breath of relief for

Tyler and the band.

"Let me tell Tyler when I pick him up from his retreat today, okay?" I rolled over and nodded my head yes as I pushed Trent's hair behind his ears.

"Congrats, baby," I whispered.

"Let's just hope this soundtrack produces just as good of numbers as the movie." He smiled.

"Stop! Would you just enjoy this moment, you brat!" I rolled my eyes and stretched my arms. Trent leaned over and started tickling me.

"Brat?" he asked as I laughed.

"Stop, you're going to make me have to pee!" I squealed as I slid out of bed and headed for the bathroom.

"What time are you leaving to pick up Tyler?" I called out to him as I brushed my teeth.

"In an hour or so. Actually, you should come with me. Tyler would love it," Trent suggested. I glanced back at myself in the mirror. I hadn't seen my best friend in quite some time. I was actually starting to really miss him.

"Are you sure you want that?" I was a little reluctant as I called back to him as I rinsed my mouth out. "Of course, baby. You just go ahead and throw on some jeans and I'll start the coffee and feed the cats. We'll be there in a couple of hours. I know Tyler will need to see you," he said as I agreed. I made my way into the closet and grabbed something to put on. Good. I needed to see Tyler just as much as he probably needed to see me.

Pulling into the parking lot of the all-too-familiar detox treatment clinic, I felt my stomach do its usual somersault.

I parked the truck and paused before opening my driver side door.

"Are you ready for this?" Trent asked me. I looked over at him with a bit of hesitation and answered, "Here we go again," as I blew out a breath, nervously tapping the steering wheel. Trent reached out for my hand and squeezed it.

"Let's go get our fragile lead singer." I laughed at the image, but secretly hoped he was stronger this time around.

Walking into the clinic, the spring season snuck up all around us as I breathed in the scent of fresh flowers. The walls were painted a calming lavender color, and all the windows faced a beautiful, serene lake with white benches scattered around the property. Trent walked over to the guest services desk to notify them that we were there to pick up Tyler Black. I moseyed over to a set of glass doors that were propped open to take in the scenic view.

As I looked around, I noticed Tyler sitting on one of the white benches just leaning back in his Soundgarden t-shirt, black headband tied around his forehead and ripped jeans staring at the lake.

I smiled, then walked through the doors and made my way over to him.

Tyler glanced over at me, then abruptly got to his feet and opened his arms wide. I picked up my pace as I ran into his arms and squeezed him so tightly.

"I missed you so much, Ty!" I said as I kept hugging him. He kissed my head, breathing in the scent of my hair.

"Oh, baby girl. I needed this," he whispered.

I stepped back and looked up into his eyes.

"You look so refreshed," I complimented him as I reached up and touched his cheek.

"I feel good, thank you," he said as he hugged me once more.

Trent walked up towards us, grabbed Tyler and just hugged him for a moment. Tears started to surface as I watched their embrace.

"I'm proud of you, man," Trent said as he stepped back and took a look at Tyler.

"You look well-rested, dude. Are you ready to head back home? I have you all checked out," Trent said as he patted him on the back while Tyler nodded his head yes.

Trent went to retrieve Tyler's bags as I intertwined my hand in Tyler's and walked him out to the truck. "I've missed you," I said as I opened the truck door for Tyler as he slid in the backseat.

"I've missed you, Alex. Thank you for forgiving me. Thank you for everything." I smiled as I walked around to start the truck up. Trent joined us as he threw the bags in next to Tyler then hopped in the truck and took a seat next to me. This felt like the time Trent and Tyler picked me up from Miami. How they both drove from Texas to Florida to save me from Gage Heston and that toxic relationship I was suffocating in, just to bring me back home. Now, I felt I was somehow returning the favor to Tyler.

I smiled as I glanced at Tyler in the rear view mirror, happy that we were all together again.

"Happy, baby girl?" Tyler leaned up against the seat asking.

"Are you ready to be happy?" I questioned as Trent grinned back at Tyler.

"Whaaat?" Tyler asked as he looked at us both.

"The movie was a hit, dude! It broke box office numbers!" Trent hollered as Tyler's eyes lit up like fireworks.

"No shit?" he asked as we just laughed.

"Did you expect anything different?" I teased Tyler as

he leaned back in the seat and just relished the thought of the movie and its soundtrack being a hit.

"No, I did not." He was pleased with himself.

The three of us drove back to Dallas with the windows down as we listened to music.

No more apologies were needed. We'd all finally moved on.

CHAPTER 28

A few days later, I was sitting on the couch at Trent's apartment as he sat on the floor digging through a box.

"Look at all this equipment I scored from that studio for sale on the West Side!" He was smiling with glee as he pulled out assorted cables and headphones as I just watched him.

"Oh, wait a minute, babe. Look at this!" He flashed me a naughty grin. I laughed.

"Whatcha find?" I leaned over, looking into the box as Trent pulled out a small handheld video recorder.

"Guess what I want to film?" Trent licked his lips as I pushed the box aside with my foot and sat down on the floor next to him.

"To hell with being in rock and roll. You're now going to be in the adult movie business?" I teased, laughing as I watched him turn the camera on.

"It works!" He was getting excited when his cell phone began to ring. He handed me over the video camera as he got up from the floor and walked away to answer the phone. I flipped the camera on as I pushed the record button and started recording Trent's place around me.

Trent hung up the phone, then walked back over to me

and sat back down on the floor, gathering everything and placing it back into the box.

"Leave that lil baby out," Trent smirked as I set the camera next to my bag.

"Why are you packing everything back up? What's the rush?" I asked as I helped him pack the box.

"Hey, the guys are all on their way over to the recording studio. Zack has called an emergency meeting with the band." I rolled my eyes.

"What constitutes 'an emergency' in music? Did an amplifier blow up?" I said as I made air quotes with my hands. Trent laughed as we both finished packing the box and he lifted it and set it down by the front door.

"Do you want me to stay here while y'all discuss this 'emergency' at the studio?" I asked as I made another set of air quotes in the air. Trent rolled his eyes.

"No babe, you'll find out sooner or later what the situation is, so why not just sit in on the meeting with us." Trent nodded his head yes as I shrugged my shoulders and collected my bag and the camera. Trent picked up the box as I opened the front door.

After locking up, we went downstairs to my truck, loaded it, then headed straight over to *Head Rush*.

Within a half-hour, the guys from WHIP all started to walk into the studio and gathered around me as I sat on the couch. One was texting on his cell, another was sipping his coffee, then Tyler walked in the door as I stuck my tongue out at him. He walked right over to me and popped a squat in front of me on the floor as I began playing with his hair while we all nervously waited for Zack's arrival.

Suddenly, the door slammed shut as Zack stood there and looked around, counting heads.

"Hell's empty, looks like all the devils are here!" he shouted as everyone started to laugh as they relaxed, awaiting his big news.

"Okay, gentlemen and lady." He glanced over at me and smiled.

"Listen up, I have exciting news!" He took a deep breath in and then released it.

"You guys have all been nominated for a Billboard Music Award for Top Soundtrack!" Everyone's eyes dilated three sizes as they all stared back at Zack in shock.

"What?" Trent was the first one to break the silence.

"WHIP is nominated for a music award!" he repeated as all the guys suddenly jumped to their feet with excitement.

"Hell yeah!" The drummer yelled out. Tyler just leaned his head back into my lap as I kissed his forehead.

"Congrats, string bean," I whispered. He then got to his feet and started hugging the other members of WHIP. I smiled as I grabbed the video recorder out of my bag and hit the record button to document the band's reaction to this wonderful news.

"We did it!" the bassist hollered out. The drummer then glanced over at me and mouthed a

"Thank you" as I blinked my eyelashes back at him, nodding my head. I then leaned back on the couch and let the pride wash over me as I watched them celebrate. *Mr. Gage Heston was not getting the last word this time*, I thought to myself as I felt so happy for each and every one of them. They all worked so hard that they really deserved this nomination.

After all the high fiving, Trent made his way over to me, took my hands, and pulled me to my feet. He then wrapped his arms around me and squeezed me tightly. I closed my eyes and held back the tears that were trying to surface.

"I'm so proud of you, baby," I whispered into his ear. He just held on to me a moment longer and swayed as I could feel the excitement radiating from his body.

"Bring that lil recorder home with us tonight. We have some celebrating to do!" I laughed as I tugged on his hair then kissed his soft lips.

After everyone settled down, Zack continued on with the meeting as he went over the dates, the flight, and the hotel with everyone. The band all listened intensely as they were all trying to digest the exciting news.

"We'll be back in Las Vegas baby!" Zack clapped his hands as Tyler and I exchanged a concerned look. "It'll be okay," I mouthed to Tyler as he nodded his head. *Oh boy*, I thought to myself. *Here we go again, Las Vegas.* I just shook my head. *We can handle this*, I reassured myself as I joined in on the clapping.

"Yay, Vegas!" I sarcastically shouted as I felt a lump rise in my throat.

Later that night, Trent and I were back at my place again.

"I love your reaction when you receive good news!" I smiled as I watched Trent setting up the video recorder.

"Are we really documenting our celebration?" I teased as I lit a few candles on the windowsill and on the bedside table.

"This is for our private collection only, Alex. I'll lock it in my safe with the gun. I promise," he said as I laughed nervously.

"Okay, as long as it's locked away. I tend to get a lil camera shy, you know," I confessed as Trent paused and looked at me.

"Act like it's not even there babe, just follow my lead." Trent pushed the record button and slowly walked over to me.

He reached for my hand then raised it up to his mouth and gently kissed it. I blushed. I completely trusted him, so I decided I was going to enjoy this. I pulled back my hand and pulled his hand up to my mouth and returned the kiss. Trent smiled. I then slid one of his fingers slowly into my mouth and began sucking on it.

"Umm," Trent said as I began to lick the tattoo on top of his hand, over his wrist and up his forearm as Trent let out a louder groan. I continued to lick up his bicep, his shoulder, then up his neck. I could feel the flush of goose-bumps rise across his neck as I licked a few more times then slid my warm tongue into his mouth. Trent devoured my kiss as the passion began to rise between us.

"You're not camera shy at all, are you baby?" Trent whispered as I stepped back and pulled his t-shirt up and over his head, tossing it aside as Trent's silky black hair dangled across his face.

I ran my fingernails down his fully inked chest until I reached for his black jeans. I unfastened them slowly as I licked my lips with anticipation. Sliding my hand inside his tight jeans, I grabbed a hold of his cock and began to rub it slowly.

"Oh Alex," he moaned, as I could feel him grow harder by the second.

I then gave him a slight push to sit on the edge of my bed as I stood between his strong legs and began to perform a little 'Vanity' striptease for him.

"I like this." Trent smiled as he gave me his undivided attention. I slowly unbuttoned each button on my shirt one by one to expose his favorite red lace bra underneath.

"Oh, my favorite lil red bra!" He smiled at me as he watched me intensely licking his lips, as he was very hungry for me. I tore the rest of the shirt off and tossed it aside as I wiggled my hips. Trent smiled.

"You're sexy, baby," he complimented me as I slowly unbuttoned my denim skirt as I swayed my hips back and forth. I lifted up the edge of my skirt to flash him my matching red panties as Trent moaned, covering his mouth. He then reached out for my hips and pulled me closer to him.

He slowly peeled the skirt off of me as I stepped out of it and turned around. I leaned my back up against his warm inked chest and grabbed his hand. I slowly guided his fingers to slide themselves into my panties and slowly rub me. Trent licked my ear as his breathing became heavier.

"You're wet for me," he said as I gently pulled down my bra and exposed my breasts as my nipples peaked with excitement. Trent pulled his hand out of my panties and grabbed them both as he slowly gave them a tug.

"That feels good, baby," I said as I pushed back harder against his chest while he tugged as I was completely turned on. I then spun myself back around and faced him as I slid down his chest, over his hardened cock and onto the floor.

On my knees, I reached for the loops from his black

jeans and slid them down his legs and off his body, tossing them aside. With his hard cock dangling between his legs, I grabbed it and slid it between my cleavage as ecstasy flashed across Trent's face.

"Oh, Alex. That's trouble," he said as he ran his fingers through my hair. I rubbed up and down a few times until he slowed my pace down a bit.

"Oh baby, I don't want to come yet." He groaned as I smiled. He gently took my hand in his and stood me back up in front of him. He grabbed my lacy panties and slowly pulled them down as he leaned into me. Licking me with his tongue, he trailed my abdomen, up my cleavage, up my neck and pushed his way into my mouth. I accepted his tongue once more as he circled it around my tongue, then pulled out and whispered in my ear.

"I want to be inside of you, Alex." I loved hearing those words as I nodded okay.

He leaned back on to the bed as I crawled on top of him, straddling him. He grabbed a hold of his stiff cock and slowly entered me as I moaned, pushing myself down on him.

"Oh Trent, you feel so good!" I called out as he held onto my hips and pushed himself deeper. I started to rock slowly up and down as Trent threw his head back.

"Baby, that feels so good." I picked up my pace, knowing I was on the right track to an amazing climax.

I then rocked back and forth as I leaned back, steading myself with one hand. Trent moaned louder. This cowgirl was definitely bull riding as I leaned up back into him, keeping pace.

"Come on, Trent," I encouraged him to thrust harder as I pushed my hips down on him.

As I felt him push deeper, I started to cry out.

"That's it! That's it baby!" He kept making love to me as I exploded with an orgasm. Trent didn't slow down one bit as he rolled me over onto my back and in the missionary position he continued to thrust inside of me. I pulled on his long hair as he leaned in to kiss me.

"I'm going to come so hard for you," he whispered as I spread my legs a little bit wider. Trent thrusted and started to climax as I dragged my nails down his damp back.

"Congratulations baby," I whispered in his ear as our little nomination celebration was coming to a close.

"Y'all need to be nominated for more stuff if we celebrate like this every time!" I hollered as Trent laughed while he slowly sat himself up and headed over to the video recorder to hit the stop button.

CHAPTER 29

"I'm so nervous about this trip to Las Vegas," I said as I sifted through the dress rack at Nordstrom a few days before the award ceremony.

"It's the Billboard Music Awards, girl! You're supposed to be excited, not fucking nervous!" Nova laughed as she held a black cocktail dress up to her body, sizing herself up in the mirror.

"You remember our last little adventure to Vegas?" I flashed her a dirty look, knowing damn well she remembered Tyler and all the drama that partying with cocaine had brought upon us.

"It's a quick trip, girl. Just keep Tyler on a short leash." Nova held the same dress up to me and shook her head no.

"I'm glad you're going to join us. You and Zack, huh? Who would've ever thought?" I teased her. She licked her lips as she fussed through another rack of dresses.

"Look, Tyler just returned from that holiday 'retreat.' I think he can handle Vegas this time around." I was trying to convince Nova that Tyler had matured, but she wasn't buying it.

"Plus, we're flying in then heading straight to the hotel, then to the awards ceremony, then back to the hotel, then back to Dallas." I paused as my brain began to swirl around in my head.

"I don't think he has time to get into trouble." I looked over at Nova who was just ignoring me as usual. She knew damn well that Tyler always found the time for trouble.

"Here, this is the one for you!" She held up a beautiful silver and black sequined dress with a scooped back.

"That's gorgeous!" I called out as I ripped the hanger from her fingers, admiring it.

"Go try it on!" Nova urged me as I turned towards the dressing room and went in to try on the garment.

As I slipped out of my cotton dress, I stepped into the sequined party dress and let out an "Ooo, this is it, girl." I turned around to look at my gothic angel wings tattoo on my back, peeking out on display.

"This is perfect!" I hollered out from the dressing room to Nova.

"Come out, I want to see you in it!" she demanded as she was trying on a similar dress in all black.

"Why are we always looking like we're going to a funeral every time we have somewhere to attend with the guys from WHIP? The only color they have in their damn color wheel is black!" Nova laughed as I opened up the dressing room door and stepped out.

"That's it!" She looked me over and repeated.

"That's it, girl." I hugged her.

"Thank you. I really want to look good on the red carpet next to Trent." I glanced in the hallway mirror one last time and made the decision to purchase the dress.

"Mr. Van Zant has some competition for the spotlight if you're going to flaunt that dress, girl!" She boosted my confidence as I wiggled my hips in the dress.

"Thank you," I said again as I swayed with gratitude.

Suddenly, I heard, "Is that you, Alexandria Leigh Rae?" I quickly turned around and saw my mother standing in the dressing room holding a few dresses of her own.

"Mama! What are you doing here?" I asked with surprise as I gave her a hug.

"Hun, I'm always here at Nordstroms, you know that. I have another dinner party to attend, so I need to get myself all gussied up for it." I laughed as I looked through the dresses she was holding.

"Oh hun, what is this that you're buying?" she asked as she nodded her head in approval.

"Mama, my boyfriend is up for a music award, so I have to look my best at the ceremony." I smiled as she ran her hand down the sequins over my hip.

"Are you talking about Trent, dear?" I nodded my head yes.

"He's a nice boy, Alexandria, but any man that is in that so-called rock and roll music that y'all call it, is not fit for a husband. It's the devil's music," she chastised me.

"Are you two planning on getting married?" She looked at me with disgust. I frowned as I watched her smooth my hair back out of my eyes.

"Actually, it's prog-industrial music, not devil music. And, I wouldn't bring up marriage and little white chapels at the moment. Alex is very sensitive about that," I heard Nova holler from the opposite dressing room stall, and I just shook my head in embarrassment, laughing.

"That's Nova in there, Mama." She rolled her eyes at me.

I then turned around to grab my hanger when my mother huffed with surprise.

"Alexandria Leigh Rae, what is that black stuff all over your back?" She feverishly spun me around.

"Mama, that's a tattoo." I was ashamed as I put my head down.

"See? That music man is no good," she said as she tried to wipe off my tattoo.

I pouted my lips, then said, "He's good to me, Mama. I created this design myself and I got the tattoo when I wasn't even seeing Trent. My boyfriend had nothing to do with it," I said sternly as I pulled away and went back into the dressing room to change my clothes.

"You know I'll have to tell your father about this," she huffed once more.

"Go ahead, Mama, and please tell him that it was my decision and that I'm an adult. I can legally get tattoos, you know. Plus, Trent is my boyfriend right now, and I would appreciate it if you would give him a chance." I swung open the dressing room stall door as my mother stood there tapping her foot.

"Well, alright then, dear. Y'all have a nice time at the award ceremony. Please be sure to call me when you get back," she ordered as I leaned in and kissed her cheek as Nova came out of the dressing room and laughed at me.

We both watched Mother turn around and shake her head in disapproval when we waved our hands and in unison said, "Bye Mama!" as she walked out.

I huffed then turned towards Nova. "Are you ready to get out of here, girl?" I asked.

"Let's go," she laughed as she took the dress from my hand and carried it to the register for me.

Standing at the register, I glanced around and noticed the men's department across the way.

"Hold up," I said to the woman typing into the cash register as I pranced over to a men's rack of clothing.

"What are you doing?" Nova hollered towards me.

"How hot would Tyler look in this?" I held up a hanger in the air.

"A fucking skirt?" Nova questioned.

"No, you idiot, it's a kilt. How hot would he look with this on over his black leather pants?" I sifted through the rack, searching for Tyler's size.

"I'm so buying this for him!" I hollered to Nova as she giggled.

"It's a skirt," she said as she rolled her eyes.

"It's a kilt!" I barked back.

"Whatever, I know he'll like it." I smiled at the saleswoman pleased with my two selections as I handed over my credit card.

I was zipping up Trent's outfit in a garment bag that the band all selected to wear tonight to the event.

"Baby, we are going to look so fly on that red carpet tonight!" I squealed as Trent carried our luggage downstairs.

"The car will be here shortly, Alexandria. You better put your shoes on." I laughed as I sat on the bed next to Beatle and Beethoven and slid on my heels.

"You boys behave for the pet sitter," I warned the cats as I patted them on the head.

"Alex?" Trent called up to me once more in the loft area.

"I'm coming, baby! I was saying goodbye to our boys."

He let out a subtle laugh.

"The car is downstairs. Are we ready for this babe?" He paused nervously as he looked around, not making eye contact. I walked up to him and softly kissed him on the lips, trying to tame his nerves.

"We were born ready, baby." I gave him a second kiss, then tapped him on the butt.

"Now, let's do this!" I locked up the loft and followed Trent out to the car.

Arriving at Dallas Love Field Airport, the car pulled over to the curb unloading zone as we quickly stepped out and retrieved our luggage. Nova ran up to greet us.

"Dudes, Zack totally booked us a private plane to take to Las Vegas, baby!" She squealed with excitement as I smiled and placed my bag on the curb while adjusting the garment bags in my hand. I just gave her a nod as I watched her jump up and down.

"I got the bags, babe. You just head in with Nova," Trent said as he was tipping the driver and collecting our luggage.

Walking through the small airport, Nova directed me to the correct gate. Tyler whistled over to me as I approached WHIP, all anxiously pacing at the gate, waiting to board the plane.

"Hi Ty. Here's your garment bag." I handed the bag over to Tyler as he unzipped the zipper to sneak a peek at his new black kilt.

"Are you kidding me, baby girl?" he laughed.

"I fucking love this!" I glanced over at Nova as she rolled her eyes.

"Do I know my boo? Or do I know my boo?" I laughed as Tyler kissed me on the cheek.

"Thank you, blondie," Tyler said as he zipped the garment bag back up.

Trent walked up to the gate with Zack as he clicked off his cell phone.

"Hey, are you guys ready?" He looked over at the band, Nova, and then at me. We all enthusiastically nodded our heads in unison.

The drummer and Tyler started singing Merle Haggard's "Silver Wings" as we all stepped onto the intimate private plane. A busty brunette flight attendant was first to greet us as I glanced over my shoulder at Tyler as he just smiled and continued to sing.

"Champagne anyone?" she asked as the band members all stowed their bags and selected a seat and started nodding their heads yes. I sat down next to Tyler and whispered, "No champagne for us. Vegas and champagne do not mix well on the Vegas turf."

Tyler laughed. "Thanks for not drinking, baby girl. I do not want to feel like the only fucking turd in the punch bowl." He buckled his seatbelt, then leaned back into the seat as I glanced over at him and laughed at his comment.

"Before we take off, guys, I'd like to make a toast." Zack stood up and held up his glass of champagne to toast WHIP.

"Thank you for trusting me as your label and manager. I know we're a small one, but WHIP has put us on the map, and I want to thank you, gentlemen. Thank you for the hours you put into the recording session and the passion you've put into performing on stage. The video is a success, 'Betrayal' is a success, and even if we don't win the award tonight..." He paused.

"You guys are a huge success to me, and I want to applaud you for it." Zack lifted his glass as Nova whistled. Me, the flight attendant, and the two pilots all started clapping our hands as we cheered for the band.

"Thanks man," the guitarist said as he toasted Zack, while the rest of WHIP all joined in returning the gesture.

"And, I might add that this award nomination wouldn't even be in our grasp if Alexandria and Nova didn't come through on the contract for us. Thank you, girls," Zack said as I blushed, glancing over at Trent across the aisle as he whispered, "It's okay."

I swallowed as I lifted my water bottle to toast the band back.

"Now, relax and enjoy the flight. We'll be there shortly," he said as he turned around and took his seat next to Nova, kissing her on the lips.

I tapped Tyler's leg while the excitement for the award show brewed within me. He placed his hand in mine and squeezed it as the plane slowly lifted to take off, heading for Las Vegas.

CHAPTER
30

LAS VEGAS

We all settled into our hotel rooms when we were given only a couple of hours to eat and get ourselves ready for the big event later that evening. Zack kept the band on a tight schedule as Nova and I had to abide by the rules if we were going along for the ride.

"You look beautiful," Trent complimented me as I brushed my hair in the bathroom mirror.

"Thank you. Are you still nervous?" I asked Trent as I watched him fuss with his necktie.

"I'm okay," he said as he shrugged his shoulders.

I sprayed myself with perfume, then gathered all my makeup essentials and slid them into my clutch. Trent unzipped his garment bag to pull out his dress jacket as he noticed that two of the garment bag hangers were stuck with one another.

"Hey babe, I think this bag is Tyler's," he said as he tore the hangers apart.

I walked out of the bathroom and unzipped the bag.

"Shit." I paused.

"This is his kilt he's supposed to wear tonight. I'm going to run this down to him," I said as I huffed.

"Okay, but be quick babe. We have to meet everyone in the lobby in thirty minutes." He tapped my butt as I laughed, zipping up the garment bag.

"I'll be right back." I slipped on my high heels, grabbed the garment bag and the room key, and hurried down to Tyler's room.

"Knock, knock!" I said as I tapped on Tyler's hotel room. Tyler swung open the door and smiled at me. "Wow baby girl, you look amazing!" he complimented me as I pushed him aside and walked over to the room's closet and hung up the garment bag.

"Here's your kilt, it got all tangled up in our garment bags," I said as I turned towards him and adjusted his black skinny tie on his neck.

"You guys are going to look so killer out there on the red carpet tonight," I said as Tyler smiled at me then leaned in and lightly kissed me. I stepped back on my heel as he tried to push his infamous barbell piercing into my mouth. *He knew damn well that that move always turned me on before.*

"Wait a minute there, pretty boy. You need to stop that," I said as I pulled my mouth away from his. He laughed as he wiped his mouth, then pushed me against the closet door and tried to kiss me a second time.

"I said stop it, Ty!" I pushed him away from my mouth.

"I can't kiss you like that anymore, Tyler. It's not fair to Trent." I pouted.

"You told me you respected our relationship. Now how

can I try with Trent if I have another go-around with you? I just have to control myself around you, and you need to control yourself around me, or this isn't going to work," I huffed as Tyler stepped back.

"I'm sorry, baby girl. I'll stop. It's so hard for me, but I'll knock it off. I'm just so excited for tonight, and I really want to celebrate it all with you," he said as I turned and unzipped the garment bag.

"You are celebrating with me. I'm here aren't I? I mean, I'm always here for you. We just need to practice self-control. If Trent saw you try to kiss me right now, that would be the end of WHIP. It would be all over for you. Do you really want to take that chance?" I pouted as I fussed with his garment bag.

"Here, Tyler, put on your kilt." I handed over the kilt as he licked his lips, grabbed his kilt then headed over towards the mirror.

"Finish getting dressed. I'll see you downstairs in twenty minutes," I said sternly as Tyler nodded his head.

"Twenty minutes, okay?" I asked him.

"Okay," he said as I left his hotel room in a huff.

Arriving at the MGM Grand Garden Arena entrance, flashes from the photographers were instantly lighting up the red carpet leading into the venue. Zack had on his black pinstripe dress suit with a black tie, and Nova was in her black sequined dress on his arm as he turned towards the band.

"Listen, you guys will walk up and stand in front of the Billboard Music Awards banner over there and pose for a few pictures, then Alexandria, Nova and I will rejoin you after. Then we'll all head into the venue together as a group to take our seats." The band all nodded their heads yes.

I excitedly watched WHIP walk together as a rock band over towards the photographers as they stopped to pose in front of the black and white banner as directed. They all looked absolutely gorgeous. Black form-fitted jackets, black skinny pants, black skinny ties to match their black dress shirts and black boots. Each one wore the infamous charcoal eyeliner as Trent's hair was pulled back into a man-bun while Tyler's was messy and sprayed up and out. I laughed just thinking how Tyler looked like one of my hair band guys as I stared at his hair and gave him a thumbs up. I admired the black kilt with a silver chain wrapped around the waist that he rocked over the fitted dress pants as I looked them all up and down.

"Oh my god, they all look so hot!" I giggled as I squeezed Zack's arm.

"They look like an award-winning band!" I said while tapping Nova's butt as she nodded in agreement, just watching WHIP pose for pictures.

Trent then stepped aside from the band and walked over and extended his hand out to me. I smiled, glanced over at Nova, then took his hand. Photographers immediately started snapping photos as I posed next to Trent on the red carpet and nervously smiled for the camera. Zack then scurried over in front of all of us and had us gather in together to take a group photo. He shook one of the photographers' hands, slid him a business card and some cash, then he stepped back into the shot, joining us. We all posed for a few pictures, then turned to head inside through a private artist's entrance as a group.

Suddenly, I felt someone pinch-twisting my arm and brushing me aside.

"Ow, what the hell?" I said as I rubbed my arm, almost losing my balance. I looked over to my left and noticed that Gage Heston was walking right past me.

"Hey, if you ever lay a fucking hand on her again, I'll make you wish you never even knew her name." Tyler defended me as he forcefully pushed Gage.

He slowly turned around and with a sinister smile he said, "Nice skirt, asshole." Tyler quickly pulled his fist back and punched him right square in the jaw. Trent immediately pushed me behind him, using himself to shield me, as photographers started snapping pictures.

"You're a pathetic asshole, Gage, you sad, miserable fuck!" Tyler called out to Gage as he steadied himself from the shock of Tyler's punch. WHIP all stepped up and got themselves involved.

"Do we have a problem here, Mr. Heston?" one called out as all five men stepped into Gage's personal space. Zack walked up to WHIP and started pushing the guys back.

"Go on inside, Gage. Get your ass out of here before you really get hurt," Zack ordered as I grabbed Nova's hand and just stood there, watching in shock.

It was a sudden epiphany for me right there on the red carpet. My ah-ha moment was so clear as I realized that all the guys all had my back. I was no longer fearful of this pathetic, weak excuse for a man, as I drove a cold stare right through Gage as he was wiping his bloody mouth with his handkerchief.

A security guard immediately came over to investigate

the little tussle as he radioed for his team to escort Gage Heston off the hotel premises right away. Trent turned around to Nova and me and asked, "Are you girls okay?" We squeezed each other's hands and nodded a surprising yes.

I smiled at Tyler and mouthed, "Thank you," as he flashed me a grin back while shaking out his bruised hand. We then all followed a second security guard into the arena as he swiftly walked us over to our seats.

Fans were whistling and screaming WHIP's name as they waved signs from two tiers up as we entered the arena. I felt like I was back at the venue in Houston with all the *Whip-ettes* screaming for the guys' attention. Their fan base was growing as their album and the movie soundtrack both continued to climb the charts. I just looked around in awe as familiar musicians and their significant others started taking their seats next to us.

I waved to Roger from the REVENUE and to his new bride, Tonya, as she ignored me.

"Why does that bitch always have an attitude with me?" I whispered to Nova as she flipped her off.

"Don't worry about her, Alex. She's probably still pissed you tried to steal her thunder when you almost married Tyler the last time we were here in Vegas." I laughed as I dismissed her attitude.

Every genre of music was represented here tonight. I felt like such a groupie myself as I nudged Tyler's arm, pointing to all my favorite artists. The rest of the guys were all exchanging greetings with other acts as the house lights began to flicker, letting the crowd know it was time to take their seats. I smoothed out my dress and selected a seat between Tyler and Trent.

A famous comedian walked out onto the stage as the crowd erupted. He bowed, then started into his opening monologue while the audience began to laugh at his jokes. He then introduced the first band to perform their chart-topping song while everyone sang along to the familiar tune. I nervously tapped my high heel on the floor.

"When are they announcing the 'top soundtrack'?" I asked Tyler anxiously as he shrugged his shoulders and fidgeted with his silver chain on his kilt.

"The show just started, baby girl. I have no clue what's going on," he said as I laughed as I was trying to enjoy the show, but the wait was agonizing.

All the guys seemed pretty laid back as they enjoyed every single moment the award show had to offer.

I tried to relax as I closed my eyes wondering was all that bullshit I endured during this whole journey for WHIP to be nominated for a Billboard Music Award, was it all worth it? I inhaled a deep breath as a trailer of events began flashing back through my mind.

It all started with the promise I made to Tyler on the lakeside steps to land this soundtrack gig for him if he kept himself straight without the drug abuse.

I cringed as I envisioned holding Gage Heston's hand while Nova shimmied out of her dress at Vanity as we got him drunk while he signed the contract for WHIP. Then I had to wrestle with him in the back seat of his car until he passed out. I swallowed hard then thought about Trent punching Tyler so soon after receiving the news that the band scored the soundtrack gig, misunderstanding the whole Gage conversation.

Then my heart felt heavy as Trent sang live with Tyler with his misguided broken heart in St. Louis, as I was in the midst of getting dumped.

I felt my pulse begin to beat a little faster as I pictured Tyler kissing me in the rain, then him laying in his bed naked with a bruised eye and severed skin while we used sex to comfort one another and help stave off the loneliness.

Then my mind flashed to the band WHIP as they all toasted me in unison at the film's executive producer's dinner, making me feel like I sold my soul for Tyler to land this stupid soundtrack.

Quickly, my mind shifted back to Trent as he sadly played on his piano in the band's rehearsal studio as we finally apologized to one another.

Then my mind swirled as I recalled the fucked up Las Vegas celebration of completing this troublesome soundtrack recording session. Tyler and I snorted cocaine and almost got married as I stood there in a white dress, lace veil, blood dripping down my nose and fainting outside the wedding chapel.

Ugh. I paused and smiled as this emotional rollercoaster flashback made me think of slapping Trent's face as he tried to help me sexually release all of my pent up anger over all this bullshit I'd endured over a stupid fucking soundtrack to a stupid fucking rock and roll film. *WAS IT ALL WORTH IT?* I pondered as I squeezed my eyes, keeping them sealed shut.

Are these two guys that important to me? I released the breath I was holding as I slowly opened my eyes and glanced over at Tyler on my left then over to Trent on my right. They absolutely were.

Zack interrupted the movie trailer playing inside my head as he announced to the row that "This is it, guys. This is the moment!" I took the hands of both Tyler and Trent into mine as each one gripped my hand and squeezed it tightly in theirs.

The actor on stage began to run through all the list of nominees in the category one by one as everything fell silent in my head, deafening me. I heard absolutely nothing but silence until he announced the words, "And the winner for the Billboard Music Award for Top Soundtrack is..." I released a breath.

"WHIP!" We all jumped to our feet, beaming with excitement.

Tyler immediately turned towards me, picked me up, and spun me around. I was dizzy as he set me down, then started man-hugging all his band mates. I turned around and faced Trent. He paused, smiled, then pulled me into his embrace and squeezed me so tightly, letting out a sigh.

"I'm so proud of you, Trent!" I hollered out while tapping his back as he leaned in towards me and kissed my lips a few times.

"I'm so happy, baby. We did it! All that bullshit we endured. I'm truly sorry baby. We did this together!!" he hollered out. I grabbed his waist and pushed him towards the rest of the band.

"Now go fetch your award!" I ordered as he laughed.

Zack started enthusiastically pulling the guys' arms one by one out into the aisle as he directed them towards the stage to go and receive their award. I sat back down into the seat next to Nova and gripped her hand tightly as we intensely watched them walk down the aisle.

"They did it! I'm so proud of them!" I cheered as tears started to surface as I watched all five men walk up onto the stage and shake the actor's hand one by one.

Tyler, who was representing the band, walked up to the microphone and tried to speak as the *Whip-ettes* went crazy on him with their screaming. Tyler paused and let the fans finish applauding as he tried to speak for a second time.

"Thank you. I'm going to keep this speech short and sweet, guys." He let out a breath, smiling as he looked at the award in his hand then back to the audience.

"On behalf of me and the guys here from WHIP"—he pointed to the other four beautiful men dressed in black on stage—"we would like to thank our record label, our kick-ass manager Zack, our girls Alexandria and Nova, and our amazing fans. Thank you." He raised the award in the air as the fans erupted once more.

I just covered my mouth with my hand as I watched all five of them standing there side by side, waving to the audience and to their loyal fans while flashbulbs lit up the stage. Nova hugged me as I couldn't pull my stare away from WHIP.

"Whoo-hoo!" she hollered. I smiled as I thought to my-self, *it was so worth it*. I wiped my damp eyelashes with my fingertips as I let out a deep breath. It was absolutely worth it.

END

ABOUT ATMOSPHERE PRESS

Founded in 2015, Atmosphere Press was built on the principles of Honesty, Transparency, Professionalism, Kindness, and Making Your Book Awesome. As an ethical and author-friendly hybrid press, we stay true to that founding mission today.

If you're a reader, enter our giveaway for a free book here:

SCAN TO ENTER
BOOK GIVEAWAY

If you're a writer, submit your manuscript for consideration here:

SCAN TO SUBMIT
MANUSCRIPT

And always feel free to visit Atmosphere Press and our authors online at atmospherepress.com. See you there soon!

Be sure to pick up
Jacqueline Grandey's other book

BROKEN RECORD

and to look out for

BETWEEN US BIRDS

Coming Soon

ABOUT THE AUTHOR

JACQUELINE always had a love for creativity, whether it was writing poetry, lyrics, or painting mixed media art. She earned a degree in Music Sound Engineering through ARTI, worked live music venues, and even sold her own line of punk rock swag.

After touring for a decade, she started to long for life at home. With her love of cats, she pursued her Animal Science degree through the University of Texas and became CVA certified through the Texas Veterinary Medical Association.

Today, Jacqueline is proud to hold the lead surgical technician position at a 'feline only' hospital as she continues to write, participate in art shows, and root for her Dallas Cowboys.

She resides in Texas with her husband and three cats Genesis, Gabriel and Iggy, very grateful for this balance in her life.

Please follow Jacqueline at www.jacquelinegrandey.com.